Never Just One

Book 2 in the Sunflower Beach Series

Dolores T Puterbaugh

Contents

Dedications and Thanks

Most of all to Gerry, my husband and best friend, for unflagging
encouragement and patience.
Thanks to Dora Campbell, for advice on the often puzzling process of
writing and publishing.
Thanks to Savannah Grace, for input on choosing the painting and
style for the cover.
In the first book of the series, I neglected to thank two important
people, who continue to be important to this project.
thank you to Trista Smith, my patient and gifted editor
thank you to Eva Polakovicova, designer, who creates beautiful book
covers out of my art

Disclaimer

When I was a child, I created an imaginary monster to scare my siblings – tales of a slimy beast that lived beneath the house and could emerge, wet and terrifying, from the sump in the darkest, dampest corner of the basement. Naturally, I scared myself more than anyone else and, as helping with laundry was one of my chores, I ended up spending a few years racing up the stairs, heart pounding, several times each day, hoping to lurch out the basement door into the warm kitchen before The Sump Pump monster could get its terrible webbed grip on me. Going downstairs was even worse, and it didn't take long before even the flap of the door of the laundry chute in the bathroom could trigger a surge of adrenaline as I rushed out before that terrible, scaly arm could reach me.

That being said...the people and situations in this book are entirely the fruits of my regrettably over-active imagination. Except, of course, for the animals: some of the animals memorialize much-loved and much-missed animal companions.

Chapter 1

The tag said it was a bear, and Beth supposed it was, although whether it was hopelessly old-fashioned or postmodern was hard to say. It was essentially two bear-shaped pieces of smooth, butter-colored cloth, not a foot tall, sewn together and semi-stuffed into a barely three-dimensional form; in that way, it resembled some antique children's cloth dolls. Its features were embroidered on, somehow wistful, and it had a few embroidered flowers across its broad, flat forehead. She held it up at arm's length with both hands, tilting her head.

"Beth! How are you?"

Startled, Beth lowered the bear and turned around. It was Veronica Quinn, smiling broadly. *Great*, Beth thought, *almost the absolute worst person to bump into in the baby department.* Veronica was holding a small shopping basket with some baby clothes and a fluffy stuffed hedgehog. "Oh, hi, Veronica. Good to see you." Beth paused. "Where are the kids?"

Veronica grinned mischievously. "With Gloria having Grandma time, so I can get some errands run. And this." She nodded toward the basket. She leaned in and lowered her voice. "Don't say anything about running into me here to Alex or Joe. Kevin and I are waiting to make the announcement for a bit."

"Announcement ... another baby?"

Veronica nodded, flushing. "Yes, we're so excited, but it's still a secret."

"So, you're picking up a few things?" Beth eyed the basket.

Veronica looked at the basket. "Yes, just a few of the basics; almost nothing survived Bobby. As you can imagine. And what did definitely didn't make it through Gina. Plus, the hedgehog." She sighed and shrugged. "I do this thing ... I always buy the first toy. And I put it away until the baby gets here, and it's sort of my secret, just me and the baby." She looked at Beth. "I guess that sounds crazy."

Beth shook her head. "No, no, not at all. It sounds beautiful." She blinked hard a few times.

"Yeah." Veronica suddenly fixed her gaze on the butter-colored bear. "What about you? What brings you here?" She grimaced. "That's not going to be a doggy toy for Solar ... is it?"

"What? Oh, no. It's for a colleague. A baby shower. At work, I mean. Just a little something ..."

"Oh, nice. They'll love it." Veronica touched the bear's flat, stitched nose. "So cute. What's in the water at that place, anyway? I think this must be the third baby shower I've met you shopping for in the last couple of years."

Beth felt her throat tighten up and managed to say, "Well, you know, maybe techies aren't as socially awkward as the rumors say."

"Ha! That's probably true! Can't judge by Jonah, I guess. No offense meant, Beth."

"None taken."

"Anyhow—gotta run. Gloria likes to fill the kids with sugar as revenge if I run late. See you soon." And Veronica was off, touching baby items like mezuzahs as she hurried past them.

Beth looked at the bear, tucked it into the small basket, and went looking for some dish towels to hide it on the way into the house. She held herself together through checkout and until she got into the car, where she sat crying and playing the radio very loudly for a few minutes. Then she wiped her eyes and drove home. Jonah was in the kitchen, chopping up vegetables.

She kissed him on the cheek. "Thanks for making such a great meal."

He looked at her sideways. "Not great yet. We'll see." He pushed the veggies from the cutting board into the skillet and nodded at the sizzle of olive oil. "How was it out there?"

Beth edged toward the bedroom, leaning over to pet Solar. "Oh, you know. Long lines. I ran into Veronica," she added casually.

Jonah grunted. His parents' best friends' children were his unofficial cousins, but Jonah wasn't close with any of them, unlike his younger sister, who was an honorary sister to their youngest, also a girl. "Find anything good?"

Beth shrugged, trying to nonchalantly move toward the bedroom. "You know, just some new dish towels. Something fresh." *He knows*, she thought, watching him shake his head and whack the knife through an innocent green pepper.

Slipping into their bedroom, Beth took the little bear out of the bag and stroked its flat, hopeful-looking face. Then she buried it in her underwear drawer, shook her head, and changed her clothes to take the dogs for a quick walk before dinner.

After dinner, they folded laundry together and watched a documentary on the Mars rover. Jonah grabbed the basket with their clothes and headed toward their bedroom. "Honey, don't bother," she called, "I'll take care of mine—"

"I got it," Jonah called back.

Beth heard drawers, first one and then another. "Jonah, leave it," she called. *Great*, she thought, *I bet he's hunting for that damned bear. He never puts away laundry.*

Jonah was giving a running commentary from the bedroom. "Beth, you really need to straighten up your dresser drawers. I mean, the T-shirts are folded fine, but the underwear. Seriously, how do you find anything?"

"Just leave it, Jonah," Beth called back. "Just let me put my clothes away my way—" It was too late. Jonah was in the doorway, holding up the bear in one hand and slowly rocking it side to side, as if it were dancing.

"A bear?" Jonah gestured with frustration, fanning out his free hand. "Beth, why are you doing this to yourself? Last time it was the purple dinosaur."

"It's a dragon, not a dinosaur," Beth interrupted. "And anyhow, it's not hurting anyone."

"And before that it was the pig. What, Olivia? That famous pig."

"And she didn't hurt anyone either."

Jonah shook his head, walked over to Beth, and put his arms around her. She felt the bear against her shoulder blade. "It hurts you, sweetheart. You're just making things harder." He stepped back. "If you get pregnant, then it's time to buy stuff. Not every time you're a few days late."

Beth felt tears welling up. "It doesn't hurt me to hope, Jonah. We've been trying for three years. We've flown all over the place meeting with fertility experts." She pulled the bear away from him and held it against her chest. "This is just hope. That's all. A little, blossomy hope."

Jonah yanked the bear back. "We agreed. Another six months and we'll try IVF." He headed back to the bedroom to put the bear away, muttering about her "stupid toy."

Beth called out after him. "And about IVF ... that's going to be complicated. And not just medically. This whole big secret thing you insist on is going to be impossible if I have to work entirely from home and run back and forth to the doctor's office on demand. We can't lie about that and pretend we're just taking expensive vacations like the other consults."

"I don't want to deal with the family knowing. You know how Catholic my parents are, especially my mom." Jonah frowned as he came back into the living room.

"Oh, please," Beth snapped. "I'm tired of this made-up story about your mom being so judgmental. Look how she loves Matt and Tim—" She realized immediately it was the exact wrong thing to say, because Jonah clamped his mouth together and scowled. Matt was a sore spot. "I'm sorry," Beth said, "I just don't think your parents will care and it would be nice to have some ... support. Encouragement." Against her will, tears started flowing down her face. "This is just really, really hard. It's really lonely for me." She bent over and picked up Anastasia, the Chihuahua-dachshund, who obligingly licked Beth's face.

Jonah sighed. "Beth, I know. You want a baby. Fine. But I don't think we have to involve the whole world."

"I thought *we* want a baby."

Jonah just turned and went back into the bedroom. Beth heard him opening and closing drawers, putting the rest of the laundry away. She waited a few moments and then went in the room and put the little bear back in her underwear drawer. She slid the drawer shut silently and went out to walk the dogs for their last evening walk.

Usually walking the dogs, two at a time, was exactly what she needed to clear her head and shake off any sadness. First Solar and Anastasia. Big, goofy Solar kept trying to get away and little Anastasia would occasionally nip his back leg if he inconvenienced her by pulling Beth too hard. Sometimes Beth took Solar out by himself, just to move quickly, but then he would decide to amble from smelling post to smelling post, sauntering and pausing to stare up into the trees. Then Apple and Mac, the rescue miniature greyhounds, all quivering nervous energy, had their walk. The dogs required a lot of focus; walking them was an exercise in mindfulness, because letting her attention go anywhere but the moment at hand could lead to mayhem.

Today, the walks failed to do their mind-reset magic. She slipped into the house, hung up the leashes, and put out fresh water for them. Jonah was watching the news; he muted it and turned toward her. "How did the walks go? Everyone behave?"

She shrugged. "About normal. Naughty Sol was all over the place and Anastasia bit him three times. Apple and Mac were ... Apple and Mac."

Jonah nodded and returned to the television.

It was late; soon they went to bed and kissed each other good night, pretending the argument about the bear and babies had never happened. The dogs settled into their usual places around the room, with Sol closest to Beth's side of the bed.

About one o'clock, Beth roused. Her belly hurt; her head ached. She slipped out of bed, narrowly avoiding stepping on Sol, who promptly got up to follow her to the bathroom. By the time she got there, she knew what she would see when she put on the light. Solar sat down on the bathroom rug, head tilted, watching her cry silently into her hands and then putting his big, golden paw on her knee. She stroked his head and whispered, "Good boy. Shh." Trying to be quiet, she took off her clothes and went for clean underwear; there was the bear. She willed herself to stop crying but the tears would not stop. She controlled her breathing but the tears rolled on, even as she slipped back into bed. Silently, Jonah reached for her, pulled her close. She rested her head on his chest and he said nothing, just stroked her hair and her damp face, now wet against his chest, until her breath was even. Then his hand slipped from her face to her breast, his other hand pulling her hand toward his groin. Beth pulled her hand away and shrugged his hand off of her. "Jonah, not now. Please."

"Come on, Beth."

"Not now, please. Jonah. Stop it."

"I thought you wanted a baby."

"It's not a good time, Jonah. Please."

"Then just take care of me. Come on, Beth."

"Jonah."

"It's not all about you all the time, Beth." Beth sighed and turned over, facing away from him. Jonah leaned up on one elbow, close enough that she felt his breath. "Sometimes you're such a selfish little brat, Beth. Go get your little toy and cry yourself to sleep."

Beth pressed her lips and eyes shut as hard as she could, waited a breath, and said, "Well, maybe I will, Jonah. Good night." Then she lay very, very still, trying not to sound as if there were tears burning in her eyes, until she fell asleep.

Chapter 2

I t was the usual second Saturday of the month coffee for the four friends, who had known each other since they were in high school. Then, they had swapped semi-formals for homecoming dances and proms; now it was the deep sharing and inside jokes of long-standing friendships. Beth arrived first, staking an outdoor table. Sol tried his best to fit underneath, but he stuck out on two ends. She rubbed her temples, trying to massage away the last of the headache from crying herself to sleep. She supposed Jonah was right; she should stop tormenting herself by jumping the gun.

"Headache again?" Beth jerked her head up. It was Courtney and her oversized tote bag. Even without the kids with her, she always had that tremendous tote with her, overflowing with every possible emergency supply, and was constantly rummaging around for something she couldn't find. Courtney was small and thin, and wore her hair natural, in an afro about as wide as her tiny shoulders. She plopped down next to Beth and reached over to rub Beth's shoulder. "You need to relax. Working too hard?"

"No. Well, yeah, but it's not work. It's that time of the month." Beth shrugged.

Courtney nodded. "It's the one thing I did not miss when I was pregnant."

Beth pulled her lips inward for a moment. She saw Courtney's raised eyebrow and took a deep breath. *She knows I'm leaving things out*, she thought. "Maybe later. Oh—here comes Kitta. I figured Izzy would be last."

Kitta came up, waving, and kissed each of them before sitting down. She pushed her chair back a bit and grinned at them. "How's everything? Courtney, you made it! Mark's got the kids?"

Courtney rolled her eyes. "The kids have Mark. When I left, he was pinned on the sofa with one on his chest and one on his legs, watching cartoons. I expect they'll still be there when I get back."

Beth shook her head. "They'll be there *again* ... you know what happened as soon as you left the driveway."

"Yeah ... raid on the cupboard: crackers, snack bars, the chocolate chips for baking ..."

"You've got *three* kids." Kitta smirked.

Courtney nodded serenely. "Yup." She gazed out to the parking lot. "And here's Izzy, late as always."

Izzy waved broadly, grinning, and hurried toward them, stopping abruptly as she stepped from between parked cars into the path of a jeep. The jeep jerked to a stop; the driver looked cranky, but Izzy just smiled and waved at him, too. He smiled, waved back, and drove off, shaking his head. Izzy sat in the last empty chair, reaching down to pet Solar. "How are you guys?" she asked. "I'm sorry I'm late." She sighed. "I guess I'm always late, aren't I?"

"It's not a big deal," Courtney said, leaning over to kiss her on the cheek. "As long as we're all together for a while." There were hugs all around, coffee requests made, and Izzy and Kitta went in to get everyone's drinks. Beth and Courtney sat quietly.

After a few moments, Courtney looked quizzically at Beth. "How's the headache? Fresh air helping?"

Beth rolled her eyes. "Fresh air as in being with you and the girls? Yes. Fresh air as in out of that damned house? Yes." Beth sighed. "I guess that's not fair."

"Everything okay?"

"Yeah, sure. It's great. All great." She paused. "The house is just a little small sometimes. Like on weekends. I mean, Jonah's ..." She trailed off. Beth felt ashamed of herself complaining about Jonah, who could be so sweet. Like last night, when he found the bear, reminding her of their plan. "Fine."

"Not so fine, then."

"Well, you know, Jonah is ... Jonah."

"Mm-hmm." Courtney nodded.

Beth rubbed her temples. "And he's like this dark cloud," she admitted. "Well, not really a cloud; they move. He doesn't. I'd like to dynamite him right off the couch or throw paint on the television screen. Anything."

"Ah. Yeah, that sounds like it's no break from work in someways." Courtney's voice was soothing. Beth tried to imagine what that low, soothing voice was like for Mark, Eva and Mikey. *Maybe I should start being softer when I speak; maybe Jonah would be less irritable.*

Kitta and Izzy arrived with their hands full of coffee drinks.

"How much do I owe you?" Beth asked Kitta.

Kitta held up her hand. "It was my turn. Next time, your turn. AND I'll be getting something huge with extra whipped cream." She smiled, a bit Mona Lisa–like, and gazed into her drink.

Beth glanced around at everyone. Courtney was surveying the table, too; Beth guessed she was figuring out how to orchestrate the conversation. Izzy was ebullient. Kitta was gloating. *It will take a lot of Courtney magic today*, Beth thought, sipping her coffee.

Courtney sat back, smiling around at them all. "Ugh, it's so good to see all of you. Sometimes it seems I'll never have a conversation in full sentences again."

Beth smiled weakly. "Oh, the kids are getting big. Isn't Eva almost five now?"

"Yes, this summer. Next year's kindergarten. And Mikey will be in the three-year-old class. Tune in for me crying up a storm in August," Courtney answered. She grinned broadly. "Okay, sorry, girls, but cute kid story. I can't help it." She looked around the table. "You'll love this, I promise." They all nodded, smiling, as Courtney leaned forward, elbows on the table. "So, last Monday, one of the kids in Eva's class mouthed off to one of the teachers. Well, that's not the funny part but I guess, yeah, it's funny, too. Apparently, she told the teacher, 'You're not the boss of me,' which technically was not a good thing to say."

"Oh, gosh," Izzy said. "That sounds like teenagers, not preschool."

"Exactly!" Courtney nodded emphatically. "And of course, Eva had to come home and try it out with me. Which was hilarious and so not hilarious at the same time."

"Of course."

"So, we had a little chat," Courtney said. "I explained that actually, right now, grown-ups at home and school are the boss of her, and it's not polite to say that to our bosses. And it seems she understood." Courtney sat up a little straighter, with a one-sided grin. "Because later on when Mikey got bossy—you know how bossy he is—Eva just got up, went over to him, planted a big noisy kiss on his forehead." Courtney made a big kiss in the air, "Mmmmmwaaah!"before finishing, "And she told him, 'You're not the boss of me,' went back to her toys and kept playing." She leaned back, grinning.

"So, what did he do?" Kitta asked. "The usual meltdown?"

"No! That's the crazy part. He just sat there staring at her for a few moments and then shook his head and went back to playing. No meltdown, no repeating himself, not even the usual whining for me to intervene."

"Okay, I need some of that," Kitta said.

Beth nudged her. "You? I'm the one. Have you met my husband, aka the immovable object?"

"Jonah's not that stubborn," Izzy protested. "At least not where you're concerned." She paused. "Yeah, well. Maybe he is. Actually."

Beth nodded. "Jonah's great, but don't try to convince him of anything if he's made up his mind."

Courtney snorted. "And that would be different from you exactly how?"

Beth grinned. "Hey! I'm just determined and strong-willed."

Courtney rolled her eyes. "Izzy? What's up with you? Looking a little smug over there."

Izzy twirled a strand of brown hair. "Oooh, nothing. Well, I met a guy."

Her three friends groaned in unison. "Seriously?" Beth asked. "Is that why you were late?" *Not another one*, she thought. *Not another so-in-love-and-then-heartache routine.*

Izzy shifted in her chair, smiling coyly. "Well, seriously worth being late over, anyhow." Then she shrugged. "I know, I know ... but this one seems different. I've known him for three weeks," she added defensively.

"And you slept over. Or he did." Courtney sounded like a disapproving mother.

Izzy looked straight at her. "Actually, yes. But it's not what you think." And everyone groaned again. Izzy held up both hands. "No, wait. Wait." She folded her arms, elbows on the table. "We talked until two a.m. Three pots of tea. Dragged out the cold pizza around midnight." She paused. "No alcohol. No messing around. Then he slept on the couch and I went to bed. He was washing dishes when I came out for coffee. Coffee brewed, waffles ready to toast, fruit cut up."

Kitta shook her head. "Yeah, right. Dream guy, deluxe model. Exactly what drug induces that dream?"

"Seriously. Girl Scouts' honor," Izzy said, holding up three fingers.

"Still ... just three weeks and he keeps you late from the most important standing event on your calendar?" Beth teased. "He had better be something special."

Izzy twirled her coffee stirrer. "We'll see," she said. "But I think he could be. Really special." She smiled, shaking her head. "Men don't usually want to talk until the middle of the night. And then sleep on the couch."

Under the table, Solar made a quiet, whining sound. Beth laughed. "Sol doesn't buy it, Iz. Tune in next month, second Saturday, to see if good old what's his name is still keeping our girl up too late."

Izzy laughed. "Fair enough. And it's Ozzy."

"NO," Courtney said firmly, in her best mom voice. "No, I forbid it. I can't go through the next sixty years having Izzy and Ozzy over for pie every Thanksgiving Day." She put her hand on Izzy's. "Seriously, girlfriend, either start calling yourselves Isabelle and ... Oswald? Or find a new guy."

Izzy laughed. "Mmmmmwaaah! You're not the boss of me!"

They all broke up laughing, and Sol peeked up over the edge of the table, lifting one eyebrow. Beth leaned over, kissed the top of his head and whispered, "Down, Sol." He nudged her gently with his nose before settling back down in the shade.

Kitta swirled her coffee stirrer in what was left of her whipped cream. "I've got a little news, too," she said, shrugging and making a nervous smile. She glanced around the table. "I think I'm pregnant."

"Congratulations," Beth said conventionally, and gave her side a discreet pinch to anchor her into this moment. She kept her gaze riveted on Kitta and smiled.

"Are you sure?" Izzy asked. "Did you use a good test or one of those cheap ones?"

"Three good ones, two days apart," Kitta said firmly. "I have a doctor's appointment next Friday." She grinned at all of them. "Then I'm going to tell Hunter!"

"Hunter doesn't know?" Courtney asked. "Why didn't you tell him right away?"

"I want to be sure," Kitta explained. "I don't want it to be iffy." She sighed and stirred her coffee more. "I'm sure he's going to be excited about it. So, if it's not for real, why disappoint two of us?"

Beth pinched her ribcage a little harder. Courtney shot her a look. "Beth? You okay?"

"Hmm? Oh, yeah. Mosquito bite. You know how pesky those can be." Beth gave a desultory scratch to her side, shrugged and placed both hands firmly around her coffee cup.

Courtney looked at her sideways before returning her focus to Kitta. "You think this will change anything? You think Hunter's going to find out you're expecting and finally propose, don't you?"

"Maybe. I mean, why not? It's been five years, and—"

"And if he was going to propose, it would've happened three years ago. Why are you wasting your time in a relationship with someone who has no intention of growing up past paying his half of the bills? If he is paying his half these days?" Courtney looked annoyed.

"Well, I've invested five years—" Kitta began.

"He's not a mutual fund! He's a guy. A nice enough guy, but a guy who has no interest in marrying you or he would have gone there already. What are you doing?" Courtney went into full mom mode. "Kitta, I love you and you are just not ... ugh! He's not the guy for you. I wish he was, but he's just not."

Kitta folded her arms across her chest. "I thought you would all be happy for me." She wiped her eyes. "I haven't told anyone else."

Beth sighed and reached out, rubbing her hand on Kitta's shoulder. "Of course, we're happy. We're talking about a baby! Who can't be happy about a baby?" Her voice cracked. "We're happy about the baby, very happy... and worried Hunter's going to disappoint you. That's all."

Kitta put her hand over Beth's. "Thanks. I know." She looked around at all of them. "I'm afraid to tell him. I'm afraid he'll leave or start talking about an abortion." She shook her head. "When his sister got pregnant last year, he pushed her to get an abortion, said that having a baby while she was still in college would ruin her life, blah blah blah. It was awful."

Izzy tilted her head. "You mean Cynthia? She had the baby, right? Wasn't that her baby we saw when we were picnicking at the beach a couple of months ago?"

Kitta nodded. "Yes, that was Cynthia, and the baby is Emily. The dad's AWOL but that's probably for the best. Cynthia's on track to graduate on time with her education degree this year, and she's going to be teaching next year. And now Hunter acts as if he knew all along that Cynthia could pull off the single mom thing." She sighed. "So, I'm sure he'll be happy when I tell him."

Izzy rubbed Kitta's shoulder and said, "So am I."

The rest of the morning was lighter, talking about babies and day-care plans. "Infant care fills up quickly," Courtney warned them all. "Sign up for as many as you can now and weed them out later." More advice, more teasing about Ozzy. Beth deflected questions beyond work and how fine everything was. As good-byes were said, Courtney leaned toward Beth and said, "Got a few minutes?"

Beth pressed her lips together and nodded. Of course, Courtney could tell. Courtney could always tell. When Izzy and Kitta had left, Kitta already practicing the pregnancy saunter she didn't need yet and Izzy gesturing with excitement, Courtney turned to Beth. "Okay. Spit it out."

"Huh?" Beth feigned innocence.

"Ah, here we go," Courtney muttered. She put a hand on Beth's shoulder. "My God, you're worse than Eva sometimes. Beth. You're upset. Really upset. Is everything okay?"

"Yes. No. Yeah." Beth burst into tears. Courtney took her elbow and guided her away, toward the little grassy area nearby, ostensibly for Sol's benefit.

"What happened?"

"It's what didn't happen. Well, did happen." Beth frowned and wiped her eyes. "I thought maybe I was pregnant ... you know, I was a few days late, and of course, no. Again." Her breath shuddered. "I don't know what's wrong with me. The doctors keep saying I'm fine, there's no reason I shouldn't be conceiving. But clearly, I'm not okay. Clearly. I mean, we're young. Healthy. If I'm in 'good working order,' like they say, every time, why aren't we pregnant? What's wrong with me?"

Courtney hugged her. "Beth, baby, everything will be okay. You'll see." She rubbed Beth's back and patted gently. Courtney took a deep breath. "Jonah?"

"Jonah's great. He wants me to stop being so sad all the time. He says give it six more months."

"Oh, okay. But what I meant was ... what about Jonah? Is he in 'good working order'?"

"Oh, yeah," Beth said, shaking her head. "He went to a urologist early on and told me everything was fine. So, it must be me."

Courtney raised her eyebrows. "I don't know ..."

"No, seriously, Jonah told me. The urologist said he was in good working order."

Courtney shook her head. "Well, nice to hear *something* about Jonah is in good working order."

"Oh, that's not fair."

Courtney rubbed Beth's back with one hand. "Well, baby girl, whatever's going on ... try to find your peace. Take joy every day. It's a gift."

"I know," Beth sighed. "I know." She paused. Courtney was such a great friend. She wondered, for a moment, if Courtney was this much ahead of them all because of being a mom, and then thought, *No; it has always been this way. Courtney's just wiser or something.*

"No, I'm not," Courtney said. Beth jerked her head up in surprise. Courtney grinned. "Yeah, you said it aloud. You might want to watch that little habit around Jonah and work. But thanks for the compliment."

Chapter 3

"You really have to learn to not let these things get to you." Beth dumped soapy water out of the measuring cup, set it down in the empty side of the sink, and starting wiping out a mug.

"You're not exactly one to talk," Jonah grumbled. "Have you listened to yourself lately?"

Beth shrugged. "I know. I complain a lot, too." She turned toward Jonah and added, "But, honey, you have to admit, you're just nonstop. It's not just work, it's everything."

"So, what are we supposed to do? Just take it?"

Beth pressed her lips and drew her eyebrows closer, considering. "I guess it depends on what the 'it' is and whether we have any influence over it at all." She felt a nudge; Sol was pushing his nose against the side of her leg. "Not yet, Sol," she said. "In a few." He made a small, complaining sound and wandered off. She heard him lie down in the living room area with a sigh.

Jonah finished putting the flatware away and slid the drawer closed smoothly so nothing would rattle out of place. He hated jumbled flatware. "The 'it' is the amount of stupidity at work. And everywhere. But at work, seriously, we're a tech company. Can't HR find non-idiots for these positions?"

"Just because they don't know everything you know ... yet ... doesn't make them idiots." Beth rinsed off the mugs and measuring cup and put them in the drainer.

Jonah nodded. "That, I understand. Don't like, but understand. But just generally, I mean. You can't buy coffee without them screwing up the order."

"They never screw up mine. Well, once. They forgot the whipped cream. But that was it."

"You know what I mean." Jonah thumped a mug down on the counter and picked up the next to dry it. "You're being deliberately obtuse."

"Yes, I do, and no, I'm not." In her head, Beth added, *And you have to get over thinking everyone who doesn't think like you is defective.*

"I mean, I get that not everyone's a genius, but I don't think responding to emails in a timely manner at work, where it matters, should be such a challenge."

Beth nodded. Jonah always vented about work and Beth tried to minimize her venting. More venting didn't seem to make things better, and Jonah was so naturally competitive that, instead of misery loving company, it became misery wants an ultramarathon of comparative misery. Better to not mention her own work aggravations except in passing. There was a pause, and she tried changing subjects.

"Do you think Mac and Apple would enjoy a trip to the dog park tomorrow? Sol and Anastasia could stay here for a couple of hours. I think we could trust them not to be too bad. Or we could crate Sol." She added, "It's supposed to be really nice tomorrow and they could use the romp."

Jonah took the bait. "I guess. Not too early? Maybe after breakfast?"

"Sounds good." She wiped her hands on a towel. "Right now, Sol's waiting sort of patiently for a walk so maybe I'll take him out by himself. Want to come along?"

Jonah surprised her by saying, "Sure," and so in five minutes the three of them were out the door for a neighborhood stroll, pace to be determined by whether Sol needed a romp or a scent-ferreting saunter.

It was a scent-ferreting saunter evening, and Sol had to investigate every mailbox post and utility pole, plus many stops in the grass along the way. They strolled in amiable silence, holding hands. Jonah squeezed her hand and asked, "How are you, really?" and looked at her sideways.

She turned, smiling unconvincingly, and, squeezing his hand, said, "Better. Thanks for being so ... you."

He nodded and said, "The walk helping?"

"Helping?"

"Helping you feel better."

"Yes, thanks." Beth leaned her head briefly on his shoulder while Sol investigated a corner fence post. *He wants sex tonight*, she thought, *and I'm not up to it.*

They ambled another ten or so minutes in comfortable silence, then Jonah said, "So, I was thinking about what you said before."

"About?"

"About not letting things get to me. And you're right, I mean, I know that. It's been a problem forever." He glanced at her. "As you know." She grinned, nodding once. "I guess I'm not sure how to do this. This, stopping being pissed off because of how other people behave."

"Maybe it just depends," Beth offered. "I mean, sometimes it really matters, and sometimes it's just an inconvenience, and frankly, sometimes it's just neutral but not to your—our—liking. Maybe it's determining which is which." She wondered why she was bothering with this conversation, which sounded like so many other conversations over the years.

"Okay," Jonah said. "But, I mean, inconvenience, that could be a big deal."

"It could," Beth agreed. "And it could be that other people have bigger stuff going on than your inconvenience. Or mine, for that matter. I mean, I don't mean you, personally."

Jonah made a skeptical sound.

"I mean, like, the other day at work. You were all upset because Dina didn't get back to you with the data you wanted for the presentation right away, but we found out later it's because the team in charge of the data pulled it back because they'd made an error in the algorithm. So, it was good she hadn't shot it right over, because you would have had outdated information, but you didn't find out instantly. You were annoyed, but within half an hour you understood why there was a delay, and it had been out of her control because, for her, it was last-minute, too." Beth shrugged and changed hands on Sol's leash.

"Fair enough. But that's an exception."

Beth sighed and said, "Jonah, I love you, and if you're going to decide to make yourself miserable because the whole world doesn't have a high IQ and think the same things are critical as you do, then that's your gig. I don't see it working for you very well."

Jonah looked grumpy and said, "Just because you're willing to tolerate—"

"Oh, no," Beth said. "We're not going there. Treating tolerating like a bad word. People do the best they can with what they have, most of the time. Fine, you have exceptional intellectual abilities. Which means different from most people's, which means you should have the grace to be a little generous in cutting people who didn't get that particular gift a little slack." She gave Sol gentle tug. "No, Sol. No digging."

"I don't think that most people are doing the best they can," Jonah grumbled. He gestured in a general way around them. "I mean, does it look like it to you? This neighborhood is a mess." He gestured harshly at the house across the street. "Crap all over the yard; can't their kids pick up their toys? And over there." He pointed to the house just ahead. "How old are those rocking chairs on the porch? And what's with the Christmas lights still up?"

Beth shrugged. "Those people's kids play outside a lot. I think it's great." She paused as they strolled past the house with the old rockers and the Christmas lights. "And those people—you know their son is deployed. They're keeping some Christmas up until he gets home. I think it's nice."

Jonah grunted.

She looked around their quiet neighborhood, older homes of varying sizes, some with wild xeriscaping and others neatly landscaped, some with kids' bicycles and soccer balls in the front lawns, others with rocking chairs on the porch, and said, "Yes, actually. It does look as if people are doing the best they can." She squeezed his hand and smiled. "And so am I. And so are you." She tilted her face up toward his and said, "And you're wonderful."

"And I wish I could see things the way you do."

Beth knew better than to challenge him about his choices in how he thought, and instead veered gently to a neutral topic. "This reminds me of a study I was reading about ... by Dr. Barry Schwartz ... about maximizers and satisficers. How maximizers are always wanting to be sure they're getting the best, the perfect, the 'just right,' I guess sort of a Goldilocks attitude, while satisficers are more content with what meets their needs and don't worry about wasting time seeking perfection in all things."

Jonah nodded. "Interesting. Makes me think of that guy at work. Bill. He can't do anything without a few days of research." He rolled his eyes. "You couldn't be around him at break for a month before he figured out which model of pickup truck to buy."

Bill was one of Beth's direct reports. "Yes, that sounds like a maximizer," she agreed, not mentioning, because, married or not, some human resources issues were not up for discussion at home, that Bill was on probation because his endless pursuit of perfection meant he was always late with projects. His projects were routinely far from adequate, despite his foot-dragging in pursuit of perfection, because he always procrastinated to the point where he was just throwing something together. Bill was queueing up strike three at present.

"So, you think I'd be happier if I would give up on maximizing so much?" Jonah continued. "That the point of your little lecture?"

"Well, I don't know about you. But I'd be happier," Beth teased him. He half smiled, shaking his head. "You know ... okay, you asked for a tall and got a grande. So what? Bill likes to talk about every model of truck in existence. So what?" She nudged her elbow against his arm. "Your sister's a pest. So what?"

"Now what?" he asked. "Does Sandy want something?"

"No, no, just an example," Beth assured him.

"Ah. I thought maybe she had some fundraising thing. Sea turtles or the aquifer or something."

"Not this week. Not so far, anyway." Beth shrugged. "But it's Sandy being Sandy. There's no use getting so aggravated about it."

Jonah twisted his mouth, looking sidelong at her. "Don't act so zen about it. She drives you bonkers, too. Remember the last time she dog-sat for us?"

Beth grinned. "Yes, I remember. I think I found one of her sticky notes yesterday, under the bathroom sink, with suggestions on natural replacements for the toilet cleaner." Beth paused. "To tell you the truth, vinegar did work really well, and I didn't have to worry about poisoning the dogs."

Jonah rolled his eyes. "Okay, one point for Sandy. One."

"You both love animals," Beth offered. Jonah shrugged and she continued. "I mean, she likes all of them, and she would rather control people than animals. Whereas you, we"—she tugged at Sol's leash—"prefer animals we can control. Sort of," she added, grimacing. "No, Sol—don't—no, don't eat that. Eeew."

"Okay, point taken. We both love animals."

Beth nodded with satisfaction. The evening light was shifting, and the breeze picked up. "I'd kind of like to curl up with a book this evening. How 'bout you?"

Jonah sighed a little. "I need to relax a little. I'm thinking I'll poke around on the mosaic. That always gets my head out of work."

"Sounds good." They walked along in companionable silence. The mosaic was Jonah's ongoing project, using bits of broken pottery and glass to create a seascape for the large, empty wall in the open living area. The guest bedroom was functioning as an ersatz studio, with the project, thus far not permanently assembled, on a large sheet of plywood on a smaller table. An assortment of open containers with like-colored pieces rested on every available flat space, including the bed. "It's going to be great when it's finished."

"I hope so." Jonah shook his head. "You know how it is ..."

"The artist's lament," Beth teased. "The fact that nothing is perfect is what makes it worth striving for. Ask your mom."

"Maybe sometime I will," Jonah said sharply, and pressed his lips together.

Chapter 4

It was a soft, mid-April evening, and the windows were open so the fresh breeze could come through the house. The dogs were mesmerized by the smells coming in, with Sol and Anastasia in their perpetual mismatch at the front window, and Apple and Mac at the sliding door to the back porch. Beth sighed contentedly and nestled a little deeper into Jonah's chest, where she was propped up, half reading and half watching the documentary he was watching. It was about as perfect as a Tuesday workday evening could be.

Her phone pinged, so she switched from the gratifyingly shallow bestseller to texts. "Huh." She tilted her head up a bit in the general direction of Jonah's head. "It's your mom."

"Uh huh." Without pausing, Jonah continued, "See, I can't believe the Germans made that sort of strategic error. I mean, I'm glad they did—otherwise, who knows how the war would have gone?" He gestured impatiently toward the television. "Luckily, the generals were all too busy kissing Hitler's butt to take the time to make sense."

"Yeah." Beth was noncommittal on the idiocy of dead German generals. "Your mom. She's inviting us for dinner next Saturday. It sounds like some sort of big deal. She's talking about an announcement." She tilted her head. "Announcement? Like what?"

She felt Jonah shrug. "Who knows? Maybe they won the lottery. Maybe ... no, they're both too young to retire. Can't imagine. Sandy can't be getting married; I don't think she's ever been on a date."

"That's not very nice," Beth scolded. "How would we know?"

Jonah shook his head. "Have you ever known Sandy to keep her mouth shut about anything? Anything at all?"

"Not particularly," Beth agreed mildly. "Still, dinner at their place at six on Saturday. Okay by you so I can confirm?"

Jonah nodded. "Fine. Look at this—I mean, I knew this but still, seeing the footage—can you believe this?" He waved the remote toward the television.

By Saturday, they had speculated on all the possible announcements: Sandy was getting married. Sandy was running away to join Greenpeace. Sandy had finally found a full-time job. "Would they have a family dinner to announce that?" Beth wondered when Jonah suggested it sarcastically. "What if it's bad?" Beth wondered. "Like an illness? If not them, then maybe your grandmother?" Jonah wondered if his grandmother was moving to Florida and quickly changed his mind. "No, the great-grandkids are up there." Then Beth breathed in sharply, Jonah sighed and frowned at her, and they both stopped talking about the dinner mystery.

The drive was fairly short, and, pulling up, they saw an extra car in the driveway. "I wonder who that is," Beth remarked.

Jonah jerked his head toward the back of the unexpected car. "Check the bumper sticker. It's probably Cody. Wonder why he's here."

Beth nodded at the bumper sticker: I believe in the Tooth Fairy. Yes, probably Cody. This was confirmed in short order when Sandy, Cody, and his twins tumbled out the front door to greet them. Marta and Sean were about nine, Beth recalled, and spent almost all their time with their dad.

Sandy hugged Jonah and Beth with equal fervor. "How are you guys? I'm so glad to see you! It's super-exciting here! Come on, come on." She whirled back toward the door. "Mom and Dad made this great meal."

"We helped," Marta added. "Hi, Uncle Jonah. Hi, Aunt Beth." She hugged them both. Beth hugged her back, hard, and smiled down at her.

"Hi, Uncle Jonah. Hi, Aunt Beth." Sean hung back just a bit, but Beth reached out and gave him a hug.

"Oh, it's so good to see you guys," she said. "How have you been? Tell me what's been going on fun."

"We did a beach cleanup this morning," Sean began. Beth caught Jonah starting to roll his eyes and shook her head, frowning; he nodded and went to his default, mildly gloomy, expression.

"A beach cleanup sounds good. I bet you found a lot of junk," Beth replied as they stepped into the house. "Mmm, it smells wonderful in here."

"We found a lot of junk AND we were watching some people fishing and they caught a stingray. A huge stingray! Even though the water is supposed to be too cold." Sean gestured, hands stretched far apart. "It was huge!"

"Of course, they let it go," Beth confirmed. "Right?"

"Oh, yeah, of course." Sean looked indignant that anyone would consider another option.

"I bet it had babies to take care of," Marta said. "It would be sad to have baby stingrays without their mom or dad to take care of them."

Beth nodded and called toward the kitchen, "Mom, Dad—it really smells great." She put down her purse. "Can I help with anything?"

Jonah's mom made her way out of the kitchen, gently touching the twins' shoulders as she went past. Alex was smiling, hair disheveled, an apron loosely tied around her neck and waist. She hugged Beth and then Jonah, and then responded, "No, not a thing. Just be here! We'll have dinner on the table in a jiffy. Your father's outside grilling."

Jonah mouthed, "Jiffy?" to Beth and she shook her head, and turned to Cody. "Cody! So good to see you. How's your dad doing these days?"

"Recovering from the accident really well, thanks." Cody was opening a wine bottle. "Actually, he's pretty much better. He's giving my mom a ton of trouble, of course, but that's nothing new." He yanked out the cork.

"It must be hard for her," Beth offered.

Alex chimed in from the dining area, "Gloria's driving him crazy. I think she can't decide whether to push him to back to normal faster than humanly possible or if she's terrified he'll overdo, relapse, and be an invalid forever. Sometimes she pushes, sometimes she tries to slam on the brakes."

Cody nodded, putting the wine on the table. "Exactly. Mom likes control and apparently, whatever else happened in that accident, Dad's controllability got reset. He used to pretend to go along. Now there's a lot more pushback." He laughed. "It's been interesting." He headed into the kitchen. "Marta? Sean? Milk or apple juice?"

"Apple juice," Sean said.

Marta added, "In wine glasses. Like the grown-ups, so we can toast, too."

"Toasting?" Jonah asked. "What are we toasting?"

Joe came in from the backyard with a plate piled with grilled steaks. "Okay! Dinner's ready! Let's go! Everyone, wash up and get ready to chow down."

"What are we toasting? Did I miss something?" Jonah whispered to Beth as they went in to take their seats. There were extra chairs pulled up. Cody and Sandy slipped into the middle two on one side, with a twin tucked in next to each of them. The other side had two chairs, so Beth and Jonah sat there, and Alex and Joe took the ends.

Beth shook her head. "I don't know. It's an announcement." She was watching the other side of the table.

"Dinner is going to be great. The steaks are all grass-fed, organic. No antibiotics, no hormones, no nothing." Sandy sighed contentedly, and then leaned forward toward Beth and Jonah, adding a bit more quietly, "Mom and Dad are finally coming around." Before either Beth or Jonah could reply, Cody winked at them and rubbed Sandy's back.

"It's going to be delicious," Cody said. Beth gave Jonah just a tap of a warning kick under the table and he flinched and then made a very slight nod. *Good*, Beth thought, *he's going to keep a rein on his tongue today.*

The table was heaped with food: a large bowl of green salad, a plate with cut-up chunks of avocado, baked sweet potatoes, the steaks, fresh from the grill, and a sliced loaf of crusty bread. Joe poured everyone a glass of wine except the twins, who were holding their apple juice–filled wineglasses in anticipation.

"Let's say grace first," Alex suggested, "And then, Joe, you can do the toast." She folded her hands and closed her eyes. Beth watched the twins adopt the same posture as Alex, as did Cody. Sandy loosely intertwined her fingers, as did Joe. She folded her hands, glanced sideways at Jonah stubbornly refusing to play along, and then reached over to hold his hand, as if this was what they always did for prayer. Alex opened her eyes, scanned the table, smiling, closed her eyes, and said the same, simple prayer Jonah and Sandy had learned as children. Everyone chimed in, "Amen."

Joe stood up, clearing his throat. *Oh, no*, Beth thought, *please don't*, and then Joe began. "Jonah, Beth, thanks for being here. Sandy, Cody, Marta, and Sean, thank you. This is a big day for your mom and for me. Well, your aunt," he added in Cody and the twins' direction. "And we wanted to share the news with you all and celebrate."

"Celebrate what?" Jonah interrupted, but his father was undeterred from what were apparently prepared remarks.

Joe continued. "We've been working at the college for a long time, and retirement looms in the next few years." Joe paused. "I guess that's redundant. Well, our nest is basically empty." Beth again kicked Jonah under the table. He looked at her in annoyance and she glanced over at Sandy and back to him; he nodded. Joe was still talking. "I've had a years-long dream of a research project, a sabbatical journey, a time to explore, learn, and gather the methods and experiences of fishing among the eastern American indigenous people, as well as the experience of modern fly fishing and other methods up and down the eastern U.S."

Please don't, please don't, Beth thought. The food is getting cold and you know how Jonah gets about cold food. She tried, hopelessly, to send telepathic messages to Joe, who had, as she'd feared, slipped into professor mode.

"Enough with the lecture, professor," Alex interrupted, smiling. "The food's getting cold. Let's rock and roll here." Jonah jerked his head toward his mother in surprise. She winked at him and then turned back to her husband, crinkling her nose.

"Oh. Right." Joe grimaced. "Sorry, folks." He lifted his glass. "To your mother. And to me, who each have a sabbatical year starting after this spring semester, and to our adventures, together and apart. Cheers!"

They all replied, "Cheers," and clinked glasses. Marta was very gentle, Sean only a little less so. "Nice job toasting," Beth complimented them.

"Thanks," Marta said.

"Aunt Alex let us practice with chocolate milk this morning," Sean added, "in plastic cups."

"Ah," Beth said. "That was smart. Good job." Sean grinned at her. Beth turned toward Joe, who was starting the rotation of serving dishes. "So, the sabbatical ... you're fishing. And researching," she added quickly. "What about Alex?"

"She's got a full agenda," Joe said, putting a small steak on Marta's plate and handing the platter on to Sandy. "She can tell you all about it; I can hardly keep it all straight."

"Mom?" Jonah asked. "You never mentioned a sabbatical. Unlike Dad." Joe nodded; that seemed fair.

Alex smiled and heaped salad on her plate, then passed the salad bowl to Jonah. "Living the dream, Jonah." She shook a loose wave of hair back from her face. "Seriously, taking some classes, doing some art, going up to the Georgia mountains for a couple of months in the fall."

"What classes?" Cody asked. "Art? I'm guessing."

"I've started one art class already. Doing some more during the summer, as well as an ornithology course." Alex glanced over at Beth and Jonah. "Don't laugh." She shrugged. "Or, heck, go ahead and laugh. It is pretty funny."

"The mountains in Georgia?" Jonah asked. "Where?"

"Outside of Helen." Alex poked a fork through a chunk of avocado. "One of the other librarians and her husband have a place up there; they're renting it to me for a song for most of the fall, so I'll have plenty of time to hike, do art, do some studying."

"That sounds fun," Beth remarked.

"Don't even think about it," Sandy interrupted. "She's already laid down the law. Almost no visitors. I did hear that already." Sandy shook her head with disapproval at her mother's unsociability, and added, "But at least Mom's getting out of her rut."

"That's not nice," Marta remarked. "I don't think Aunt Alex is in a rut."

"Thank you, Marta," Alex said mildly. "Sandy thinks doing things the same way twice qualifies as a rut."

"Ouch," Sandy said in mock indignation.

"Dad? What about you?" Jonah interrupted.

"Me? I have a whole road trip planned, up the Eastern Seaboard and then back south, just trying to stay ahead of the worst of the winter. Unlike your mother"—he nodded down the table toward Alex—"I am encouraging participation. So, if you'd like to fly up and join me, or drive up, let me know either where, and I'll let you know the when, or when, and I can tell you the where." He poured a little more wine into his glass, adding, "I expect to have the itinerary worked out by the end of May. Objective: head out in late July."

"Any chance you'll be spending much time in the Carolinas?" Jonah asked. "I wouldn't mind a bit of that." Beth turned to Jonah in surprise. He caught her look and made a quick, questioning face as if to wonder why she would look astonished.

Joe nodded. "Yes, but I'm not sure if I'm going to head north first, so I can get to Maine before it's miserably cold for fishing purposes, and then work my way south. I might be doing New England in the fall and hitting winter and early spring in the south."

"I'll be here by Thanksgiving, so Dad's planning a sabbatical break at home from Thanksgiving through New Year's, and then off on the road again," Alex chimed in. "Sean, do you need more bread and butter?"

"Yes, please," Sean replied. "Will I be able to go fishing with Uncle Joe?"

Joe tilted his head toward Cody, who looked down at Sean, grinning. "You think you'll like hanging out with a bunch of us old guys, fishing and telling ghost stories around a campfire, huh?"

"Oh, yes," Sean said.

"Well, then, we'll make it work," Cody said. "Uncle Joe, just guessing ... Dad's been pestering Mom about being ready for a fishing trip; confirming that this is it?"

Joe nodded. "Yes."

"So, Bob's really is doing that much better?" Beth asked. "I'm so glad to hear it."

"It's a relief," Cody agreed. He turned toward Jonah. "Do you think you'll want your dad to yourself, or would you mind company?" He glanced at Sandy, adding, "Aidan will want to go, no doubt, but he'll have to work around school holidays. Probably spring break next year for the public schools."

"Aidan is ...," Jonah started.

"Rachel's boyfriend," Sandy finished. "He teaches history. Dad's going to love spending lots of time with him without interruptions."

"Ah." Jonah nodded. "Okay. So, Uncle Bob will take some time, you and Aidan ..."

"Count on Matt and Tim, too," Alex added. "They go fishing with the old guys regularly."

Beth glanced over at Jonah, watching him try to put on the placid face he used when he was annoyed but trying to be polite. "Well, Dad, maybe I'll decide to just tag along with Cody and Aidan, or maybe get you all to myself."

Beth sat a bit straighter, surprised; she'd never heard Jonah show interest in one-on-one time with either of his parents. "That would be nice," Beth offered. She waited a moment and turned toward Alex. "So, you're not going to be den mother for this one, huh? Nice."

Alex tilted her head and raised her eyebrows toward Joe's surprised face, grinned, and said, "You are absolutely right, Beth. As a matter of fact, those were almost my precise words."

Joe shook his head, smiling sheepishly. "Well, I guess we boys will have to figure out how to take care of ourselves. Which probably means"—he waved a forkful of arugula—"not many fresh veggies."

Sandy rolled her eyes. "Dad, seriously. You can get organic produce on the road."

"And you can get cola, donuts, and fries, too," Joe said, leaning back and patting his belly. "Yes, indeed."

Everyone laughed, even Sandy. The rest of the evening was pleasant; while Joe, Jonah, and Cody stepped out back to talk about the trip, and Sandy was busy playing catch in the twilight with the twins, Beth helped Alex with cleanup.

"So, a sabbatical is a big deal," Beth opened. "I don't know about Jonah, but I'm surprised. In a good way, I mean."

Alex smiled, rinsing off a plate and putting into the dishwasher. "Me, too." She laughed up at Beth's surprised face. "I mean, I'm surprised I actually pulled it together. You should have seen Joe's face." She rolled her eyes. "For some reason, even though I'd brought it up months ago, and more than once, he acted as if it were a complete shock to him that I would want my own sabbatical instead of being, well, as you said, den mother to a bunch of overgrown boys pretending to do research while they're just going fishing." She rinsed off another plate. "I mean, not that there's anything wrong with just fishing. But we all know what this is really about."

Beth nodded. "It sounds great." She turned toward Alex, leaning on the counter and still holding the spoon she'd been using to put leftovers away. "Are you worried about ... I mean, are you sort of looking forward to, you know. Having time by yourself."

"Absolutely. I need it. I need that time in nature, that time to just ... breathe." Alex paused. "I'm going to miss Joe, and Sandy for those two months, but it's the perfect time." She tilted her head, studying Beth's face. "You know, Beth, if you decide you need a few days in the mountains, you let me know." She grimaced. "I had to make a firm boundary with Sandy. For heaven's sake, otherwise she'll be up there on some nature campaign, and I'll never get rid of her. Save the rare spotted milkweed beetle or something."

Beth frowned, snapped a top on the container she was holding, and asked, "Is there a rare spotted milkweed beetle?"

Alex shrugged. "Who knows? Does Sandy actually need evidence of a problem to try to fix it?"

"I heard that," Sandy announced, walking in. "Mom, I can't help it if people don't take things seriously enough."

Alex kissed her cheek and said, "Sandy, you are so full of wonderful, intense energy, and I love that about you. And I think it will serve you better if you focused it through a laser sometimes, and didn't always scatter it through a prism."

Sandy nodded, barely pretending to sulk. "Okay. So, Mom ... Cody's going to head home. Bedtime for munchkins."

"And?" Alex asked.

Sandy glanced quickly at Beth and said, "Well, I was going to head over, too, for a while, but if you'd think it's better that I hang out and visit ..."

"Oh, don't worry about us," Beth interrupted. "The dogs are near the end of their tolerance. We won't be here too much longer, either."

After Sandy had left, Beth glanced sidelong at Alex. "So ... is that what I think it is?"

Alex nodded, closing the dishwasher firmly. "Yes, I believe so. Sandy really stepped up to help with the twins after Bob's accident. Gloria had been babysitting all the grandkids, but especially the twins because, well, Cody's pretty much a hundred percent single parent. But Bob's been a full-time job for Gloria, or at least she's treating him that way. So, with Sandy around all the time, yeah, it seems to be what it looks like."

"Nice," Beth replied. "I don't think I ever would have predicted that match in a hundred years, but seeing them, now it seems obvious." She shook her head. Cody, so steady and dependable, and Sandy, bouncing off the walls with more energy than Cody's twins. Still, the way they looked at each other. The way Cody looked at Sandy ... Beth pressed her lips together tightly.

Alex wiped her hands. "Yes, yes, it does. I guess we'll see what unfolds. Shall we go see what the boys are up to?"

Chapter 5

Beth backed out of Joe and Alex's driveway carefully, gave a wave, and pulled away. Jonah, sitting in the passenger seat, gave his usual grudging wave and then leaned his head back. Beth glanced at him; his eyes were closed.

"Sleepy?" she asked.

He shook his head. "No, tired, not sleepy. That was definitely not what I expected. In any way."

"Me, neither," Beth agreed. "It was a lot of good surprises, but still, all a surprise." She paused. "Sounds like you could have fun with your dad."

"Yeah … as long as I'm not camping and fishing with Matt and Tim, not for a million dollars. It would be all kumbaya and helping strangers find firewood and telling ghost stories around the fire with those two."

Beth sighed.

"I have to think about all of it," Jonah continued. "It's a lot to take in. I think my dad planning a months-long fishing trip is the least surprising thing about it." He paused. "But my mom has apparently gone bonkers and I don't even know what Cody's thinking. I mean,"—he turned toward Beth—"Sandy's just impossible."

"You mean because she obviously knew about all this beforehand? With the remark about your mom laying down the law?"

"No. I mean she's Sandy. Like she always is."

Beth shook her head. "Sandy's very smart, very energetic and full of enthusiasm. Cody seems to like her well enough. Maybe he's kind of an anchor for her, and she's uplifting for him. Perfect system, right?"

Jonah grunted. "Maybe. But my mom … maybe this is some sort of post-menopausal breakdown? Librarians don't go hiking around in the wilderness with binoculars and sketch pads."

Beth laughed. "Oh, come on. We've been wondering for months about your mom. 'What's gotten into Mom? Why doesn't she want to walk our dogs on her lunch break? What was up with the purple hair?' Well, that was Sandy and the beet juice, but anyhow, we've been wondering about your mom being different for months. I guess this was all in the works."

"Well, yeah, but still. My mom? Hiking around in the mountains? Painting and drawing and writing about birds and nature? She's a freaking librarian." Jonah looked out the side window. "People's moms don't just go off and live in the mountains like some hippie hermit."

Beth frowned at him sideways. "What is this thing about looking down on librarians?"

"What, like sitting around pointing to books all day is hard?"

"You know that's not what she does. Besides, she works in a college! She has to know enough about every single subject to help students organize their research! Do you think that's nothing?" She glanced at Jonah. He was staring stonily ahead. Beth took a deep breath and continued. "And she was an artist and biologist before she was a librarian."

She shrugged. "I mean, really, Jonah, you know that. And you know that's where you got your artistic talent, for all you keep it locked up and out of sight."

They pulled into their driveway. Stepping out of the car, Beth added, "I don't think you realize how much you're like your mom. Neither one of you says anything until you're pushed to the wall. You're both very sensitive and artistic—"

"Oh, no. We are not going there tonight," Jonah cut her off. "Don't even go there. I am a lot of things, and like my mom is not one of them, not ever. Beth, I'm tired. I want to relax and get some sleep. Let's just get the dogs walked and call it a night."

Beth shrugged and hung the keys by the door. "Fine. Do you want Sol and Anastasia this time?"

The rest of the evening was quiet. Beth ruminated about the dinner. She wondered about Alex; what had happened? She had never seen her like this: Had Alex ever interrupted Joe in his professor mode at the table before, or seemed so relaxed? And the way Alex had just seemed to put her finger on Beth's need to have some quiet time, as if she could see right through her.

The next morning, Beth got up early, walked the dogs, and then retreated to the back with a cup of coffee. The morning was just breaking; the birds were singing. A blue jay, curious, landed just four feet away. "You're a little beggar," she told it. "You know I don't put out your food until I'm having my breakfast." It tilted its head, making a whiny sound, and she sighed. "Fine." She went in and came out with a handful of sunflower seeds. The jay, now up in a branch, watched as she sprinkled them about ten feet from her chair. Before she was in her seat, it was on the ground with the seeds.

She watched it absent-mindedly, sipping her coffee and pondered the visit with Jonah's parents. *The change in Alex,* she wondered; *what if it isn't a change at all? What if this is what she was always like—and then a lot of responsibilities crushed her?* Beth wondered about herself; *am I changing? Am I turning into some shell of me, just going through the motions and trying to make other people happy? Why does it feel sad to think about what Alex is doing for sabbatical?* She wondered about Jonah's annoyance at her last night, comparing him to his mother. She knew Jonah thought of his mom as weak, as not particularly smart, which was ironic, given she was the one with two bachelor's degrees and a master's degree in a third, entirely different subject area, when everyone else in the family clung to one lane of expertise.

The door opened behind her; Jonah stepped out with a cup of coffee. "Good morning," he said. "Been up a while?"

"Good morning," she replied. "Yes, an hour or so. Little walk with the pups, just for business, and then out here."

Jonah sat down. "It's a beautiful morning," he said.

Beth nodded. "It is. I've been out here enjoying it. And thinking about last night." She looked at Jonah curiously. "Do you think you'd really like to meet your dad somewhere along the way?"

"Yeah. To tell the truth, that whole thing with Uncle Bob's accident shook me up. I mean, that could happen to anyone. And I haven't spent much time with my dad." He shot a sideways look at Beth. "And I know that's my fault. He keeps asking and I keep coming up with excuses." He shook his head. "And I don't really know why."

"You're not the biggest fan of fishing," Beth offered kindly.

Jonah sighed. "It's not that. Dad's been great—anything I want to do? Road trip? Projects? Anything? He's like a puppy, so eager to please. It's kind of annoying, I guess ... I don't know. I always feel busy, and it always seemed like someday there'd be more time. But maybe not. So, maybe now." Jonah shifted. "But still, when I think about listening to him yammer on about history for hours, then maybe not. I don't know. The whole professor thing just grates on me."

"Well, you're kind of a history expert, too. Just not officially."

"Well." Jonah shrugged, looking pleased. "And the old man does keep trying."

Beth nodded. It was true; Joe kept the door open for Jonah, keeping him in the loop, asking if they could get together, anything Jonah wanted—but Jonah always had some reason to decline. It didn't seem useful to remark about it herself. "Well, any part of the country particularly interest you?"

"The Carolinas sounded good. New England in the fall sounds great, just getting up there and seeing fall foliage, enjoying the season. That sounds best. Otherwise, I'll take early spring because it's tax season." Beth made a confused face and he added, "Matt and Tim won't be going anywhere during tax season."

Matt and Tim were accountants. "Oh," she said, and added cautiously, "it sounds like you've been thinking a lot about last night, too." *Better to not poke at his irrational dislike of Matt now*, she told herself.

He nodded, turning his coffee mug in his hands. "Yes, a lot." He turned toward Beth. "What about you?"

"What about me?"

"You know. About last night. About thinking about parents' mortality. Whatever." He shrugged. "I mean, your parents ... we don't see them very often."

Beth sighed. "They're in Maui this month, at their condo. And next month they're flying to Scotland to spend some time with their friends. Golfing. They thought they could pass through, on their way to Scotland, but it turns out that Dad's business partner's daughter is getting married in Maine so they're going there instead." She paused.

"My mom texted about it. She said she was so sorry, but she was sure we'd understand. Maybe they'd be around in late summer." Beth pressed her lips together. "Same old, same old." She shrugged, then turned straight to Jonah and took a deep breath. "I don't think you know how lucky you are. Parents-wise, I mean."

Jonah stared at her.

Beth shook her head. "I'm sorry. I don't know. I mean, look at your parents. They love you so much, and they're so nice."

"Can we not start the 'how nice my parents are' thing?"

Beth frowned at him. "They're normal. Kind. I mean, look at Cody's kids." Her voice cracked. "They're at ease with them. Cody, everyone. Sheesh, have you ever seen what it's like to go anywhere with your mom? Everyone talks to her. She's the one who should be the psychologist. The woman can't buy a loaf of bread without learning someone's life story. She's just ... nice. No, better than nice. She's a really kind person." Beth looked up at the sky. "And it was good to see her seeming like ... I don't know, maybe the real her, the one who was a crazy wildlife biologist and artist back in the day."

"I guess." His voice was clipped. He paused. "Well, poor little Bethie, should I make some breakfast? I'm starved ... how about I make up some pancakes? Blueberry?"

I'm not taking the bait, Beth thought, staring hard at the back fence. She nodded, rising. "Sounds good, thanks. I'll make us more coffee." They went inside.

Later, when they had finished cleaning breakfast, walked the dogs again, and were ensconced on the couch with their books, Beth looked up to watch Jonah reading. He was frowning one moment, quizzical the next; she smiled. The real him, the one not so carefully curated to keep people at bay, always showed up on his face when he was reading. She reached over and tickled his foot. He flinched reflexively, looked up, half smiled at her. "Nothing," she said. "You're just so cute when you read."

He shook his head, smiling, said, "You, you're the cute one," and went back to his reading.

"I'm thinking," she said, and he looked up. "I'm thinking,"she repeated.

"Which you are always doing," he finished.

"No, I'm thinking about putting in to have my job partly remote. Work from home, I mean. Maybe half-time."

Jonah put his book down on his lap. "Work from home, or are you planning to run away to the mountains with my mom?"

Boy, he pays attention more than you'd think, Beth thought. But aloud she said, "No, here, with the dogs. Maybe a little less stress will help with ... you know what they say. Just relax, you'll get pregnant." She sighed. "Plus, if we do end up having to go with IVF, it will be easier to navigate if I'm working from home. The schedule is crazy and completely unpredictable, all lab-results driven."

"Is it doable?" Jonah wondered.

"I'm sure we can work something out. I really need to rest, to get healthier."

Jonah frowned at her, closing his book. "Oh, come on, Beth. Here we go with the babies again. We have a perfectly nice life, lots of freedom, dogs for my mother to fuss over. It's not like you need to recreate your perfect childhood."

"Jonah."

"Fine, fine. Work at home. Whatever. Is it doable? Will the company go for it?"

"I sort of put out feelers a while ago. Since I'm director of a couple of locations, I'm never on-site for anyone all the time, anyway. Plus, that means they can use my space for flex for other people. We've been adding staff and there's not enough space for everyone."

Jonah nodded slowly. "It sounds good. I guess see what happens. It'll make things easier with the dogs, for sure." He lifted his book, opened it, and added, "Just don't turn into some crazy hermit, okay? Dye your hair purple and lose your comb, you know?"

Like your mom? Beth wondered, but aloud she just said, "I'll give it my best shot." She stared at her book but the words on the page were blurry; she sighed and closed the book, standing up. "I think I'll go check on the laundry."

Jonah just grunted, not looking up.

Chapter 6

It was impossibly hot, and it was only May. Beth grimaced as she readied Sol and Anastasia for their midday walk. *No wonder Alex gave up helping out with this,* she thought. Aloud she said, "Okay, guys, this is going to be short and sweet. Just business. We can have fun this evening." Sol snorted and Anastasia nipped his back foot. Shaking her head, Beth stepped out into the day.

This was an advantage of working from home; no rushing home at lunchtime, figuring out which of them was more available. Besides the more leisurely mornings, this was probably the main time advantage. Then there were the chores. Being home all day meant stealth chores: the laundry in the washer just before the 8:00 a.m. meeting, the quick transfer to the dryer during the stretch break. The overall effect was that their evenings were less stressed: hers because the chores were mostly done, Jonah's because now Beth was doing a majority of the chores.

"But you're doing the hermit thing," Jonah had complained last night. "You even blew off the Saturday coffee two weeks ago, for, what? The first time ever?" Beth had shrugged it off; she reminded him how tired she'd been and that it was just once. He had shaken his head, making his annoyed but concerned face.

Now her phone pinged softly in her pocket, but with two dogs at a time on a walk, there was no checking it. Returning home, she saw to her surprise it was Jonah's sister, Sandy. *Now what*, Beth wondered. *Some sort of charitable thing for animals?* To Beth's surprise, it was just a quick message:

Hi, Beth, hope everything's good with you guys.

Beth shrugged.

Yes, great, how about you?

Sandy must have been free at the moment.

All good here. Just wanted to say hi, see if we could get together sometime. Just catch up.

Weird, Beth thought, *but, okay.* She texted, *Sure. Have to work around my job. When were you thinking?*

Maybe later this week? Thursday after work? Or Saturday?

Could Friday work? Beth typed. She put Apple and Mac's leashes on them.

I have the twins until seven Friday. Otherwise it's good.

Interesting, Beth thought. She checked the calendar; neither she nor Jonah had anything on the calendar for Friday.

Friday at 7:30; what were you thinking?

How about ice cream? It's hot.

Meet you at Mr. Twisty next to the pizzeria on 49th? 7:30?

Sandy replied, *Great. See you then.*

Beth sent a smiley-faced bear, tucked her phone in her pocket, and stepped out with the greyhounds, shaking her head.

Jonah was incredulous at supper that night. "Seriously? Sandy? What does she want?"

"To catch up, she says," Beth replied, drizzling olive oil on her salad. "I can't imagine." She looked at him, quizzical. "Do you think she's just settling down? The whole responsibility thing? Because it's normal to be friendly with your only brother's wife."

Jonah tilted his head and squinted at his plate. "I don't know. I mean, yeah, it's normal. But Sandy and I, we're not close."

"Maybe that's an artifact of you being older and a different kind of gifted. Maybe the age difference and the difference in ... styles? Strengths? Shouldn't matter anymore. Or not so much."

Jonah nodded slowly. "Well, it could be. It always drove me crazy that she didn't know how to do stuff. When I think about it, she usually caught on about a year or so after I did." He grimaced. "Which means she was actually younger than I was for those achievements." He scowled at his salad.

"Yup," Beth said.

"I wonder why that never occurred to me before," Jonah remarked. "Odd, really. So Sandy is smart, yeah, but you have to admit, she's more than a little bit weird."

"Weirder than us, with four dogs? With a work schedule that revolves around dogs? And a spare bedroom turned into a mosaic workshop? A dresser jammed full of sad stuffed animals?" Beth sighed. "I don't think we're in the best position to judge weirdness." Jonah reached out and put his hand on hers. Beth just sighed and gently pulled her hand out from under his. She speared a leaf of arugula and studied it, blinking hard.

By Friday, Beth was wondering why she'd agreed to meet with Sandy and spent the lunchtime dog walk coming up with perfectly legitimate excuses—reasons, really, she assured herself—to just call it off. Maybe Sandy wouldn't react to a cancellation like her Saturday morning group, with a barrage of concerned texts and calls. In the end, she had a salad with Jonah while he ate supper at six thirty and then headed off to meet Sandy for ice cream.

Sandy was standing at the edge of the sidewalk in front of Mr. Twisty. It was one of those crazy, ice cream cone–shaped buildings with only outdoor seating, a too-close-together cornhole game and a small play area. The two teenaged employees were dutifully playing the owner's preferred music—a sort of soft-rock medley from forty years ago. Sandy waved enthusiastically, hair flying, and Beth found herself smiling.

"How are you?" she asked as she hugged Sandy, who hugged her hard back.

"Great! A little tired ... five hours of twins." Sandy shrugged. "Of course, it's way more fun than Cody's twelve hours of dentistry. Well, ten hours." She turned to look at the long list of flavors. "What are you having?"

"Oh, probably just some soft serve chocolate. Maybe a small sugar cone. You?"

"Well ... I'm sure it's not organic or anything, and the cows probably ate all sorts of processed crap ... but ... a chocolate-dipped waffle cone with chocolate soft serve and rainbow sprinkles. If I'm going non-healthy, I'm going for gold."

Beth grinned and shook her head, stepping up to order. When they were seated—the May sunset was just a few minutes away—Beth leaned her elbows on the table, closed her eyes and let herself take a deep breath of evening air, rich with the smell of flowers, ice cream, and the pizzeria across the parking lot.

"Isn't it great?" Sandy remarked. "Perfect evening after a great day. At least, for me," she added. "How are you? How's work? How's my ever-elusive big brother?"

Beth grinned. "In reverse order ... Jonah's fine. He works too hard and he's incredibly jealous that I'm doing remote work a few days a week." She paused, savoring her ice cream. "He's glad I'm out, just because he's afraid I'll become a hermit."

Sandy rolled her eyes. "As if. You guys are always on the go."

Beth shrugged. "Not for a while, looks like. Things will be quiet. How about you? Work? Everything?" She wasn't quite sure how to handle the Cody question. While it was obvious from the dinner at Alex and Joe's house that they either were, or ought to be, a couple, you never knew. What was obvious to everyone else might not have sunk in; Sandy had a history of being oblivious.

"Work is good; I've gotten some extra tutoring and it looks like it's going to be just about full-time. And of course, I'm with the twins a lot. And editing the dissertation." Sandy paused, rotating her cone and eliminating a few near-disasters of melt. "Aunt Gloria's up to the eyebrows with Uncle Bob, and the twins need caring for, so naturally, I've got the time. At least until school starts in August."

"Ah." Beth worked on her ice cream.

"And you know, spending time with Cody." Sandy suddenly seemed very intent on her ice cream. She looked up at Beth. "What do you think?"

"Huh?"

"You know. About Cody. And me. You know us both, but you didn't grow up with all of us." Sandy fidgeted and it struck Beth how young she could look. "You know. Is it too weird?"

"Weird how?" Beth shrugged. "You both seem happy, and comfortable with one another, and the kids clearly love you. So ...?"

"So being practically cousins. Honorarily, I mean," Sandy added quickly, then burst out laughing. "Can you imagine Jonah if it turned out Matt was really his cousin?"

Beth barely contained a snort that would have spewed ice cream out her nose. "Oh, my gosh. What a thought." She paused, sucked in her lower lip, and then asked, "What's the deal with that? I've never been able to get an answer that makes any sense out of Jonah when it comes to Matt. I mean, I can't buy the personality conflict story since elementary school."

Sandy shrugged. "Everyone loves Matt. Everyone but Jonah. That's all there is to it. Jonah apparently thought, from day one, that since he was the smartest, it meant he was the best ... and when everyone, from kids to teachers to the cafeteria ladies, always liked Matt better, it just got under his skin. And now," Sandy paused to tend to her ice cream, "now, you still can't talk sense into him. Believe me, I've tried."

I can just imagine how that went, Beth thought, but aloud she said, "So it really is just as simple as that?"

Sandy nodded. "Yeah, which is weird because when Jonah isn't being that way, he's fine. Well, okay. Really." She leaned forward conspiratorially. "You know how he is. He always hates any situation where he isn't the best. Like, when he was little, he was really good at drawing. He could draw animals, plants, even buildings." She paused. "And buildings are hard because if they're not right, it's obvious. You can fudge trees and mountains," she added knowingly. "But once people started comparing his work to other people's and saying how he was taking after Mom, he just stopped." She shook her head.

"That's sad," Beth offered. *Interesting*, she thought. *He's the same way about work, and cooking, and just about everything else.* She knew he was secretive about his art, but he'd always justified it as not wanting everyone asking him all the time. No one in the family knew precisely what he did for a living, and if they knew he did art, he asserted, they'd just ask about that because it's something they could understand. As far as Beth could tell, Jonah operated on the belief that his parents and sister were fairly bright but not really up to his level.

Sandy shrugged. "Well, as you know, having fallen in love and married him, he's really a good guy at heart. But for whatever reason he's in hot competition with the whole world." Sandy grinned. "Well, not me. He thinks I'm a loser and dumb, which is kind of fun, in its way."

Beth realized she was enjoying this conversation more than she'd expected. When she and Jonah married, Sandy was still in undergraduate school, preoccupied with her studies, and they'd never really gotten to know one another. The Sandy who populated her head was an environmentalist flake, painted in vivid clarity by her brother, and, to be fair, the real-world Sandy had done a pretty good job fulfilling the description. That time she'd dog-sat for them and labeled all their environmentally incorrect items with sticky notes would live in infamy. "Thinking it's funny that he thinks you're a loser and dumb, that's pretty philosophical of you."

"I guess so. But ... okay, I know husbands and wives aren't supposed to have secrets but it would be better if Jonah doesn't know this one thing." She paused. "It's not a bad thing, but Mom and I have agreed that, well, it would just keep the peace."

Beth furrowed her brow. "Yeah, I don't keep secrets, but if it's some little good thing between your mom and you ..."

Sandy leaned on the table and looked around to see who might be listening. Beth smiled encouragingly and Sandy said, "Okay, so the official family mythology is that Jonah's the smart one and I'm the not-smart one, even if he's the one with a four-year degree and I'm wrapping up my doctorate. But, it works for him and I don't care. Well." Sandy sat up straight. "I guess I do care, sort of, or I wouldn't be putting this out there. Anyway, the truth is, well, I'm not dumb."

"Well, I know that." Beth was confused. *What sort of announcement is this?*

"I mean, really not dumb. I'm in the Triple Nine Society." Sandy paused. "But seriously, Mom knows. Cody knows. We didn't tell Dad because he would just blurt it out in the middle of a lecture."

"Triple Nine Society?" Beth squinted. "What's that?"

Sandy shrugged. "It's like Mensa, that high-IQ club. Except Mensa is sort of like the top two percent of IQ, like one out of fifty, and the Triple Nine—TNS, we call it—that's the top .1%, so like one out of a thousand." She paused. "I mostly joined just because I could, frankly, but the annual meeting is going to be in Florida this summer and so I'm going, and Cody's going to be my guest. Mom belongs too, but she isn't going. Getting ready for those Georgia mountains." Sandy rolled her eyes.

Beth stared at Sandy. She knew the whole family was bright. She knew Jonah had been in the gifted programs at school, but it hadn't occurred to her that Sandy had that sort of intellect. In her mind, smart people did STEM subjects and less-smart people resorted to soft subjects.

"Yeah, I know," Sandy interrupted her, and Beth winced, realizing she'd once again thought out loud. "I know. Psychology, environmental stuff, everyone thinks if I were really smart, I'd have gone into engineering or something." She shrugged. "I flatlined the aptitude tests—equally able to do well across the board—so I went with my gut." She smiled. "My mom's awesome—she was entirely behind me. At least until she found out that it was going to be hard to find a job in environmental psychology."

They chatted a while longer, made enthusiastic promises to get together again soon, and Beth headed home. It was nearly nine o'clock, and Jonah was stretched out on the couch with Anastasia on his belly.

He waved at her when she walked in. "I'd get up but I have Her Majesty," he apologized.

Beth smiled and leaned over to kiss him and then Anastasia. "No worries. How's the evening?"

"Great. Lazy. How's Sandy?" He was absent-mindedly massaging Anastasia's shoulders and neck.

"It was fun. Interesting," she added.

"I bet." There was a tinge of sarcasm. "Did she lecture you about anything?" Jonah stroked Anastasia's ears.

"No, not at all," Beth replied. "You're spoiling her. No wonder she never wants to let me get anything done." She shook her head. "Did you walk the dogs for bedtime yet?"

"Not yet."

"Don't get up—I've got ice cream to walk off." Beth added to herself, *And I've got some thinking to do.*

Chapter 7

"I was thinking," Jonah said lazily, leaning his head back over the arm of the sofa so he could see Beth in the kitchen. He had put the documentary on space travel on mute.

Beth grinned over her shoulder. "What? You? Thinking?" She tossed her head. "Crazy talk."

Jonah laughed at her. "Smartass. Seriously, I was thinking." He hoisted himself upright and knelt on the sofa, arms on the back as if he were behind a podium. "Why aren't we having more fun?"

Beth put down the spoon she'd been using to stir chili and turned to him, slightly stunned. "I'm sorry? What?"

"Fun. Fun. *Fuuuuuun.*" He stretched out his hands like a jazz dancer. "You know. Fun. I mean, if you get pregnant—"

"When. When we get pregnant," she interrupted.

"Right, right, WHEN we get pregnant, everything's going to change. In a good way, I mean, but this is it. The time when we can do whatever we want and not have to be, you know, with kids. Otherwise, we'll be my parents' ages and talking about sabbatical adventures like elderly college seniors."

"Oh, that's not nice," Beth said reflexively. "And it's not fair. To them, I mean. Or to us." She folded her arms and leaned back against the counter, head tilted. "Are you saying we don't have fun? That I'm not fun?"

"No. No, that's not what I'm saying. I mean, we should be having the kinds of adventures best had, well, now. When we're young and healthy and unencumbered."

"Except for four dogs and our jobs." Beth turned to stir dinner again. "So ... what exactly would be fun?" She felt her eyes starting to burn. *Here we go, another litany of complaints about me.*

Jonah got up, walked closer, and leaned on the breakfast bar. "Beth. I didn't mean we don't have fun. I meant ..." He sighed. "We always do this."

"I'm not doing anything. You said we should have more fun. Or you asked why we're not having more fun, and I'm waiting to hear what that means, exactly. Or sort of. What it means, sort of, that's a start." Beth kept her back turned, blinking back tears. *Now I'm no fun,* she thought. *He wants to watch endless documentaries and collect dogs, and I'm the boring one.* She had that familiar tight, shaky feeling in her chest.

"Beth. I want a do-over." Jonah paused. "We have a great life, and I think we ought to have more fun." She turned to see him making a puzzled face. "We should be ... mindful. That's it. We should be deliberate about how we have fun. How we spend our time." He gestured loosely over his shoulder at the frozen television screen. "Like this. It's all right, but ..."

"But you're the one who put it on," Beth said shortly. "Meanwhile, in the past two months, I've mentioned the beach, the parks, paddleboarding, kayaking, cycling, seeing a movie, taking a cooking class … oh, and an outdoor jazz concert at the city park." She gave the chili an angry poke and was punished with a splatter across the stovetop. She ticked off her fingers, "And it was no, no, no, no, no, no, no, and no." She shook her head. "I guess I don't come up with fun suggestions, huh."

"That's not what I meant," Jonah protested. "Beth, honey. You know what I mean."

"No, I do not know what you mean, Jonah. Maybe I'm not smart enough to understand."

"I mean … we talk about fun stuff, but it never happens. I'm saying let's just make a plan, a real plan, instead of coming up with a vague idea and then not turning it into a plan."

Beth whirled around. She took a breath. *Control yourself*, she thought. Aloud she said, "Fine. Any given evening between now and the end of the month, you plan something and let me know. I'm free. And any Saturday except the second Saturday morning. You go first. Because I'm tired of suggesting things and being shot down." And she turned back to the chili, turned off the stove, and added, "Dinner in ten minutes."

"Okay. I will." Jonah was subdued.

Dinner was quiet. They talked about work and whether Apple and Mac were getting enough exercise in the cooler parts of the day this time of year. Jonah was excited about a new work project; Beth encouraged that line of conversation. It wasn't her project, but one of her staff was involved, and it was helpful to hear how things were going. She poked at her chili and wondered if Jonah was as bad at communicating at work as he was with her these days. She'd broached the subject, somewhat awkwardly, with the peer who managed Jonah.

"My husband ... Jonah ...," she'd begun, as they prepared their cups of coffee for one of her few in-office appearances—a command performance for all managers at her level and above. Arthelle had grinned. "Ah, Jonah. Yeah. He's a good guy." She laughed at Beth's face. "Seriously. Are you surprised or something?" Arthelle tore three packets of sweetener and dumped them into her cup. "This coffee is swill," she remarked, and then turned her attention back to Beth. "He's a good worker, creative, willing to put his ideas out there. Not always the best at collaboration."

Beth smiled. "Yeah, that's not a big surprise."

Arthelle nodded. "How do you two even navigate chores? I mean, does he ever work with you, or do you just divide and conquer?"

Beth sighed. "We've always been the perfect team for divide and conquer. Working together ... I dunno." She half smiled. "We can't even put up a tent together without bickering."

Arthelle tilted her head and looked Beth straight in the eyes. "I say this as a friend. And as someone who's been married a long, long time. That's going to get old really fast, honey. Especially when the babies start coming." Beth was sure Arthelle saw her flinch but graciously said nothing—just gave the small, pressed-lip smile that signals pain has been truly seen and understood. Arthelle went on, "So either you two get a rowboat or get a marriage counselor. One or the other. Or it's going to be a long fifty years."

"Rowboat?"

"Sure." Arthelle stirred two creamers into her coffee and turned to go to the meeting. "Either you learn to row together, or you get into trouble. There's no 'every man for himself' in a rowboat. Rowboat or therapist, Beth. Trust me."

Jonah had wrapped up a story about work and looked at her quizzically. "Beth? Are you there?"

She smiled blandly. "Yes, sorry. Got sidetracked about work. You mentioned Rocco and I was thinking about Arthelle. His boss. Your boss."

Jonah nodded. "Yeah, she's really sharp. I don't think she misses anything. I mean *anything*."

"What makes you say that?" Beth figured getting Jonah to talk would lead him off track from asking her what they'd discussed.

"Oh, you know. Some project will be not quite right. Like the presentation about benefits for new employees, and she just zeros in on the place in the video portion that's not quite smooth or the only typo in the handouts. But she always points it out ... gracefully. Yeah," Jonah finished, "Gracefully."

"Mm-hmm." Beth nodded.

"And you? What about you guys? I mean, I understand, management and blah blah blah ..."

"Oh, yeah. We were talking before the meeting this morning, getting coffee. She was talking about rowboats." She paused.

"Yeah, well, that's pretty arcane." Jonah shook his head.

"Maybe. Maybe it was metaphorical or maybe literal. She said people who can't get along, can't work together, it's like ... they need to learn to row together, so they don't just spin in circles or go nowhere or something ..."

Jonah frowned. "Oh. Like us." He looked straight at Beth. "Maybe we should go rowing."

She looked down and stirred what was left of her chili, topped with a few strands of melted cheese just cool enough to congeal. "Maybe so." Then she looked up and asked, "So ... when are you going to arrange that?"

He blinked a few times. "Oh, yeah. Right. Maybe week after next? If the weather's okay."

Beth nodded, lips pressed together. *Always, always,* she thought, *this is always how it goes.* "Sure. Let me know," she said aloud, and stabbed a kidney bean with her fork.

Chapter 8

Beth sipped her first cup of coffee, staring at the calendar on the kitchen wall. They hardly ever used it, but Alex had put together a calendar with pictures of the family, their dogs, and local scenery as a Christmas gift, and it seemed wrong to not at least hang it up. May featured Beth and Jonah with all four dogs. She grimaced, turning and shaking her head. *Happy Mother's Day to me*, she thought, and blinked back the automatic wetness in her eyes. She'd skipped the monthly coffee the day before Mother's Day—too much to take, she thought—but had that ice cream outing with Sandy. Late May was dragging by, the endless days and work weeks that seemed to be ten days long, followed by weekends that seemed to simultaneously drip with inertia and zip past.

She got Solar and Anastasia ready for their long morning walk. The Florida summer always arrived early, and the mid-day and later-day walks were shorter. "Come on, kids," she said quietly, and slipped out the door.

It was not quite light. The birds were singing. The mockingbird in their hedge was going through his drill of calls, repeating each twice and then repeating the sequence. "Nice work," she said as she passed, and was rewarded with the renewed sequence. The air was thick with the scents of plumeria and night jasmine, the sky just beginning to turn pink in the east, and the brightest stars and planets still visible in the lightening sky. It was Beth's favorite time of day—quiet, peaceful, and it always felt as if it were some secret she was a part of, the beginning of a new day. She had never understood why people didn't pour outside to see this. "They miss the whole thing! How can they stand it?" she had wondered aloud to Jonah, and he had grumbled, "They're smart enough to get up when it's daytime, that's how," and rolled his eyes at her. Jonah was not a morning person.

Beth strolled along, letting the dogs set the pace. There was no hurry; she had two hours before she had to sign in at 8:00 a.m. and needed to walk all four dogs and have a clean shirt and makeup on in time. Actually, she thought, no makeup needed; there were no meetings online today. Still, just in case ... she'd been caught with five minutes' notice for an all-management video meeting before, with just enough time to barely resolve her bed hair and change out of a yoga shirt.

She wondered about Arthelle's remarks. She didn't think Jonah would go for counseling. She suspected he'd say something sarcastic about his sister and Rachel, Sandy's best friend, a guidance counselor, and suggest maybe she, Beth, should get some help. She sighed and Solar paused, looking up, one eyebrow raised. She smiled and petted his face. "Good boy," she cooed, and he went back to the business of investigating the smells of dawn. Beth wondered about counseling, about what good it would do. Jonah had sulked and rolled his eyes through their entire required premarital session, when the counselor went over their questionnaires—all about parenting, faith, money, expectations for marriage, family of origin—as if it were a waste of time and treated the premarital retreat the same way. "What a bunch of tripe," he had complained on the ride home. "I thought it was good," Beth had said mildly. Jonah had pressed his lips together in a flat line and nodded as if that meant something.

"What's that supposed to mean?" Beth asked.

"Huh?"

"The little grimace and the nod. Like you suspected I would think it was good. And like that means something."

"You're imagining things," Jonah had answered, and she had dropped the conversation.

As she recalled, the counselor who worked with the church had told the pastor he gave them a "yellow light" for marriage—no real red flags, but he thought that the groom needed to grow up a bit, that he didn't seem to appreciate the degree to which marriage was a two-way relationship. There were also questions on the groom's openness to children, but Jonah had written him off as an idiot, Beth had flared up with defensiveness for Jonah, and the pastor had shrugged and gone forward without asking them to wait and do a bit more thinking about this.

Beth sighed and looked up at the sky, now streaked with ribbons of pale light that blurred into the deep blue. "What was I thinking?" she said aloud, and this time Anastasia nudged her. "Good girl," she said, bending to touch her, and they strolled on. She'd been defending Jonah since before they were even a couple, since her first days in the computer engineering program.

Beth had been seventeen when she started as a sophomore at the state college; Jonah was two years older and in the same cohort. Two of the other women students, Alicia and Tameka, asserting their seniority and social acumen, took Beth under their wing, helping her navigate the demanding world of the engineering program. They let her know which professors took attendance only at the beginning of class, and which took attendance at the beginning and again at the end; which textbooks were worth buying new and which new ones had only one or two minor editorial changes that wouldn't impact anything but price; and which of the male students were to be avoided. They'd been sitting in the café on campus, sipping overpriced, fancy coffees, and Alicia and Tameka were setting Beth straight on the boys in the class, as they put it. A number of the men of their cohort were obligingly scattered around the café, so Beth's guides could indicate, with a look and a nod, who they were describing.

Two of their male classmates went past. One was dressed neatly, as if he expected to be transported directly into an engineering position, with a tucked shirt and khaki pants, short, curly dark hair, and glasses; he carried his stack of books and walked crisply, almost military style. The other, in jeans and a T-shirt, also with dark curly hair, walked at the same pace but somehow seemed to be sauntering, as if he had all day to get nowhere in particular. They were barely past their table when Tameka leaned forward a bit and nodded in their direction. "Okay, Beth. The nerdy one is Aaron and the other one is Seth. Steinberg. They're the twins in the program." She waited to see Beth's surprise. "I know, right?" Tameka went on. "They're actually identical twins but they decided to bifurcate just to be told apart." She turned to Alicia. "Should we tell her?" Alicia nodded. Tameka added, "It would be kind of fun not to ..." and Alicia laughed aloud.

"Tell me what?" Beth wondered. "Are they axe murderers? What?"

Tameka grinned. "No. They're Aaron and Seth. And today Aaron's the nerdy one. Tomorrow it might be Seth. They switch roles, nerd and surfer. Drives everyone crazy. Their dad's a rabbi, and apparently he doesn't know whether to think it's terrible or hilarious. Great family. Their mom's an artist and their big sister's a pediatric surgeon. But you might want to think twice about dating either of them if you're not into, well, confusion."

Beth shook her head. *Engineering boys are complicated*, she thought to herself. A tall student sauntered their way, pausing to grin awkwardly at Alicia and say, "Hey, Alicia." Then he gulped and added, "Hey, Tameka. Beth, right?" The women all nodded and smiled, saying hi back, and Alicia added, "See you in class, Phil." Phil reddened and loped off.

"And Phil?" Beth asked.

Alicia grinned. "Phil's had a crush on me since we were in third grade." She looked at her coffee and looked sideways at Tameka. "And I think I might be ready to have a crush on him. I mean"—she poked her elbow toward Tameka half-jokingly—"he *has* grown into his looks. You have to admit."

"I admit nothing," Tameka said firmly. "He's all yours, babe. Help yourself."

Alicia shrugged, said, "Well then, maybe I will," and took a sip of coffee.

Tameka leaned in again, voice quieter. "Okay. Beth. Look over to the left, all the way over at the wall. No, you dope. Don't make it obvious. Just kind of look over there. See that guy?"

"The one with red hair?" A Viking in blue jeans was eating a burger the size of his head.

"No. The other table. The guy with the light brown hair and needed glasses." Tameka jerked her head to the side and Alicia rolled her eyes, barely containing a cackle.

Beth glanced over. A slim, medium-height young man, wavy light brown hair, dark round glasses, was sitting alone, with a coffee cup and his schoolwork in front of him. "The guy two tables away from the Viking?"

Alicia laughed. "The Viking is Michael. He's actually Irish, at least that's his story. Irish by way of Norse invaders or whatever. But yeah, two tables away. That's Jonah Bonhall."

Beth tilted her head. "And? He's the class axe murderer?"

Tameka laughed. "No, nothing like that. That would be easier to deal with, actually. I mean, at least with an axe murderer, you know it's a bad, bad thing. No, Jonah's the class jerk."

"Weirdo," Alicia added. "Not like, dangerous weirdo. Like Tameka said. He just thinks he's smarter than everyone else. He barely speaks to us, he makes nasty little sotto voce remarks in class, and forget group projects." She sighed. "The professors figured out pretty quickly they had to do random assignments because no one in their right mind would work with Jonah more than once. He's that bad."

Beth looked at him sideways. He seemed harmless enough. "But what if he is? I mean, what if he is smarter than everyone else in the class? Someone has to be."

"Says the sixteen-year-old who's a sophomore in a computer engineering program." Alicia laughed.

"Seventeen. As of last month," Beth added in concession.

"Plus, the rule of smarts is, the smarter you are, the less you talk about it. The really smart ones don't advertise. They just do smart, not talk about smart," Tameka said firmly.

"He doesn't look mean," Beth offered. "Maybe he's just awkward. You know, like everyone says engineers are. Like they say we all are."

Alicia gave her a look that was almost a pat on the head. "Maybe, Beth, maybe. But watch yourself."

Solar tugged at the leash; they were nearly back at the house. *That's when it all started*, she thought. *I've been defending and protecting*

Jonah since before we actually met. She slipped into the house, took Solar and Anastasia off their leashes and leashed up Apple and Mac for their faster-paced walk. Stepping back out, she forced herself to go back to the issue of defending Jonah.

Have I been making excuses for Jonah all along? she wondered. She answered herself, *Of course I have. I've been explaining for him, covering for him, and going along with his mystifying secret-keeping.* She never could figure out why they had to lie to his parents about their trips, pretending they were jet-setting around and not telling the truth about consulting with fertility experts, or why his artwork was a secret from his family. *I don't think I have the energy to keep protecting Jonah from the world,* Beth thought, startling herself with the idea. *I want Jonah to try to take care of me for a change. But he thinks he does take care of me.* She shook her head.

She quickened her pace, accommodating the needs of Mac and Apple. The morning was in early daylight now, and birdsong filled the air. "I can't believe people are in bed or inside with the television on, missing all this," she said to the dogs, who glanced up and then went back to a mix of hurry and sudden stops for curiosity.

For some reason, she thought suddenly of Jonah's mom and wondered what Alex would think of all this, Alex who just turned her life around, emptying closets, buying new clothes, changing her hair, getting back into her hobbies, and going on sabbatical—and suddenly speaking up. She recalled the sabbatical announcement dinner and the surprise of seeing Alex speak frankly to Joe instead of silently seeming to defer and then sulking in the kitchen, slamming cabinet doors and pretending she wasn't angry. *Something's going on with me,* she thought. *Maybe I should have lunch with my crazy mother-in-law.*

She texted Alex when she got home with the dogs, before Jonah was even awake. She knew Alex would be awake, had probably been for a while already, savoring the early morning just as Beth did.

Hey, it's Beth. How are you?

It didn't take long for a reply.

All good; how are you two?

Beth grimaced.

We're good. Wondered if you were free for lunch sometime. Just the two of us.

Sounds great. Where/when? You're the working girl.

Always considerate, Beth thought.

Tomorrow? Noon? The Greek restaurant?

Perfect. See you there.

Beth sent a smiley face, put down her phone, and started coffee for their breakfast.

Chapter 9

The neighborhood Greek restaurant was family-owned; the women in the family worked the lunch shift, and after school half the employees would be high school students. The front room doubled as a bakery storefront; a larger dining room had tables, booths, and a large mural, which had grown over the years, with whimsical additions by various talented members of the family. At some point, twinkling lights had been added to the lighthouse, some three-dimensional effects had been attached, and there was a slow creep of mural around the edge onto the back wall. When Beth walked in, she saw Alex, already seated, smiling and waving. Beth smiled at the hostess. "My mother-in-law's already here; I'll join her." She headed over. The hostess followed, carrying an extra menu.

Approaching, Beth felt again the small surprise she'd felt at the dinner where Alex and Joe had announced their sabbatical plans. She'd known Alex for years, but she seemed different—younger, and happier. She had sun streaks in her brown hair; the purple dye was faded and growing out. She looked, not thinner, but fitter, and wasn't wearing her old clothes. She seemed, at first glance, almost like a different person, but she looked much more like the Alex in the old photos reproduced in their kitchen calendar, when Jonah was about ten and Sandy eight years old.

Beth leaned over and Alex kissed her cheek. "Hey,sweetheart, good to see you."

"You too," Beth replied, sliding into the other side of the booth.

The hostess placed the menu on the table, smiling. "Hi, I'm Nicki. I'll be serving you today. Today's lunch specials are moussaka with a side of our Greek salad, and that includes a beverage. Non-alcoholic, that is. And dessert, either baklava or tiramisu. Or, we have a gyro platter with spanakopita, a small Greek salad, non-alcoholic beverage and dessert, same thing, baklava or tiramisu. I'll let you have some time to decide. Can I get you anything to drink to start?"

"Unsweetened iced tea for me, please," Alex said.

"Me, too," Beth added. "I'm ready to order, actually. You ready?" Alex nodded, and Nicki took her pad out of her pocket, pencil poised. Beth glanced at the menu and said, "I'd like the main-dish size spanakopita with the side Greek salad, please."

"And I'd like the same," Alex said, smiling. "It's the best."

"Absolutely," Beth agreed.

"Yeah, we all love it, too. Never any left at the end of theday." Nicki patted her flat belly. "I'll have that right out for you. Salads first?"

"Sure," Beth said, and Alex nodded. Nicki left them, soon to return with their teas.

"How have things been?" Alex asked. "Working at home, I mean... on the one hand, it sounds great, and on the other it can be a little isolating." She scanned Beth's face.

Beth tried not to flinch at the searching look. *Alex doesn't miss much*, she thought. *She can probably tell things are a little uncom-*

fortable with Jonah. She hesitated. *Focus on the question*, she reminded herself. "I like it even more than I thought I would." Beth shook her head. "I'm getting more done, and the days I do go in it becomes apparent how much useless chatter goes on. I never noticed it when I was there all the time."

Alex nodded and sipped her tea. "Hard to imagine Jonah immersed in useless chatter. To tell you the truth, he never says much about work, at least to us. We have no actual idea what he does."

Beth grinned. "He's not a big talker, is he? He talks about projects and coworkers to me. I don't have much of that latitude." She shrugged. "You know. Manager stuff."

Alex sat back and pushed her hair away from her eyes, fixing her gaze on Beth and tilting her head. "I don't mean to be nosy. Well, maybe I do, actually. But don't feel obliged to answer this ... but, really, how does Jonah handle it, you being higher up the ladder than he is? I mean, well. When he was a kid, God forbid anyone be better than him at anything. Thank goodness Sandy was born second, and he got to reach all the milestones first."

Beth paused. She'd kind of intended to go there, to talk to Alex about Jonah, but the way Alex just zeroed in on things, as if she had been waiting for Beth to crack the door open for this conversation, was unnerving. *I guess that's why I called*, she thought, recalling yesterday's impulsive decision to set up lunch with Alex. "Yeah, I guess ... well, wow. This is kind of past due." She pressed her fingers into the edge of the table and looked straight back at Alex. "I guess ... I guess I want to know about Jonah. When he was a kid. Probably something I should have asked about before we got married." Jonah had warned Beth about his mousy mother, pontificating father, and flaky sister, so she'd been aloof throughout their courtship and, really, until now. The Bonhalls, however, had always been welcoming. Every time they got together with his parents, he would complain, and she would ask Jonah, "What was so wrong?" Jonah would only shake his head as if she were too stupid to see.

Alex nodded slowly. "Well, Jonah's kind of ... private, I guess. And he kept his romance with you pretty private, too. Except for knowing you were in school together, we don't really know how it all started. It seemed you were in the engineering program, you graduated, and before very long, you got married."

"It seems that way to me, too," Beth said quietly. "Truth betold, well, that's all there is to it."

Alex sipped her and then looked up; Nicki was back with their salads. "Beautiful, thanks," Alex said, and Nicki smiled. "Grace?" Alex asked; Beth nodded, and Alex said a quick grace, crossed herself, and lifted her glass and her eyebrows. "To Jonah. A man we both love and who drives us both bonkers."

Beth laughed and clinked her glass against Alex's. "To Jonah," she agreed. Putting her glass down, she added, "And he does drive me bonkers. I don't know, this whole thing about ... I'm not sure how to put it." She paused. Alex nodded. "The thing is, when I first met Jonah, well, before we met, actually, the girls at school told me he was ... difficult. Not like, mean, directly. But that he thought he was smarter than everyone else and they needed to know he was smarter."

"Not news to me," Alex remarked, spearing some lettuce.

"And, I mean, in an engineering program, everyone's smart. Really smart. Not bragging," she added, "but most of us were around the top of our graduating classes, so it's not like we were a bunch of dummies and there were just a few Einsteins, you know?"

"Mm-hmm," Alex said, taking a chunk of cucumber.

"But I figured they were just jealous of Jonah. That they didn't get it because, you know, when you're really, really smart other people usually think you're weird."

"Absolutely," Alex agreed, and Beth felt a twinge of surprise, and then remembered Sandy talking about her high-IQ society and the pact with her mother to not mention it to the boys. She wondered, for a moment, about the little secret brainiac society in the Bonhall household, where the girls were the brains of the outfit and let the boys believe they were clever because it kept them happy.

"So, I sort of defended him at the time, before we even met. And then started defending him in my head during classes, that sort of stuff. And then when I saw him being left out of things, looking like a sad little puppy with those floppy bangs and big glasses ..."

"You rescued him like a beagle at the shelter," Alex finished.

"A beagle? Oh. Well, yes. I did. I decided I would protect him and take care of him."

"And you still are and you're burning out," Alex said gently. "Is that about it?"

Beth glanced up; their entrées arrived, beautifully toasted on top, generously filled with feta and spinach. "Thanks, Nicki," she said, and Alex chimed in with her thanks. They waited while Nicki refilled their teas and then Beth said, "Well, it's getting exhausting. I mean, was he always like this? If it's not his idea it's not good enough, that sort of thing? Thinking other people are dumb?"

Alex laughed aloud, a real laugh. "Oh, gosh. I could tell you stories. Yes, for whatever reason I could not discern, Jonah latched onto his intellect as his ticket to approval and felt like anyone who didn't know what he knew, or think the way he thinks, was stupid." She cut into her spanakopita with her fork. "Don't get me wrong; he was very gifted, even as a small child. Reading before kindergarten. But Sandy was reading chapter books at four, and before she was five, she'd figured out she got along better if she read in her bedroom because Jonah would find her reading a book he struggled with and get angry at her, start picking at her. Jonah could be intense." She took a bite and was quiet.

"What about Joe? How did he manage Jonah?"

"Joe is very kindhearted and sweet. He sees the best in everyone, and he's so ... in the air, in his own head." She waved her hand as if it were a butterfly, fluttering from her shoulder up over her head. "I don't think he noticed so much, and when he did, he'd just have a little chat with Jonah and think everything was fine. And for Joe, it was fine. For whatever reason, Jonah didn't feel a need to spar with his dad very much. It was mostly Sandy and me, and of course the kids at school." She hesitated. "And the teachers. And the assistant principal. And just about everyone."

"Yeah, and what's the deal with his cousin Matt?"

Alex took a deep breath. "That goes back to day one. Jonah's extremely bright, and he figured school was about being smart and then it turned out that, well, being smart about book stuff wasn't the only kind of smart. And Matt, well. You know Matt." Beth nodded. Alex went on, "Everyone at school loved Matt: the boys, the girls, the grown-ups. And it drove Jonah crazy, because he felt that since he was better at academics, and that was the reason to be at school, that he should be the favorite. And you couldn't get him to let go of bludgeoning everyone with what he knew."

Beth nodded thoughtfully. "So that's it? No big feud? No fights?"

Alex shook her head, smiling sadly. "No, nothing but the imaginary competition in Jonah's head. He couldn't even succeed in making Matt dislike him; Matt would keep trying to include him in things when no one else would, and Jonah would absolutely refuse." She sighed. "I love him, but I really do not get where he got this attitude. We always tried to praise effort, not outcomes, but nothing was ever enough for Jonah." She looked right at Beth and added, "Well, except for you. He's happy with you."

"Yeah," Beth said, but the word hung flat in the air.

It was silent for a bit. Beth felt the softness of Alex's unblinking gaze for a few moments. Then Alex swirled her iced tea and said, "So… change of subject. Joe's putting his schedule together for his road trip. Any particular weeks you'd like to offload your husband? Maybe send him off for some quality time with his dad?"

"Oh, gosh. We don't have anything planned anytime soon … whenever, I guess. When are the other guys going?"

"Well, Bob needs to recover a little more; he's thinking about going when Matt and Tim go, so the boys are along if he needs a bit of help. Aidan is going in late July, after he gets home from Ireland, before school starts, and I think Cody will go along with Aidan. Joe will have company just after he starts. That way Rachel and Sandy can tag team with Marta and Sean. Although those two with the twins … well, that will be interesting. Anyhow, I would say, anytime will work, except I'd avoid overlapping with Matt and Tim."

"Did Joe figure if he'd hit the Carolinas in the early fall or in the spring?"

Alex tilted her head. "I think he's leaning toward spring. The Carolinas are a magnet for hurricanes and I think he's planning to avoid that during the peak of the season."

"I'm guessing Jonah will want the spring, then. That works; Matt and Tim will be up to their eyebrows in tax season." Beth grinned. "Of all the people to choose for a nemesis!"

Alex nodded in agreement. "Yes, Kevin or Cody would have made more sense—but being angry with Matt is like being angry at a kitten or a baby bird. And Tim … well, that's just as preposterous. It's pretty silly but, hey, we all have our quirks."

"Indeed." Beth worked on her food for a bit.

"And Cody and Sandy are …" she said, breaking the silence.

"Almost definitely an item," Alex finished. "It's not official, per se, but it's obvious."

So she's not sure. Interesting. "How are you with that?" Beth asked. "I mean, the families being so close and all. And the age difference."

"It's seven years, which doesn't matter at this age. And Sandy needs that."

"For the maturity?"

"No, for the brains." Alex was quiet for a moment, and then said, "It works better for very smart women to have a partner who is a little older. The head start in knowledge helps, plus when there's an age gap there's less competition. Assuming the guy has his head on straight. And Cody does."

"Oh." Beth crinkled her face. "It sounds like Sandy must have studied a lot of this stuff in psychology classes, huh? I mean, all this tuff about intelligence, and all that."

Alex smiled. "Mm-hmm."

"And you? How's sabbatical?" Beth asked, suddenly feeling an urge to get far away from anything that would touch on Jonah, or the needs of smart women.

"Great, enjoying the art class and the online ornithology class. Getting in shape for serious hiking and being able to carry art supplies around in the woods." Alex rolled her eyes and playfully flexed her biceps. "Loving it. I am just really enjoying immersing myself in the things I love."

The rest of lunch concerned birds, hiking, and Beth's long morning walks with the dogs. They agreed, not for the first time, that people who slept in missed the best time of the day. Beth commented that the birdsong was better than usual this year and Alex concurred. They parted ways, agreeing to do this again, and soon.

Beth wondered about Alex, about her role in that family. She seemed to have a different perspective on each of them. *I wonder what she thinks about me*, Beth thought, and shook the thought off. She needed to get home before the team meeting with her staff.

Chapter 10

"Seriously? Lunch with my mom? Since when is that a thing?"Jonah looked annoyed.

Beth pretended not to notice he was annoyed, continuing to massage Solar's ears while the dog made his best retriever Zen smile. "Since I'm working from home and had the time."

Jonah shifted his weight on the other end of the sofa with a bounce, as if to underscore his annoyance. "So, how is the crazy bird lady?"

Beth sighed. "Jonah, seriously. Can you go five minutes without being mean?"

"Just kidding. Sheesh, where's your sense of humor, Beth? It's not like you think she's up for the Nobel Prize for brilliance."

"And neither are you, Einstein."

Jonah turned toward her. "Beth, seriously. You've been joking about my mom the loon for years."

"No, *you* have. I just haven't argued with you about it. If you recall, once in a while, I ask you why you say those things, and you act like I'm an idiot for not seeing how stupid or ditzy or whatever she is." She caught herself being a little too enthusiastic with Solar's ears; he gave a gentle whine, and she stroked him, giving him a coo, and he raised one eyebrow.

"Same thing," Jonah grumbled.

"No, not the same thing. I was just weak," Beth shot back. "And yeah, I had lunch with your mom and we had a nice chat." She looked at him sideways, hoping to lighten the mood. "She told me all sorts of stories about what a little terror you were. So now I know all your secrets."

Jonah slid closer on the sofa, sliding one hand up her arm and around her shoulders. "Oooh ... all my secrets?" he asked, wiggling his eyebrows, and she laughed. Solar whined in complaint about Beth's distraction from him, and Anastasia nipped Solar's tail, distracting him from their humans.

Later, as they walked the dogs together in the early evening, Jonah revisited the lunch date. "So ... how are my parents, anyhow? The whole sabbatical thing?"

Beth nodded, giving Apple and Mac a gentle tug. They were too interested in a rabbit in the neighbor's front yard. "Doing great. She thinks your dad is going to be in the Carolinas in the spring, but you might want to lock that down with him. No one else can go in the spring, except maybe Aidan during spring break, and Bob, so it's wide open for you."

"Nice. That sounds good, actually."

"It does. Nice to have time with your dad while you can."

Jonah glanced at her. "That sounds morbid."

Beth shrugged. "Well, like you were saying after their announcement. The close call with Bob last year ... kind of a big deal." She paused. "And you really are lucky to have ... your parents. Warts and all, I mean."

"You have your parents."

"Oh, please. Can we not pretend this is the same thing?"Beth scowled. He always did this, switching topics and minimizing things that mattered to her, she thought. "My parents? My job is to be their perfect little narcissistic projection and the extent to which I succeed at making them look good is the extent to which I get their approval. End of story."

"Fine. Sorry." Jonah was quiet for a few minutes. *Of course*, Beth thought, *that will be it. Either he thinks this is enough of an apology and/or he'll sulk for the rest of the night because I didn't let him bully me.*

"Yeah, you just said that out loud," Jonah interrupted, and Beth gasped. Her morning habit of talking aloud sometimes had burst out unexpectedly. "So that's what you think is going on? Thanks a lot."

"I'm sorry you heard that," Beth offered. "I really am. Jonah, really. But you do shut down and just shut me out whenever a conversation doesn't go the way you'd like. And since you're not talking, I don't have much choice other than to either not care or try to sort it out without your input."

Jonah was silent. She looked up at him; his lips were clamped shut and he had that flattened expression that meant no conversation would be forthcoming. She nudged him in an attempt at playfulness; he pulled his arm away and his next steps brought him further away on the sidewalk.

"I hate to point out that you're kind of making my admittedly rude point," she said, straining to find a light tone. She felt her belly starting to twist. Still nothing, not even a glance. She nodded resignedly, and they finished the walk wordlessly.

The evening unfolded exactly as she'd predicted: Jonah was stonily silent, uttering only the absolute requirements. She, meanwhile, did what she usually did. She pretended everything was okay, chattering about the state of their various dog kibble supplies, whether or not Isabelle was going to take that cruise to Alaska this summer, and did Jonah think they should try to get tickets for the summer jazz series this year? Even the direct question about the tickets merited only a shrug. She glared at the back of his head from the kitchen, where she was prepping the next day's dinner. Stacking containers for the refrigerator, she said, as nonchalantly as possible, "Okay, I'll take that as a yes and if you don't want to go to any of them, I'll see if one of the girls is free." She paused and added, "Or maybe I'll invite your sister. Or your mom," and was rewarded with a slight twitch of Jonah's head. Otherwise, Jonah's head remained perfectly still. She shrugged, cleaned up the kitchen, and went to read in bed, kissing the top of his head as she went by. He didn't move, except to keep gently stroking Anastasia, who was settled into his lap.

The next morning was still tense. Beth spent two long dog walks pondering the situation. If past performance was any indication, she thought grimly, Jonah would keep up the chilly routine at least through the morning, and then go to work, leaving her home with her job, the dogs, and a sick stomach. She was looking forward to coffee with the girls on Saturday, but she thought she might reach out to Courtney; she was married, so she'd understand the need to be discreet about advice.

She had a long, mandatory training—the usual annual set of trainings explaining how important it was not to sexually abuse or harass employees. *Ugh*, she always thought, *have you seen my employees? Is this even a risk?* She muted her microphone, used her avatar on screen, and, after a few feints, called Courtney.

"Hey, Beth! How are things?"

"All's good ... how are you and the crew?"

Beth heard Courtney's smile through the phone and felt her belly unwind just a little. "Oh, you know ... never a dull moment. Well, actually, it's naptime. And they're napping. Swim lessons are the secret to real long naps."

"Ah, sounds good." Beth doodled on a piece of paper, swirling circles as if she were diagramming springs.

"And you? Really?"

"Yeah, not good. Needed a little married woman advice, I guess."

"Mm-hmm."

"So ... do you ever find yourself being, you know, just perpetually annoyed at Mark? Like everything he does just sets you off?"

"Well, no, mostly. Well, okay, yes, but. Usually the last two weeks of pregnancy, yeah. Of course, then I was impatient with everyone. But day to day ... no, not a thing. What's up?"

Beth sighed. "Well, you know. Jonah's being Jonah. I just can't tell if he's being more Jonah or if I'm just in a bad mood."

"What is it with you tech people? All that coding leads to thinking everything's a binary system or what?"

Beth rolled her eyes. "Oh, please, it's not that. It's just, well. It's just—"

"Just what? Beth, baby girl, maybe it's both. Or a bunch of things. I mean, Jonah's the way he is." There was a pause. "So ... what's going on?"

"I don't know. I got annoyed with him and said the quiet part out loud, twice. Once when he complained we need to have more fun, which just set me on fire. I mean, how many times do I have to suggest something and have it shot down or postponed or grunted at? And then I accidentally said he was probably going to sulk all evening aloud while we were walking the dogs yesterday. Major screw-up."

She explained the whole conversation, his evasion and trying to always pretend his family were these horrible people, as if the stork had accidentally dropped him, the completely fabulous, into a house full of fools.

"Oh, you're on fire all right," Courtney concurred. "And?"

"Well … yeah. He's been sulking ever since. Minimal response to speech this morning, no response to my mid-morning text."

"So, you were right." Courtney laughed. "That's the problem, Beth. You and I know Jonah has to be right. But that's Jonah, since day one. I mean, no surprise." There was a pause. Beth kept scribbling circles, over and over. "Beth? You there?"

"Yeah."

"Are you doodling?"

Beth rolled her eyes. "No. Well, yeah, circles."

"Okay, circles. As in going around and around with Jonah, huh?"

"Okay, Freud," Beth said. "Yeah. Better than mean faces. That was earlier today."

"Yeah, I figured," Courtney replied. "Okay, so you want old married lady advice, is that it?"

"If you've got it, I'll take it," Beth said, but her voice sounded hesitant.

"Fine, but you're not going to like it."

Beth groaned. "That bad?"

Courtney's voice was smiling. "Not entirely. So, there's a plan A and a plan B."

"I'll take plan A."

"You'd better take both."

"Fine. Ready." Beth paused. "I'm not doodling now. I'm ready to write."

"Right. Here goes. Plan A. Start trying to notice everything Jonah does right. Even half right. Even a quarter-right. Let him know you noticed. Pay attention to small things. Take a daily inventory of things about Jonah you're grateful for. Maybe jot them down in a notebook, five or so a day."

"Okay," Beth said, jotting, *Be grateful. Notice what he does right. Praise.*

"And plan B, if that doesn't work, is see a marriage therapist."

"Oh, no. Not gonna happen. Not in a million years."

"Why not? Jonah? You?"

"Yes and yes." Beth started scribbling hard, dark lines crisscrossing the crazily spiraling circles. "Can you imagine? I can't even get him to go kayaking. And you know how he is about his sister."

"Oh, yeah." Courtney sighed. "Well, I know a guy. Will Garnette. I'll text you his contact info."

"Garnette?" Beth was hesitant. "Like, you know him? Or know of him?"

Courtney's voice was firm and upbeat. "They say the first five years after the first kid are the hardest on a marriage. So. Mark and I agreed before baby number one that we'd get some tips to handle things and stay connected before we were on fire. We met with Will before we were parents, and again afterward. Here and there. You know, just some coaching."

"Coaching," Beth repeated. "Coaching."

"Yeah, call it relationship coaching if you like. And if Jonah absolutely refuses, go yourself."

"Why should I go by myself for marriage counseling?" Beth was annoyed. "I'm not the problem. Well, not the only problem, anyway."

"Hey, you're the systems engineer. Change one part of the system and ..."

"The system will change," Beth grumbled. "But the change is unpredictable."

"So is life," Courtney retorted. Her voice softened. "Beth, it won't get better by itself. Jonah will be more and more ... Jonah, and you'll be more and more bitter, and then you'll be miserable. And feel stuck."

"Bitter and stuck." Beth rolled her eyes.

"I heard the eye roll," Courtney said teasingly. "Seriously. Get some coaching on this. Try plan A first, see how it goes."

"You're the best," Beth said. "Thanks."

"Anything for you," Courtney replied. "And I hear the kiddos getting restless. Gotta go. See you Saturday?"

"Sure, thanks. And, you know ..."

"I know. My lips are sealed. See you then."

Chapter 11

For three days, Beth executed plan A with the same determination she brought to every project. She tried to focus on everything Jonah did that was thoughtful, or helpful, or just not unpleasant. She thanked him for being so nice to Anastasia. She told him how much she appreciated him stopping for groceries on the way home. She wrote down, acceding to Courtney's experience, all the things she was grateful for about Jonah at the end of each day. She kept reminding herself that Jonah was just being Jonah, after all, and times were stressful for both of them.

Unfortunately, by the end of the third day, Jonah was still, well, Jonah. *Look at him. He's not even trying. All his big speech to me about us not having enough fun and there he sits, watching documentaries.* Beth found herself angrier than she'd been before. She wondered if she should hold off on plan B until she'd checked in with Courtney. *Maybe I'm doing something wrong,* she thought. *Maybe I'm focusing too much on looking for big things.*

Jonah had stopped overtly sulking but had not initiated any of the fun he had complained they should have more of before babies arrived. Beth reminded him over dinner that she'd be seeing the girls for their usual second Saturday coffee the next day.

He nodded. "Yeah, rolled around pretty quick," he said. "That should be nice. Get you out of the house."

"Mm-hmm," Beth responded. She sucked in her lips, briefly, and then decided to stay quiet.

They ate silently. *Let him talk first for a change*, Beth thought. *Look at him. Just shoveling food. Could he at least look up? Like I'm actually here?* Unfortunately, that very moment was when Jonah chose to look up, catching her sullen stare.

"Beth? What's wrong? You look royally pissed."

"Huh." Beth stabbed at her chicken. "No, not at all."

"That means that yeah, you're pissed and it's a secret. Well, I don't feel like digging today." He took a sip of water. "Stay pissed for all I care."

Beth felt her chest tighten inside and her neck felt hot. "I'm not pissed. Well, I wasn't, anyway."

"Could have fooled me," Jonah said. He shrugged and leaned back, folding his arms.

Beth pressed her lips together and took a deep breath. "Okay, I am pissed. I'm annoyed, maybe. You said we should have more fun. And it's been weeks, and you haven't come up with one suggestion so far."

"Weeks. Like, two."

"Still weeks." Beth twirled her fork into her food, pushing quinoa in swirls. "And I've been trying to be nicer. You know, after being a little ... blunt the other day." Jonah sat there, implacable. She took another breath. "Anyhow, I was thinking. I think we need some ... coaching. You know, for our communication."

"You mean a marriage counselor. What, some different brand of flake from my sister?"

Refuse to take the bait, Beth thought, *just refuse*. She feigned a light attitude. "Well, maybe. Or maybe not a flake. Maybe someone who can just give us some ... tools. You know. So we do this"—she waved her hand in a loose circle over the table—"in a better way."

"Oh. And I'm guessing you talked to ... who? Sandy? My mom?"Jonah paused, tilting his head. "No, probably one of your friends. Courtney, I guess."

"Well, yeah. Actually, she suggested it, not me. She knows a guy. Well, they know a guy."

"And we're just supposed to go talk to some guy about ... what? That we don't communicate the way you'd like?"

"Do we communicate the way *you* like?"

There was silence. Beth stared down at her plate and then looked up at Jonah, who was eating placidly again, as if nothing in particular had happened. She felt a little insane, as if maybe she hadn't said anything, had just imagined the whole thing. It occurred to her that this was how things went; she would be quiet, he'd either ignore it or poke at her, and then, if she started talking, he'd flare up and she'd shut up. *Flare up, shut up; flare up, shut up*. She wondered why she hadn't noticed this before, hadn't seen this pattern.

They finished eating in silence. She said, aloud as if to the whole house, "I'm going to take Anastasia and Sol out for their walk. I'll get Apple and Mac after," and the house did not respond, nor did Jonah, except for a grunted, "Thanks," from the recesses of the couch. The dogs all made their sounds of acknowledgment.

The dogs were treated to long walks. Beth hardly noticed the evening, just occasionally blowing a mosquito off her arm, her hands full of leashes. *This pattern of flare up, shut up, flare up, shut up*, she thought, and it was as if a slide show of episodes from their relationship flickered through her mind, all the times she'd tried to push back at something and then just decided that Jonah's disapproval wasn't worth it.

Somehow it hadn't seemed important when they were dating. She thought hard; right now, it seemed as if that was impossibly long ago. It occurred to her, in retrospect, that they hadn't dated so much as just gotten into some sort of fuzzy, vague habit of being together all the time. She thought it was odd that she couldn't actually remember Jonah ever pursuing her; he'd been rather passive about the whole process, as if she could be there if she liked. Yet he could be so affectionate sometimes, so gentle. She shook her head.

Other things joined the slide show in her head. She thought of how his mother had walked their dogs every day on her lunch break for all that time and how both Alex and Joe seemed to cave in almost every time Jonah demanded anything of them. She remembered, with a wry smile, how infuriated he had been that time they'd stopped by on a Saturday morning to drop off the dogs to find Joe, his Uncle Bob, and Matt and Tim there, ready to go fishing, and been told his mom was not available; that she, too, had plans. Jonah had grumbled about the unfairness of this for weeks.

Everyone in Jonah's world tiptoed around him, Beth realized. Even his sister was so tuned in that she played along with the ruse that Jonah was the smart one, because no one wanted to deal with what might happen if Jonah realized someone else might be smarter, especially someone he'd looked down on as a fluffy-brained idiot.

Both leashes jerked; the dogs were alert. Beth shook herself out of her thoughts and was surprised to see Jonah approaching with Apple and Mac bouncing ahead. It was nearly dark and for a moment she doubted her eyesight. "Jonah?"

"You were gone a long time and these two characters got restless," Jonah explained. He gave a gentle tug to the leashes and the greyhounds stood still for a quivering moment.

"Oh. Well, thanks. I was going to take care of them. I don't mind walking in the dark." She paused. "Another turn around the block, maybe?"

"Sure." Jonah came alongside. "Let's see if we can keep these characters from tangling up." His voice was light, as if they hadn't had a fight over supper.

Beth wondered if he felt as relaxed as he acted. She didn't say anything, not trusting herself. She felt that shaking feeling in her upper chest, as if something was going to burst out, and suspected it wouldn't be good, whatever it was.

After a few moments of silence, Jonah cleared his throat. "I was thinking."

Beth turned toward him briefly and nodded in the twilight. "Mm-hmm."

"And I was thinking, well, you're right in so far as, I haven't taken any initiative for us to have fun."

In so far as, Beth thought. *Isn't that nice? I get a little concession that I could be right about one small data byte.*

"And I thought maybe we could start planning some things over the next couple of weeks."

"Such as?" *I'm not going to bail you out by making suggestions for you to either accede to and then blame me when it's not fun or to shoot down*, she thought.

Jonah glanced at her sideways. "Well, I was hoping you'd have some suggestions. Since sometimes what I think is fun isn't quite your thing."

"What? Like watching documentaries?"

There was a long silence. They were nearly home when Jonah finally spoke. "Well, yeah. I like learning."

"Oh, and I don't?"

"That's not what I said."

"But it's what you *meant*. Always the digs, always the little, 'Oh, you're the dumb one, Beth.'" Her voice cycled up.

"Shh," Jonah hissed. "Voices carry. You want the whole neighborhood to hear?"

"Hear what? That you're a snob and you think you're the smartest person you know? Well, you're not. No one thinks so except you." Beth had a vague thought fly by to stop, just stop talking, but the shaking feeling exploded into words, words that spilled out in terrible clarity in the evening breeze. "You have some sort of superiority complex and you never entertain anyone else's ideas. You think everyone's dumb, or at least not as bright as you. You're a fountainhead of put-downs and sneers. I'm not stupid, except for putting up with this crap day after day and week after week. I'm the systems engineer and director, Jonah. I'm the one with the bigger salary and more vacation. I'm the one who figures out how to juggle most of the things that make this household run." They had reached the house and she swung the door open, marching in first and not even glancing back to see if he'd caught the door or been hit by it. She bent to let Sol and Anastasia off their leashes. Sol scrambled away and hid behind the loveseat. Anastasia jumped up on the couch and sat, head cocked, watching her humans as if it were a play put on for her entertainment.

"At least we're inside," Jonah grumbled, letting Apple and Mac off their leashes. "The whole neighborhood probably heard your little rant."

"I doubt it. It's air conditioning season. And it's not a rant. It's the truth." Beth flicked a mosquito away.

"What, that you're in management? Yeah, I got that." Jonah shrugged, kicked off his sandals, and settled down next to Anastasia.

Beth folded her arms across her chest. "Do you even listen to me? Ever? You think that was the point, for me to remind you about the organizational chart at work?"

Jonah picked up the remote control and looked at her blandly. "That was the point, right? That you must be smarter than me because you're higher up the ranks? Is that how it goes?" He snorted. "What about that idiot Claymore? That go for him, too?"

Beth threw up her arms. "We're not talking about ranks or Claymore. Are you actually this obtuse or are you messing with me? Trying to get me to shut up? That's what you always do, just act like a jerk until I shut up." Jonah opened his mouth, and Beth threw up a hand like a traffic cop. "No. No more. I'm done. You want me to shut up? Fine. I shut up."

She turned and went to the kitchen, tended to the dishes and the dogs, and went through the rest of the evening in silence. She pretended to be asleep when Jonah came to bed, carefully breathing slowly and evenly, hoping her hair had fallen across her turned face sufficiently to hide wetness in the dim light. Jonah leaned toward her and whispered, "Beth? Beth—are you asleep?" She kept still, breathing slowly. She heard him sigh deeply, and felt him turn away, curled up. She squeezed her eyes shut, willing herself to just breathe calmly, fighting the urge to turn and curl up against him and pretend again that everything was okay.

Chapter 12

Beth was up early. She took the dogs for their walks, fed them, packed up her things, and left. She thought about leaving a note and then figured, *No. He knows where I'm going; he's the one who said it was good I was getting out of the house.* Then she reconsidered, thinking it would be just fuel for the fire to act as rudely as Jonah. She scribbled on a napkin, "Gone to meet the girls. See you later!" with a smiley face and left it by the coffeemaker. She stared at the note and then put his mug out and made sure there was water in the coffee maker. She put his favorite coffee in the maker, ready to go, nodded, and slipped out the door.

She arrived first, as usual, and staked out a table in the shade. It would be a warm morning, but outdoors was better. Fewer listening ears. She wrapped her hands around her cup, letting the heat sting, and sighed.

"Hey, there," Courtney said. Beth startled, looking up. Courtney was grinning, weighed down with her usual tote the size of a small suitcase. "Off in dreamland?" she asked, putting her coffee down and setting down her bag.

Beth grimaced. "Nightmare land is more like it." She got up and hugged Courtney, who hugged back, hard, and then put her hands on Beth's shoulders, holding her at half an arm's length and eyeing her, head tilted.

"You've been crying. A lot. Either that or you're allergic to your contact lens solution," Courtney surmised. She gave Beth's shoulders a squeeze and sat down. "Jonah, I'm guessing?"

Beth nodded, sitting down. "Yeah, big fight last night. Two rounds. I said a bunch of mean stuff I shouldn't have said."

"Uh oh. Like?"

"Like how he thinks he's smarter than everyone else and he doesn't listen and he's the one who complained we never have fun and then he didn't come up with anything fun. Like that."

Courtney rolled her eyes. "And the part that's mean? That's not glaringly true?"

"None of it. Except. Well." Beth sighed. "I realized that we have this pattern and then I realized that everyone who deals with Jonah has the same pattern. I speak up, he flares up, I shut up. Everyone. The other side of it is, everyone just doesn't tell him things so he doesn't get upset."

"Mm-hmm." Courtney nodded. "Yeah, that seems to be the case. It's been that way all along."

Beth looked at her sharply. "You saw this all along? Why didn't you say something?"

Courtney shook her head. "Beth. I did. We all did. You didn't want to hear." She glanced up. "Here comes Izzy. Can't believe she's not last today." She waved broadly at Izzy, who was sauntering across the parking lot. "More on this later, okay?"

"Thanks. I'd rather not share right now. I mean, you're married, so you get it."

Courtney nodded. "Yup." Then, standing up, she called, "Izzy! You're early! Woo-hoo! What is up with that?"

Izzy came over and hugged Courtney and then Beth, who stood up, too. "Oooh, just ready for the day, I guess," Izzy said. "What are you guys having? What's good? Do I smell mango? I'm going to go get my stuff. Can I get you anything else?"

Beth and Courtney didn't need anything. Once Izzy was safely indoors, Beth turned to Courtney and said, "I really appreciate you keeping this quiet. The whole Jonah thing, I mean."

Courtney nodded. "It's because you want me to, Beth. I don't think keeping it a big secret from Izzy and Kitta is necessary. Or useful, frankly. But I get it." She shrugged. "I'm not sure all this keeping things close to the vest is doing you any good."

"What's that supposed to mean?"

Courtney glanced at her and then scanned the parking lot for Kitta. "I mean that you pretend everything's fine. Funny how you do the same thing you used to complain about your mother-in-law doing. Acting like everything's fine and then, kaboom. Everyone acts stunned."

"Hey," Beth began, but Courtney interrupted her.

"Kitta! Right here!"

Beth looked in the direction of Courtney's focus. Kitta was approaching. Her walk was a bit slow. Beth whispered, "Something's not right."

Courtney attempted to whisper back through a smile. "Just a couple of texts this month, no news. But yeah, something's not right." She stood up to hug Kitta; Beth did likewise. "How are you?" Courtney asked, and then added, "I mean, both of you?"

Kitta smiled and blinked hard. "Fine! We're fine!" She hugged Beth. "So good to see you guys! So, Izzy's last as usual?"

"No, you won this time," Beth replied. "Izzy's inside."

Kitta sat down with a sigh and dug a large water bottle out of her bag. "No caffeine, obviously. And it's too hot for cocoa." She looked at Courtney and Beth. "And how are you?"

"Great," Courtney said. "Tired! The mom complaint du jour ... but all is well. You?"

"Oh, good. Super tired. I fell asleep trying to fold laundry yesterday. Thank God I was sitting down so I just face-planted on the couch. And a little ... barfy. Didn't expect it to be so pervasive." Kitta grimaced.

Courtney nodded. "It's hard to explain how different it is from regular nausea. How's Hunter handling things? A good help?"

There was a short silence. Beth almost held her breath. Kitta put her water bottle on the table, hid her face in her hands, and began weeping. She was quiet at first and then sank into the tabletop, great heaving sobs shuddering her shoulders. Courtney and Beth sighed in unison and moved in close, each touching her shoulder and arm, and Courtney gently brushed Kitta's hair back from her face. Their eyes met over her back; it was what they'd all feared and what they'd expected, given Kitta's silence the past few weeks.

Izzy came back to the table, coffee in hand. "Oh, my gosh. What's going on?" Her eyes bounced from Courtney to Beth and back. Beth shook her head silently. Courtney mouthed, "Hunter," and Izzy put down her coffee and sat, reaching a hand out to rest on Kitta's upper arm. The women sat and waited until the tears subsided. Kitta took a long, deep gasp of air and sat up, wiping her face and looking up and around at her friends.

"I'm sorry," she said softly. "I know I should have let you guys know." She paused, looking down and then around. "I was so disappointed. Hurts so bad. And yet ... well, you know. You were right." She looked specifically at Courtney. "You were right. He was never the guy for me. When I told him about the baby, I really did think he'd think about his sister and how wrong he was, and he'd be happy for us." She shook her head. "That's not what happened."

"Did he just"—Beth hesitated—"leave? Just walk away?"

"First, we had a huge fight. Lots of yelling. The neighbors came up and banged on the door to see if I was okay, that's how loud he was. He said some awful things." Kitta shuddered. "I thought ... I really thought he loved me. But he said we had a good thing, and I used to be fun. Fun! I was a really good time for a pretty long time, he said. But he wasn't in it for the long haul. He said, he's not a long-haul sort of guy and he'd never promised anything."

"What an ass," Izzy said indignantly. "What's five years? Nothing?" Beth shook her head at her and Izzy looked puzzled.

Kitta continued. "Which is true. He'd never actually promised anything, he just stuck around and I just, well, I just assumed." She looked around at all of them and added, "And no jokes about 'when you a-s-s-u-m-e.'" She smiled weakly.

Good, thought Beth, *a little spark of humor, being Kitta after all this. Always the fighter.*

Courtney rubbed Kitta's back and stroked her hair. "So, did he leave? Are you alone?"

"He left two weeks ago." Kitta patted her tummy. "And I'm—we're—not alone." She sighed. "I have a lot of deciding to do."

"About?" Beth asked. "You have a doctor, right?"

Kitta wiped her eyes and sat up straight. "Oh, it's been a busy month. I have my OB-GYN, I started making plans for childcare—you can't imagine the waiting lists, it's crazy. Courtney, you were so right on that one. I have to find a lawyer, and then sit down with my parents, my sister, and the lawyer in a couple of weeks."

"Lawyer?" Courtney wondered.

Kitta nodded. "Apparently, I don't have to identify the father for the birth certificate and Hunter would have to go to court for parental rights. I need to decide about that, whether I want to just keep Hunter out of the picture." She took a deep, shuddering breath. "He wanted me to have an abortion. So maybe he's not father material, right? I mean, it's not like we're kids. If he doesn't want to be a dad, maybe I don't want to put up with him for the rest of my life. And co-parenting guarantees that. And I'm going to have to figure out who gets custody if I die and all that stuff."

Beth felt a twist in her belly. "You can do that? Just leave Hunter out of the picture?"

Kitta smiled wryly. "Apparently, yes, since we're not married."

"Whoa." Izzy shook her head. "Whoa." She gave Kitta's arm asqueeze. "We're here for you! Don't leave us out of the loop. All you had to do was let us know."

Kitta nodded. "I know. And I also know you have all been warning me about Hunter all this time."

Courtney waved her hand in the air as if brushing away a mosquito. "Never mind all that! I know a really good childcare center, great infant care. One adult to two babies, separate room for infants, great camera access all day for parents. A rocking chair for the grown-ups, great toddler rooms, too."

"But the waiting lists," Kitta protested.

Courtney winked. "I know a guy. Well, a gal, actually. Let me know."

"And I know a lawyer," Izzy offered.

"Really? Who?" Beth asked.

Izzy smirked and shrugged. "Ozzy."

"Ozzy?" Courtney's voice cycled up a notch. She nodded slowly. "Ozzy's still around. Interesting!"

"What kind of lawyer's named Ozzy?" Kitta asked. "I mean, nothing personal, but it's kind of an edgy name. Not lawyer-ish."

Izzy nodded. "Actually, it's Geoffrey Hamish Griffin Oswald III, Esquire." She said it liltingly, as if it were the first line of a tune.

"Ah," Beth said. "Yeah, Ozzy. Okay. College nickname?"

Izzy shook her head. "No such luck. The story is ... well, he had a train set when he was a kid, and he was sort of obsessed with it for a while. He made all sorts of elaborate adventures, a train around the mountain by piling up living room furniture, around the lake on the edge of the bathtub, and his dad started coming home each night and asking his mom what was the latest on Ozzy and the crazy train." There was silence. "You know ... Ozzy ... Crazy Train? The anti-war song?"

"Is this a joke? Are you just making this up to cheer me up?" Kitta wondered. "Because this story is that stupid."

"Which proves it's true," Izzy replied, slapping the table. Then she looked at Courtney and grinned. "You might want to get used to a lot of years of Izzy and Ozzy. It's possible."

Courtney shook her head in mock horror. "Aunt Izzy and Uncle Ozzy! Too much!"

They all laughed. Then the conversation turned to more problem-solving for Kitta, talk of a baby shower, and then updates on Eva and Mikey. As they finally got up to leave, Beth glanced at Courtney, who nodded slightly. The friends hugged their good-byes, eliciting promises from Kitta to not go silent until next month. Walking away slowly, Beth turned to Courtney. "Do you have a little more time?"

Courtney nodded. "I figured you needed some time. Mark and the kids are visiting his parents for the morning." She paused. "More coffee? Just a little walk?"

Beth glanced up at the sky. "It's pretty hot. Maybe some shade." They found a seat in the shade. Beth turned to Courtney. "So, I need that name. The counselor. You'd mentioned the name, but you didn't text the contact info ..."

"Sorry! Mom brain. Will Garnette. Here, I'll text his number now," she said, and she did. "He's really good. I think that him being male helped Mark not feel ganged up on, you know? Otherwise, it feels like it's going to be two women telling him it's all his fault. And it's never all one person's fault."

Beth shrugged. "Well, no, but ..."

Courtney shook her head firmly. "Beth, baby girl. No buts. You picked Jonah, you put up with him, you let him get away with treating you however it is you've now decided is intolerable. If you don't own it, you can't change it." She put an arm around Beth's shoulders and squeezed. "It's going to be fine."

Beth sighed. "But you and Mark seem ... perfect. If you guys are having trouble, there's no hope."

Courtney laughed. "And you and Jonah look perfect from the outside. Mark and I are about as perfect as can be. But we had to work out different ideas about parenting styles. I had to get past thinking he had to be a second mom when his job is to be dad, and he had to be okay with some of my style, too. Then there was just figuring out how to keep the grandparents from driving us bonkers and where the boundaries were. Normal stuff. Just ... life stuff." She shrugged.

Beth sighed. "Jonah and I had to take whole classes in that stuff before we got married. Half a day on parenting, half a day on communication, half a day on family of origin and how it influences our life. In theory, we should be prepared for everything."

Courtney snorted. "There is no such thing. Besides, do any engaged couples take that seriously? Or were you just checking off the boxes to get it done?"

"I took notes." Beth sighed. "Jonah kept messing with his phone the whole time, actually."

"Meaning that whatever he was doing on the phone was more important than learning how to solve life's problems with you, before you were even married. Oh, that's a great sign," Courtney said sarcastically.

"We also learned that sarcasm is bad," Beth remarked, and elbowed Courtney with a grin. "Just so you know." Then she sighed. "Yeah, you're right. There were warning signs all along. I don't know what to do."

"Just call Will," Courtney suggested. "And then just do the next right thing. Nothing's on fire here. Just give yourself time and space to think."

"I will," Beth promised. "I will."

Chapter 13

The weekend couldn't end quickly enough, and Beth breathed a sigh of relief when Jonah left for work Monday morning. They hadn't maintained silence, of course; at first, he'd acted as if nothing was wrong when she came home from coffee with her friends, and she'd obligingly pretended things were fine, even offering a few tidbits of news.

"Kitta and Hunter broke it off," she mentioned during dinner. He'd looked up, sharply, and then nodded when she continued, "Apparently he was never in it for real, and once he found out she was pregnant he took off."

"Oh," he said. "Well, she's better off, then. But it's going to be hard."

Beth nodded. "Yeah, we spent most of the morning on that. Talking about childcare waiting lists and all the legal decisions. You know, wills and stuff. Being a parent and all." She paused. "And Izzy's been dating the same guy for two months now. Some lawyer."

Jonah rolled his eyes. "Oh, great. You know how they are."

"How are they?"

"Pompous asses. There's a pompous ass potential section on the LSAT, isn't there? Because it seems that's how they pick them." Jonah frowned and jerked his head in the general direction of the back of their house. "Like our asinine new back neighbor. The one with all the names."

"I never pay attention. That's what the fence is for, right?"

"The dumbass got on my case about Sol barking. Apparently, there's an ordinance about how long a dog can be outside barking? Whatever! I don't need Ozzy Geoffrey Hamly whoever the hell he is to boss me around about my dog."

Beth gasped. "Seriously? That's the new neighbor? Geoffrey Hamish Griffin Oswald?"

Jonah stared at her. "You know him?"

Beth shook her head. "No, not yet. But I will." She sighed. "That's Ozzy. Izzy's boyfriend." She paused. "How long was Sol outside barking? Why was he outside barking?"

"He was driving me crazy. I was watching this space documentary and he kept pestering me, so I just put him outside and the next thing I know, there's knocking on the door and this Ozzy character is asking me to take care of my dog."

"It's hot and Sol was outside for a couple of hours, wasn't he? Without water? Just crying outside?"

"I guess. I was busy."

"Too busy to let Sol inside?"

"Beth, so what? Not a big deal."

"It was too hot for him to go with me and sit outside in the shade! I left him here so he would be comfortable, and you left him crying outside for hours?"

"I don't know how long it was. But that Ozzy jerk showed up at the door."

"And then what? Ozzy threatened you with lawsuits?"

"No, he just let me know the dog had been barking and said something about it being bad for the dog and against the law. And I said, and what are you? A freaking lawyer? And he said actually, yes, but, jeez, he looks like a bum and I was like, yeah, right, surfer dude, you're a lawyer. And that's when he pulled out the multiple names."

Beth put her hand over her forehead. "I don't believe this."

"And you're on the lawyer's side." Jonah pushed away from the table. "Great, this is going to be great. Just great." Jonah shook his head as he left for the living room. Beth rubbed her temples and prayed for Monday to come.

"I'm on Sol's side," she called quietly, but there was no answer.

The rest of the weekend was quiet.

By Monday, she'd planned to call Will Garnette five times and decided against it four times. Then she thought about postponing the whole thing and seeing if her having a more appreciative attitude would help Jonah increase his positive behaviors and decrease his negative ones. Then she thought about Sol and decided, no, her track record with behavior modification wasn't good, even for a golden retriever.

She thought she'd call at lunchtime, because then she could leave a voicemail and then postpone the conversation. Much to her chagrin, someone answered the phone. "Dr. Garnette."

She cleared her throat. "Hi, I'm calling for Dr. Will Garnette."

"Speaking. How can I help you?"

"Oh." Beth hesitated. "Um, I'm calling about marriage counseling."

"Sure. Can I ask a bit about what you're looking for help with? To be sure it's in my wheelhouse?"

Beth doodled on a pad of paper in desperate circles. "Um, we have problems with communication. And fertility issues. And I don't think my husband will want to come in."

"Well, it would be better if he does, but if not, we can start without him. Any danger?"

"Huh?"

"Are you safe? Is he safe? Any abuse or threats to safety?"

"Oh, no," Beth said hurriedly. "No, nothing like that." She wondered if that was a normal question to be asked. *Do I sound that unhappy?*

They discussed possible times, set an appointment, and she gave Dr. Garnette her email so he could send paperwork and confirmation. When she ended the call, she got up and walked around in circles, Apple and Mac right behind her. She looked down at them. "How about a walk?" she asked. "Let's just go for a walk."

The warm air hit her face, and the sun felt good. "It's hot, kiddos," she said, "so just a quick trot around the block. A big walk again tonight, when it's cooler for your paws." She was hoping it would clear her head. Around the block, behind their house, she glanced at the back neighbor's house. Funny that Izzy hadn't mentioned that Ozzy had just moved by them, but then Izzy had long since stopped sharing much information because of her friends' dismissive attitude about her tumultuous dating habits. It was, like theirs, an older home, well-maintained. A University of Florida banner was stuck in the flower bed next to the front door. The garage door was open, and a man was working at the tool bench beside the door. It was clearly a workshop; the SUV was parked outside and could not have fit into the garage, which was full of tools, a bicycle, a kayak, and a paddleboard. The man happened to look up. He smiled and waved.

She waved back. "Welcome to the neighborhood!"

He stepped outdoors. "Thanks! Just been here about a month." He jerked his head toward the garage. "It's chaos, all the way down. Taking a few days off to impose some order. I'm putting some shelves together for the pantry closet."

"Nice," Beth said. She moved the leashes to her left hand and extended her right hand. "I'm Beth. Beth Bonhall." She paused. "My husband and I and our dogs live right behind you."

The man nodded slowly. "Oh, yeah. I think I met your husband the other day." He grimaced a bit. "Sorry about that. One of the dogs was barking for a really long time."

"Jonah told me. I'm sorry. I was out with my girlfriends for coffee, and he let Sol out for way too long. I guess he lost track of time."

"I'm Ozzy, by the way. Well, last name Oswald. Ozzy for short." He looked down at Mac and Apple, who were fidgeting. "Nice dogs. May I?"

"Oh, of course. They're Apple"—she nudged Apple—"and Mac. Our other two are Solar and Anastasia. Sol's a golden and Anastasia's a little dachshund-Chihuahua."

Ozzy was squatting down, petting Apple and Mac. "They're beautiful. Very friendly."

Beth studied him. Tall, quite a bit taller than Izzy—over six foot. Not too thin, with sort of a distance runner's build. Tanned, brown hair with sun streaks, maybe early to mid-thirties. Covered in sawdust, old T-shirt, frayed shorts, flip flops. Not pretentious looking at all. She wondered what Jonah had seen or heard that set him off about Ozzy. "They're good dogs, but a lot of energy."

Ozzy stood up, nodding. "It's a big commitment, all those pups." He pushed his hair out of his eyes. "Maybe I'll get to meet the other two sometime."

"I expect so," Beth said. *Probably sooner than you think,* she thought, wondering if Izzy had mentioned the picnic the friends usually co-hosted each summer.

"Maybe at the picnic," Ozzy said. "Beth? Right? I think Isabelle mentioned you. And two others ... Courtney? Kitty?"

"Kitta, yes," Beth said. "Yes, I recognized your name but didn't want to intrude."

"Oh, no intrusion!" Ozzy laughed. "Izzy was here Saturday, I guess right after your coffee. She was going to tell you I had moved in behind you—small world, right? But Kitta was sort of the focus."

Beth nodded. *It wasn't secrecy, it was tact. Nice job, Izzy.* "Yes, it was a big morning." She smiled up at him. "Well, I hope no hard feelings about poor Sol! Sorry about that."

"No hard feelings at all. Looking forward to seeing you again. Hopefully I'll be less dusty." He flicked a few splinters off his sleeve. "I'll get back to my shelves and you probably have to get back on the clock, right?"

"Right! See you soon!" she replied and headed off for home. *So that's Ozzy,* she thought. *Just a regular guy—tools, sporting equipment, and a lawyer. He doesn't seem pompous, but maybe it's hard to be pompous when you're wearing a sweaty T-shirt and sawdust.*

By the time Jonah came home, Beth had rehashed the conversations with Will Garnette and with Ozzy multiple times. She wondered which one to bring up first. There was some brief chat about the day. There was leftover pizza and salad for supper. Sitting down to eat, Beth took a breath and said, "So, I met our back neighbor while I was walking Apple and Mac at lunchtime."

Jonah poked at his salad. "Attorney Oswald? Wasn't he supposed to be at court suing someone?"

Beth counted to ten silently, willing herself to sound calm. "Well, it seems he has a few days off to unpack. Just moved in a few weeks ago."

"Mm-hmm."

"And he's not a suing type lawyer. He does like, family law. Wills and elder care and trusts and stuff. Which he didn't tell me. Izzy did."

"Izzy?"

"That's Izzy's new boyfriend. Ozzy. I told you over the weekend." *Of course you don't remember. You probably remember the documentary you were watching, though.*

Jonah put his fork down, hard. "Seriously? That's Izzy's boyfriend? Can it get any worse?" He frowned at Beth. "What is it with your friends? Kitta gets knocked up by her loser boyfriend. Izzy picks up some asinine lawyer. And what's Courtney doing? Raising free range kids? Can you even have a normal friend?"

Beth's face felt hot and the inside of her chest started shaking. "No, Jonah. Apparently not. I specialize in collecting not normal friends. Including you." She slammed her hand on the table so hard the glasses rattled. "And that is why I had to call a marriage counselor today. The appointment's Thursday at five. I'll send you the paperwork and the address and you can meet me there after work. Or not." She got up and left the table.

Jonah was behind her as she went into the bedroom. "Marriage counselor? One fight and we have to have counseling? Beth, what is wrong with you?"

Beth whirled around and Jonah took a step back. "It's not one fight. It's a thousand fights you never noticed we were having. It's you thinking perfectly normal people are messed up and not as good as you. It's you being wonderful sometimes and most of the time an arrogant jerk. And it's me letting it all happen and pretending I'm happy when I am not." Beth folded her arms, glaring at him. "You have me gaslighting myself even more than you gaslight me." She stepped around him. "I'm going for a walk. I'm taking Sol by himself. He needs the exercise and attention."

"I'm coming, too."

"Suit yourself." She knelt to put on Sol's leash, and tousled Anastasia's head. "Not just now, girl. In a bit. Sol needs a big boy walk." She straightened, hand on the doorknob. "I'm going. Follow or not."

She stepped outside, Sol right beside her. It occurred to her, for a moment, that Apple and Mac would be at the table, eating the pizza. *Oh, well*, she thought. *Who cares? I'm not hungry.* Jonah stepped up beside her and Sol. She glanced at him sideways; his face was flushed and his jaw tight. She looked ahead. *Let him talk if he wants to*, she thought. *I've said too much already.*

Sol kept glancing up at her and she kept making reassuring sounds. Sol would occasionally glance toward Jonah and then quickly back at Beth, one eyebrow raised. *I'm right with you, buddy*, she thought. Finally, apparently assured that things were okay with his humans, Sol eased into his usual behavior, pulling to try to greet a neighbor across the street, stopping to investigate the smells around a fence post, occasionally trying to eat something off the sidewalk.

"Sol, no. No dead lizards," Beth said reflexively, giving him a little tug.

"He's naughty," Jonah said, in a strained attempt at lightness.

"Mm-hmm," Beth agreed. *Here we go; you're going to act like nothing happened. Well, I'm not going to make it easy for you this time*, she thought. *Not going to just give in and play everything is okay.*

"So ... this marriage counselor," Jonah said. She caught, in the corner of her eye, his head turn towards her but kept facing forward.

"Dr. Will Garnette."

"And you found him how?"

"Courtney and Mark saw him a few times to work out stuff with parenting and handling grandparents. She said he was really good at being fair, which sounded important."

There was silence. She glanced sideways; Jonah's jaw muscles were flexing. Finally, he said, "And so Courtney knows we're having problems?"

"She knows that I think we could be better at communicating. Which seems like a fair assessment." Beth paused. "It's not like I told her some big, dark secret."

"I don't like the idea of other people knowing our business."

"She's my best friend. And she doesn't know our business." Beth sighed. "Besides, she gave me a big lecture and told me what I should do differently, too. It's not like I just went whining about you being a pain, Jonah. Honestly, it's not always about you."

"Oh, great," Jonah muttered. Beth looked at him sharply and he jerked his head forward. "Not at you. Look. It's the Izzy and Ozzy show."

Beth looked ahead. Izzy and Ozzy were in Beth and Jonah's driveway, waving at them as they approached. Beth waved back, smiling. She whispered, "Jonah, please," and Jonah waved halfheartedly.

Izzy was smiling broadly, petting Sol and then hugging Beth and then Jonah, who gave her a stiff one-armed hug in reply. "You guys! You both met Ozzy! Isn't this great? Neighbors! I would have told you Saturday but, well. We were sort of busy."

"Hi, Izzy, Ozzy." Beth smiled. "Great to see you! Yes, what a surprise! We're just back from a walk. Obviously." She glanced at Jonah. "Care to come in? The house is probably a mess—we forgot to pack up leftovers, so Apple and Mac probably had at them."

"Good to see you," Ozzy said. "Beth, Jonah. And this is Sol, the golden. Good-looking dog." He grinned at them. "Sure, we can step in, if it's not too much trouble."

Jonah was silent, pulling the door open and barely looking at the rest of them as they paraded in. Izzy was apparently oblivious to any problems, almost immediately squatting to greet Apple, Mac, and Anastasia. "You guys! I have missed you so much! Ozzy, aren't these the cutest dogs?"

"Very good-looking dogs," Ozzy agreed. He turned toward Jonah. "How do the greyhounds do? How much running do they need to keep from being too edgy?"

"Enough," Jonah said.

Beth cringed. *He is going to be that way*, she thought. *Great.* Aloud she said, "Anyone want some iced tea? Lemonade?" Beth glanced around the kitchen. The pizza box was empty and there were chewed-up crusts all over the floor. Both paper plates were half eaten. *Oh good, I'll get to clean up the vomit later. I wonder where they'll do it this time.*

Ozzy glanced up from petting the dogs. "Lemonade sounds great, thanks."

"Me, too," Izzy said. "Let me help."

"Jonah? Can I get you something?" Beth asked.

Jonah was already on the couch in his usual spot. He didn't turn his head her way, but he did answer. "Just water."

Izzy sidled up to Beth in the kitchen, taking glasses from Beth and putting them on a tray. "What's Jonah's deal?" she whispered. "Are we in the way here?"

Beth shook her head. "No. Did Ozzy tell you? The guys met on Saturday."

Izzy nodded. "Yeah, Ozzy mentioned that. But seriously, that's what Jonah's upset about?"

Beth shrugged. "I don't have a clue. And," she added quietly, "I'm tired of guessing."

Izzy's eyes widened but she said nothing, nodding and heading into the living room with the tray. Beth followed with a bowl of pretzels.

What followed felt, to Beth, like the longest one-hour chat in recorded history. She, Izzy, and Ozzy had what should have been a great conversation, talking about the dogs, kayaking, and paddleboarding. Izzy announced that Ozzy did competitive paddleboarding, which was something Beth didn't know existed. Izzy was full of enthusiasm about learning, although she admitted her first lesson involved a lot of falling off the board. Jonah made a few comments but mostly sat silently, occasionally reaching out and touching his phone or the remote, as if both had a magnetic pull on his hand, and then pulling his hand back. Beth told herself she should appreciate the effort, and then told herself he was being a jerk; after all, he was the one who'd neglected poor Sol, leaving him out crying in the heat for hours.

Ozzy finally announced it was time to leave; he appreciated the hospitality and it was great to spend some time. Izzy hugged Beth and Jonah, and they left, promising to get together again soon.

"Bye! Thanks for coming by! See you soon!" Beth called after them, and then closed and locked the door. By the time she turned to the living room, Jonah had the television on and was scrolling through the menu. "Jonah?" she asked.

He tilted his head in her direction. "Yeah. Thank God. I thought they'd never leave."

Beth gathered up glasses and the half-full bowl of pretzels. "It was just one hour, just enough to be polite but not too long." She kept her voice as mild as possible. She went back to the kitchen, hearing Jonah's grunted reply. She sighed and prepared to take Apple and Mac for their walk. Anastasia would get her short, solo walk afterward, just before bedtime.

"I'm taking Apple and Mac out," she said. "Want to come?"

"No, thanks. We might run into more people and have a party. I'll stay here," Jonah replied.

Beth just said, "Okay." *Don't take the bait*, she thought. *Just let it lie.*

The evening was quiet, and she went to bed while Jonah was watching a documentary on Mesoamerican history. He came in later; she tried to pretend to be asleep, curled up on one side facing away from his side of the bed, but today he wasn't fooled. He pulled up close to her, pressing his face against her shoulder and throwing his arm over her. He whispered, "Beth."

It was no use pretending not to hear. "Mm-hmm?"

"Beth, honey. I'm sorry I was a jerk before. You know how I hate ... spontaneous stuff."

"Mm-hmm." *You hate people*, she thought, *not spontaneity*. "Well, we couldn't very well tell them to go away. So, now we know more about Ozzy." She kept her back to him but turned her head to respond. "And he seemed very nice. Nothing too pompous. Seems like he really likes Izzy."

Jonah rubbed her arm and reached around to her breast. "Yeah, well. Not my type of person."

She tried to bend away from his groping hand. "No," Beth said quietly. "I know." She turned her face to stare straight ahead toward the nightstand. "Good night, Jonah." She squeezed her eyes shut and, to her dismay, tears started flowing.

"Come on, Beth." Jonah moved his hand down to her hips, tugging at the elastic of her underwear. "We had your little party. When is it my turn?"

She jerked away, folding her knees up to her chest. "Good night, Jonah."

She was sure she heard him mutter, "Bitch," as he flung himself over to his own side of the bed.

"Jonah. I'm sorry. Really. I'm just so tired and stressed out." She turned toward him, touching his shoulder.

"Yeah, you're always tired. Maybe a little sex would be good for your stress, Beth. But, hey, you're the director."

"Jonah, stop it, please."

"Fine."

Beth rolled over again, her back to Jonah, knees up to her chest. After a few moments, Jonah whispered, "Good night," threw an arm over her, pushing his face again against the back of her shoulder, and seemed to fall almost instantly asleep. Beth lay awake and very still, her face wet, not wiping her face for fear she'd move and wake Jonah. She didn't want to explain why she was crying, because she was having trouble figuring out why. Besides, it would only make Jonah angry.

Chapter 14

Beth pulled into the parking lot and looked at the building: a nondescript multistory office building. A few outdoor signs, but no Garnette. Entering the foyer, she found it as Dr. Garnette had described: the elevators on one side, the bank on the other, and a large sign with all the floors and the various tenants. There was Garnette: William F. Garnette, PhD. Seventh floor, Suite 703. She looked around—no sign of Jonah. Sighing, she pressed the elevator bell and headed up.

She entered, taking a seat. No receptionist, just a common waiting area. The table had multiple card holders; she leaned forward. Garnette's was there, as well as a couple of accountants, a realtor, an insurance agent, a home health care agency, and someone named Moonrise, who put her photo on the business card and described herself as a life coach and Zen finder. Moonrise had a green and silver halo around her head and the card mentioned aura readings. Beth rolled her eyes and wondered if it were too late to just leave, pretend this appointment had never been planned. She glanced at her watch. Two minutes to go. No Jonah yet. She glanced at her phone. No texts. Now it was 4:59.

"Hello! Are you here for me?" said a vaguely familiar voice. Beth looked up, startled. The speaker grinned and put out his hand. "Will Garnette.I never say names out here. If it wasn't you and I said your name, I'd blow your confidentiality straight away."

Beth smiled nervously, standing and pulling at her sleeve before taking his hand. "Beth. Thanks. Nice to meet you." She gestured broadly and said, "My husband. Jonah. He's not here yet ..."

Dr. Garnette nodded. "Well, he'll find us. Let's start on time, shall we? This way." He stepped around the corner, opened a door, and held it open. He gestured towards the office, saying, "Sit anywhere; no assigned seats."

Beth looked around. It was a large office, with a row of windows from floor to ceiling on one wall, facing north. There was a desk, filing cabinet, and bookshelf there by the window; closer to the door was a full living room set, with sofa, loveseat, and two big armchairs in a 'U' shape, open to the door. There were end tables with lamps and coasters, and a low coffee table with some folders and a bowl of polished river rocks. The lighting was soft; lamps on the tables and floor lamps directed light up to the ceiling. The effect was, overall, very peaceful. Beth breathed out gently and sat down on one end of the couch, leaving space for Jonah to sit right next to her.

Dr. Garnette sat across from her in one of the armchairs. As he sat, she assessed him. Probably fifty-ish, she thought. Red hair, lightly salt and pepper. A beard, grayer than his head. Shorter than her by an inch, making him about five foot five. Very lean, almost like a child. He reminded her of the boys who ran cross-country in school. Dr. Garnette sat on the edge of the chair. He seemed to quiver with energy, but his face was calm and curious, his eyes twinkling green. He waited, seeming to absorb her taking him in. When she sat back, easing herself into the sofa, he nodded and began to speak.

"Well, Beth, I'm glad you're here. I got your paperwork." He lifted a folder. "Thanks for completing that online." He paused. "I haven't received anything from your husband ... Jonah, right? Let's just start even if he's just running late."

Beth nodded, pulling her lips in for a moment. "Sure, yeah. Well, he wasn't happy about this idea, so maybe he won't be here. I don't know." She turned and stared toward the window. The summer sky bore down, bright blue; no weather excuses for lateness. She turned back to Dr. Garnette. "Sure. Yes."

Dr. Garnette nodded. "So, I'm Will Garnette. You can call me Will, or Dr. Garnette, or Garnette. Whatever works for you. Some people are more comfortable with first names, some people like the honorific."

"Dr. Garnette, I'd recommend you just go with doctor for us. My husband's sort of a ... he's an intellectual snob. He's going to try to prove he's smarter than you anyway, but maybe the 'doctor' will dissuade him."

Dr. Garnette grinned. "Okay, fine. We'll see." He glanced at her paperwork, put the folder aside, and leaned forward. "So, Beth, you're here. What can I do for you?"

"My friend, Courtney. Well, you can't say you know her but whatever. She recommended you. We need to communicate better. A lot better."

"Communication. Okay. That's a big category. You told me no violence. Just verifying: You're safe? Jonah's safe from you?"

"Absolutely."

"Okay. So, communication means different things to different people. Some people have endless bickering matches. Some people don't talk very much at all. Some people are really destructively mean, some in overt ways, some in covert ways."

"Covert meanness?" Beth asked.

Dr. Garnette's eyebrows raised briefly. "The sneaky stuff. The little put-downs you hardly notice or feel silly bringing up. Sarcasm. Unnecessary corrections, especially in front of other people. Criticizing little things that shouldn't even matter. Gaslighting. Sins of omission: You know, not doing something big and terrible but neglecting all the little things, not following through, that sort of thing."

Beth felt her face and posture crumble. "Oh, gosh. You cut right to the chase. Yeah, that's our life." She looked up bleakly. "Jonah thinks he's the smartest person around and he's at war with the world. Or at least everyone who doesn't see how endlessly brilliant he is."

Dr. Garnette nodded. "And is he? The smartest person around?"

Beth opened her mouth to defend Jonah, reflexively, and then slammed her lips shut. She thought of Sandy and her high-IQ society; she remembered her lunch with Alex and Alex's quiet expertise about extreme giftedness; she thought about the fact that she'd graduated from high school early and was higher up the corporate ladder than Jonah. She sat up straighter and said, "No."

"No, and?"

"No, and he doesn't know. He doesn't know his sister is smarter and probably his mom, and the girls in the family have a little protect-Jonah's-ego pact where they let him believe he's the smart one in the family. And I'm above him on the corporate ladder." She sighed.

"Interesting. So, you and the other 'girls,'"—Dr. Garnette wiggled his fingers like quotation marks—"have a communication problem when it comes to Jonah."

She stared at Dr. Garnette.

He nodded. "I know, you're saying you and Jonah have a communication problem. Maybe you do. I don't know. But so far, you're telling me that you, and his mom and sister, all have communication issues when it comes to Jonah. Well, they're not here. But you are. So that's on the table." He paused. "What makes it so hard to talk to your husband?"

Beth sighed. "I guess he's so miserable and punishing, that silent treatment and then pretending everything's fine later, it just makes me crazy. I start feeling this shaking feeling." She pointed to her chest. "And I just want it to stop."

Dr. Garnette tilted his head. "The shaking feeling. That must be upsetting. What emotions go with that?"

"Oh, I'm freaking out."

"Sad? Scared? Angry?" Dr. Garnette shook his head. "What kind of freaking out are you having when you have that awful shaking feeling in your chest?"

"Afraid. Angry. Sad happens later." Beth was surprised at her own response.

Dr. Garnette didn't look surprised. His voice was softer when he asked, "Beth, can you remember the first time you ever had that feeling? Not necessarily with Jonah, but the first time ever? Just take a few moments to see what comes up in your memories about this feeling."

It was quiet for what felt like forever. Beth stared down at her hands. Snippets of film flashed across the front of her brain: quiet times when she hid in the bedroom or kitchen from Jonah and his icy silence; the time in high school when she realized the girl she thought was her best friend had spread a rumor about her and the chemistry teacher; the unfair accusation that she'd cheated when she'd earned an A on a history test and had to prove herself by retaking the test orally in front of the assistant principal and his secretary. She shook her head.

"Just relax, Beth. Let yourself relax." Dr. Garnette's voice was quiet and calm.

The films changed, and she was seeing her parents as they'd seemed when she was a child, the family dinners where she was interrogated on school, on friendships, on piano practice. Her father's disapproving frown if she had not had a perfect performance; her mother's harangues on how to better herself and not settle for less than the best and being sent to her room after supper. She remembered slipping out of her room to squat in the dark at the top of the stairs, listening to the adult conversation below.

Her parents were entertaining two other couples. They were all talking loudly. Beth had frowned, knowing that loud grown-ups in the evening meant cranky grown-ups lashing out at her in the morning. One of the ladies, Mrs. Anslow, was asking about her.

"And your little Elizabeth? How is she? Such a darling child."

Beth heard her mother chuckle. "Oh, I'm sure it seems so from outside. Good God, you don't live with her."

"Oh, come on," Mrs. Anslow replied lightly. "She's a beautiful little girl and so delightful. Such nice manners, and her piano playing is wonderful. This time of year when the windows are open, I love hearing her practice. So dedicated."

Beth's mother laughed again. "Oh, well, she needs all the practice she can get. She's just ... I don't know. Such a little disappointment. Always not quite good enough. She has, what? One or two friends? She can't even make friends well."

Mrs. Anslow's voice changed. "Brenda, you can't mean that. She's a lovely girl, and better to have two true friends than a lot of so-called friends." Her voice had been sharp, but it cracked as she said, "Sam and I would give anything for a daughter like Beth. You don't know how lucky you are."

Beth's mom replied flatly, "Well, easy for you to say," and then paused. Apparently, she had decided that the conversation was over, because Beth heard her say, "Andrew! Darling! See if anyone needs a refreshe on their drinks, will you? You boys aren't discussing politics again, are you?"

Beth had crept back to her room, closing the door silently and slipping back into bed. She pulled her stuffed unicorn close and rocked it back and forth, trying to quell the silent shaking in her chest.

"Beth?"

She looked up at Dr. Garnette and realized her face was wet. "Oh. Gosh. I checked out."

"No, I think you checked into something. Comfortable sharing?"

Beth nodded and launched into a description of the episode at the top of the stairs. Dr. Garnette made it easy; he asked a few questions and led her into the other memories. She told him about high school, and Jonah, and all the times she went off silently to escape.

"But you don't really escape, do you?" Dr. Garnette asked.

"No, it's always the same. I come out and behave, and then we all pretend nothing happened." She leaned forward a bit. "Until now, that is. I mean, making this appointment was terrifying. And telling Jonah more so."

Dr. Garnette nodded. "It sounds as if it must have been. How did you get to that point? Why now? I mean, if it's been this way for years, what's the reason that now is the time?"

Beth was silent. Her mind swirled, all sorts of mixed-up memories; the good times and the lonely ones, the frustrations and the tension. She shook her head slowly, finally fixing her gaze toward Dr. Garnette. "I don't know. Maybe it's the fact that we have to make a decision about IVF. Maybe I've just had enough of being … patronized? I don't even know what to call it. But something has just clicked."

"Clicked. Puzzle pieces fitting into place, maybe?"

"Just starting."

Dr. Garnette smiled and reached for his calendar. "Should we set something else up? Maybe two weeks?"

Beth shrugged. "I'd like to, but with Jonah not even showing up ..."

"How about we set something up in two weeks, same time, and you check in with Jonah. Offer to have him come solo if he likes, so it feels fair, or come in together, or use the appointment yourself. Just cancel at least two days in advance if you're canceling altogether. Otherwise, there's a fee, as you saw in the paperwork. How would that work?"

"Good. Thank you." *Jonah won't come by himself*, Beth thought. *He wouldn't even come for me.* But it was worth a try.

Driving home, she rehearsed what to say when she went in. Should she just say nothing and see what he said? Ask what happened to keep him from making the appointment? Bring it up at dinner in a desultory way? She ran through the possible dialogues. She imagined Jonah barely glancing over as she came in, not even bothering to mute whatever he was watching, and saying something sarcastic like, "So how was Dr. Freud?" Or maybe she'd bring it up at dinner and he'd say, "And did the great Dr. Garnette go like this," and lean back, chin tucked against his neck, steepling his fingers, "and say, mm-hmm, mm-hmm, to everything?" Beth sighed. She couldn't imagine a way for it to go well.

She decided to go for acting normal, as if nothing had happened, and see what Jonah did. She took a slow, deep breath, and stepped in. The dogs bounced up and down, eager for walks, fresh water and food, and some attention. She petted their heads and rubbed their faces, greeting them and heading toward the living room. Jonah was on the couch, and barely turned his head to say, "Hi, in here."

She forced a smile. "So I see." She paused. "How was your day?" She leaned over to kiss him on top of his head.

He glanced up with a small smile. "The usual."

"The usual?" *Not letting you off the hook that easily*, she thought. *Whole sentences, please.*

"You know," Jonah said crankily, shifting his weight. "Project running late. Rob dropped the ball on part of it. My boss is on fire over the whole thing. Idiots."

"Ah. Idiots dropping the ball." Beth nodded. "Well, I'm going to start the usual dog walking routine." *Dropping the ball*, she thought. *Like missing marriage counseling appointments? That kind of dropping the ball? Or not even apologizing or explaining or having the spine to say, no, I'm not going?*

"Thanks," was all Jonah said.

Beth turned away, blinking hard. "Come on, Sol. Anastasia, come on, girl. No Apple—no, Mac. You guys go next. You know the drill." She leashed Sol and Anastasia and stepped out into the still-hot Florida evening.

Chapter 15

Jonah didn't mention the appointment and Beth decided she was not going to cave in this time. Instead, she decided she would just act normal. That was the plan, but despite her best efforts the most normal she could pull off was being unusually quiet, so much so that after a few days Jonah commented on it.

"You're awfully quiet," he said. "What's going on?"

She looked up, feigning mild consternation. "Hmm? What do you mean?"

Jonah pressed his lips together and his eyebrows drew closer. "Beth. You're doing that almost-silent thing."

Beth sighed and put her book down in her lap. "Meaning I can't be quiet without it being something wrong? Unlike, say, you. Who might grunt instead of speaking in sentences based on the type of day you had at work."

Jonah shook his head. "You know what I mean. Stop being obtuse. You're not talking." He rubbed his temples.

Beth tilted her head. "I am talking. I talked at breakfast this morning. I talked when we took the dogs to the park. I talked in the pet supply store and I talked at dinner. I distinctly remember discussing the upcoming picnic, whether or not to invite my parents to stay with us when they're in the area next month, and asking how your project at work is going since Rob dropped the ball and your supervisor's on fire. So, no, I don't know what you mean."

Jonah crossed his arms and sank further into the couch. "I mean you usually try to, you know, talk. Not just superficial stuff. And you've been assiduously avoiding anything but superficial stuff."

"Very astute of you, Sherlock Holmes. It turns out I don't have anything but superficial stuff to discuss."

"What's that supposed to mean?"

"It means what it means."

"Beth. Seriously."

"Jonah," she echoed his parental tone. "Seriously. It means that I don't feel inclined to have non-superficial conversations with you right now. I'm sure I will, but not right now."

"Why?"

"I guess that's your next mystery to solve," she said shortly. "Maybe when you get done bingeing on the buried mysteries of the past you can spend a little time trying to figure out why I don't feel like chatting." Beth lifted her book up and pretended to resume reading. The inside of her chest was shaking; she tried to do slow belly breathing to relax herself enough to behave normally.

Jonah stared at her for a moment, then clamped his mouth shut and turned back to the television. Beth kept her face tilted toward her book and glanced up at him. He was staring at the television with his jaw muscles clenching and unclenching. After a few moments he lifted Anastasia up from the couch and held her up to his chest, her head peeking over his shoulder toward the kitchen; she could barely see his profile. Her heart melted. *No, Beth,* she thought. *Don't do it. Don't. Just ... don't, but—*

"Jonah? Everything okay over there?"

A brief silence, and then a quiet, "I know. I know, I missed the appointment." He stroked Anastasia's back and then leaned his face around to look toward Beth. She winced inside; his face was crumpled. "I just, I just couldn't. It's too hard."

"What's too hard?"

He grimaced. "I know how these things are. I've heard it at work. It's always the guy's fault. Yeah, I know. I know I'm hard to live with and I know I talk a good game about doing stuff and then just"—he paused—"just sit and stew, I guess." He frowned. "I don't need to pay an expert a chunk of change to tell me so."

Beth pressed her lips into a flat line and took a deep breath. "Well, it wasn't like that. He offered to see us together, or just you, to even things up, if you prefer, next time."

"Next time?" Jonah's voice spiraled up.

Beth tried to nod matter-of-factly. "Absolutely. I think that us being better at communicating is critical, especially because when a baby comes, we won't have time for this kind of tune-up work." She paused. "I mean, frankly, he mostly had me talk about me. My history. It wasn't a venting session about you." Jonah didn't respond so she added, "If you don't want to go, I'm going, because I need to do a little work on myself."

Jonah slowly put Anastasia down on his lap and swiveled his shoulders to face Beth more directly. "What does that mean, exactly? Work on yourself?"

Beth shrugged. "I don't know. Talking with Dr. Garnette ... I really saw a pattern from the way my parents treated me, like I wasn't good enough, to school and work and, well. I want to see where it goes. And see if understanding this a little will make life better."

"Well, I don't like it." Jonah frowned and rubbed his forehead. "Isn't this how my mom went crazy this past year? She decided to work on herself?"

Beth put her book down and folded her arms. "Jonah Bonhall, exactly what is your deal with your mom? She didn't 'go crazy,' she stopped walking our dogs every day at lunch and planned a sabbatical. Where's the crazy?"

"You know what I mean."

She leaned back, tilting her head. Something in her felt different; the shaking was almost gone and she felt what seemed to be, to her amazement, just a touch of amusement. "No, actually, I don't know what you mean. Why don't you enlighten me?"

He scowled. "You're being difficult."

She raised her eyebrows and suppressed a smirk. "Am I? Or are you? Being difficult, that is? Throwing out criticisms without any evidence and then acting superior when I don't know your rationale? What, are you five? Maybe you should call me a poo-poo head and go back to your little cartoons or whatever you're watching." *Oh, crap,* she thought to herself. *What did you just do? Beth, be quiet.* She pinched herself discreetly on the side of the ribs, trying to anchor herself, but there was something about Jonah's behavior that suddenly clicked in as juvenile.

Jonah stood up, dethroning Anastasia. His face was red. "Beth, you're being ridiculous. You sit around giving me the silent treatment all weekend—"

"Not true, Jonah. Stop lying."

"—and you want to pretend my mom's behavior is perfectly normal—"

"Which it is, as a matter of fact." Beth paused, and added thoughtfully, "A bit late in returning to normal after a long absence, apparently, but definitely normal."

"How can you call all that craziness normal?"

Beth sighed. "Your mom decided to take a sabbatical and pursue her own interests instead of being trapped in that godawful college library, walking our dogs during her lunch break. Tell me the crazy part, Freud."

"And you're insulting me."

"Not true, either, unless having your sulky, demanding behavior described accurately is an insult." Beth was surprised at how calm her voice was, and she realized, to her surprise, that she felt very calm inside. No shaking in her chest, no quivering in her throat. It was as if she was seeing Jonah for the first time, not as a polymath, not as the tender-hearted man she so seldom saw, and not as a wounded, misunderstood genius. She was seeing one of his facets in blazing brightness: his spoiled, juvenile side, demanding and inflated with a sense of superiority. She felt sorry for him but didn't feel compelled, not just now, anyway, to rescue him from discomfort.

"What is wrong with you?" He was angry and his voice was getting louder.

Beth unfolded her arms and placed her hands on each side of her knees on the edge of the couch, looking up at him placidly. "Nothing in the world is wrong with me right now. As a matter of fact, I feel remarkably clearheaded for a Sunday evening ... despite having work tomorrow." She paused. "Actually, I think I'd like a cup of chamomile tea." She stood up and headed to the kitchen. "Can I get you anything?" When she glanced back to see, he was just standing there, staring at her, arms at his sides, his mouth slightly open, frozen. She tilted her head. "Jonah? Want anything while I'm here?"

He slowly shook his head. "No. No." He sat down, facing the television again.

No, thank you, Beth thought. She brewed her tea and stepped to the window with it to take in the evening sky. Behind her, the narrator's voice rose and fell. A mockingbird swooped over the backyard, looped back, and perched on the fence between their house and Ozzy's, playing through his series of songs, and Solar gently nudged her hip with his nose before tilting his head up to rest his chin on her belly, gazing up at her. She smiled and stroked his ears with her free hand. "Everything is okay, little buddy," she said softly.

Solar kept his gaze on her and raised one eyebrow.

Chapter 16

The picnic was originally planned to be at the park. Beth had reserved a shelter next to the playground, but on Wednesday Courtney suggested they have it at her and Mark's house, so the kids could go to bed on time and then the adults could hang out later. Saturday dawned a good summer day: sunny, a few fluffy clouds, a breeze, and a low chance of passing storms. Beth smiled as she put together the veggie and cheese tray. It would be good to see everyone, and a chance to ease the tension that had hovered over the house since their argument last Sunday.

Jonah came in with Apple and Mac from their morning walk, shaking his head. "These two," he muttered. "How do you stand them?"

Beth glanced over. The dogs were, as usual, pacing around and a bit hard to unleash. "Why? What did they do?"

Jonah grunted. "Oh, they want to chase every rabbit. And there are a lot of rabbits in the morning."

Beth nodded and covered the tray. "Yes, they have good instincts. It keeps me focused." She lifted an onion. "Vidalia or yellow for the potato salad? Onion, I mean? Any preference?"

"Vidalia. But, these two. I mean, I thought Solar was a pain in the ass. But these two."

Beth shrugged and leaned back from the onion as she peeled it. "I guess I'm used to them." *Maybe if you walked them more*, she thought, *it wouldn't come as a surprise that they act the way greyhounds act.*

Jonah hung up the leashes. "What time do we have to leave?"

"One-ish. We're supposed to be there at one, but a few minutes late won't matter." She paused. "We could see if Ozzy wants to carpool."

"No." She didn't have to turn to see Jonah to know that his face looked as tight as his voice sounded.

"Okay," she said lightly. "No prob. I just threw that out there."

"We'll have to come back for the dogs," Jonah said in a sudden burst of apparent appeasement. "It might not be convenient for him. And Izzy."

"Good thought," Beth said, scraping onion into the bowl. "What do you think? Shredded carrots? Or no?"

"Sure," Jonah said, and threw himself on the couch. She heard the television and sighed. *At least we're going*, she thought, *without any arguments or real complaining so far.*

The drive to Courtney and Mark's was less than twenty minutes. Beth glanced at Jonah as they backed out of their driveway. "Any preferences on music?"

Jonah shook his head. "No, whatever. Quiet is nice." He slouched into the seat, arms folded across his chest. "Anything I should know? Any potential landmines to avoid?"

Nice, Beth thought, *he's thinking about other people.* Aloud, she said, "Well, Kitta's pregnancy is out in the open now. But the whole boyfriend thing is off limits. Hunter's gone AWOL and she's investigating her rights." She glanced at Jonah.

He half turned in his seat. "Her rights? What's that mean?"

Beth shrugged. "You know. Her rights. She doesn't have to name the father on the birth certificate. Then he'd have a certain amount of time to apply to be recognized as the father. She could just cut him out entirely rather than deal with a halfhearted deadbeat dad."

"That's bullshit." Jonah was nearly shouting. "What the hell? Just cut him out? No discussion?"

"That's not what happened. They talked. A lot. And he just moved out—disappeared. No responses, nothing. For weeks." Beth sighed. "Believe me, Kitta tried. So did Hunter's sister and mom. He's furious with Kitta."

"Still," Jonah grumbled. "It seems like women have all the rights and men just have to go along."

"Just the opposite," Beth said, trying to sound calm. "It took two to make that baby. Hunter can bow out and the baby will still be here. Kitta is going to have a baby. Whether she keeps it or gives it away, I guess, is her right. Or whatever. But obviously she's keeping the baby. Besides, Hunter can petition for his right to be named and have responsibility, and rights. He knows this. He just helped his sister get through the same thing a while back."

"Okay," Jonah said, sounding mollified. "Any other catastrophes?"

"Well, no, not a 'catastrophe.' You know about Izzy and Ozzy. And Courtney and Mark and Mikey and Eva are all fine." She glanced at Jonah and said teasingly, "Eva's been enthusiastic about calling people out on bossiness, so you might want to be on your toes around her."

Jonah smirked and nodded. "Fair enough. Maybe I'll try bossing her around and see what happens."

"Suit yourself. Hope I'm there to watch," Beth said cheerfully.

They pulled up to Courtney and Mark's house: a big front yard, a fence around the back. The front porch had four rocking chairs: two large, two small. A huge stuffed bear sat in one. "What's with the bear?" Jonah wondered as he stepped out.

Beth nodded. "It's ridiculous. Mark gets Courtney the biggest, tackiest stuffed animal he can find every year for Valentine's Day. Which she hates. It's an ongoing joke. That's this past year's treasure." She reached into the back for the huge container of potato salad. "Would you grab the veggie tray and the bag with the crackers? Thanks."

"A houseful of monster animals," Jonah muttered.

"Oh, no. She gives the old one away at the end of the year. It's part of the deal." Before Beth could say more, the door burst open and Eva and Mikey spilled out, yelling, "Aunt Beth! Uncle Jonah!" The children half tumbled down the porch steps and lunged into a group hug of Beth's legs that almost tackled her. "You guys! Eva! Mikey! It's so great to see you! Big hug!" and she hugged them as well as she could with one arm full of food.

The kids hugged her and then moved to Jonah, who hugged them back. Beth watched. He was able to hug the children with apparent sincerity. *Good*, she thought, *he's not completely checked out today*. They headed into the house. "Hey!" she called.

"In the kitchen!" Courtney called from the back of the house. "Come on in! Jonah! How are you? The guys are out back fighting about the correct way to grill burgers." She rolled her eyes. "Is this some law of the universe? The more people present, the harder it is to just cook burgers and hotdogs?"

Jonah put the bag with the potato salad on the counter. "Courtney. Good to see you." *He's being sort of friendly, anyway*, Beth thought. "I guess I'll head out that way."

Beth hugged Courtney. "How are you? Everyone else here?"

Courtney grinned. "Eva, let go of your Aunt Beth and go see if Daddy needs anything. Yes, everyone else is here. Kitta and Izzy are trying to set up cornhole so the kids can play. Or they're playing." She glanced toward the backyard and grimaced. "No, they're sitting on the grass talking. Kitta gets tired and just plops down wherever she happens to be."

Beth sighed. "How is she?"

"Oh, you'll see. Mostly good. I think she's found a way to start grieving the years she spent imagining Hunter would grow up." Courtney went back to stacking slices of cheese for burgers. "Speaking of which ... have you talked to Garnette yet?"

"I did." Beth's voice was clipped.

Courtney's eyebrows went up. "From which I infer Jonah didn't go."

"No. He was a no-show. And no commitment for the next appointment this coming week."

"Well, you go then. You could use it."

"What's that supposed to mean?"

Courtney sighed. "Beth." Beth looked up. "It means what it means. You go. You've been married to Jonah for years. He hasn't changed that much. But he seems very unhappy and so are you." Courtney folded her arms. "Is he depressed?"

Beth's forehead puckered. "Depressed? Jonah?"

"You know. Irritable. Uncommunicative. Doesn't seem to enjoy anything. Sulky. No initiative. Negative. Not fun to be around."

"That's depression? I thought that was just his personality."

Courtney shrugged. "I'm not a therapist. Just saying. Look it up on any psychology website and see what you think. Maybe you need to figure out how to live with a depressed person."

"Huh." Beth didn't have a chance to finish; Ozzy stepped in. "Oh, hi, Ozzy. How are you?"

"Beth! Good to see you! All good, thanks. Looking forward to having our neighbors over to see the place now that it's set up more." He turned to Courtney. "Mark wants to know when to start cooking."

"Anytime, thanks," Courtney said.

When Ozzy had stepped out, Beth said, "*Our* neighbors? Does that mean what I think it means?"

Courtney shrugged. "Sounds like. Our girl Izzy has been unusually close-lipped this go-round." She wiggled her eyebrows at Beth. "You'll have to go to visit and fill the rest of us in."

Beth grinned. "Absolutely! Wouldn't that be great? If Izzy finally found the right guy? No more heartache?"

"Too good to be true." Courtney nodded. "Give me a hand bringing things out to the back porch."

The large, screened-in porch was set up with a regular picnic table and a few other seating arrangements. Another table was pushed against the wall for the buffet. Beth and Courtney arranged the food dishes. Beth straightened and looked over the yard: the little inflatable children's pool, the patio and the grill, all three guys standing around it. Mark was waving a spatula, Ozzy was laughing, and Jonah was shaking his head, arms folded. Izzy and Kitta were trying to get Mikey and Eva to play cornhole, but it wasn't going well. "This is a perfect yard," Beth commented. "Love the little pool."

Courtney nodded. "It is perfect. Maybe, when the kids are bigger, we'll have a pool put in. Waiting on that decision." She rolled her eyes. "The cost is prohibitive and then there's the maintenance."

"You have a neighborhood pool, right?"

"Yes, and it doesn't require any chores, chemistry, or a childproof gate in the yard. That makes it perfect for now," Courtney summarized.

The afternoon was, in Beth's opinion, delightful. The annual picnic was a treasured tradition already, and this year having Ozzy join the crew more than made up for Hunter's absence, to Beth's thinking. Hunter always ended up drinking too much and slipping into inappropriate-for-families humor, and then Kitta would have to gracefully take possession of the keys and talk him into leaving early. This year, no one had to leave early.

The only blemish on the day was the nagging thought planted by Courtney: Was Jonah actually depressed? Was that the reason behind his sulky, lazy behavior? Beth found herself discretely watching Jonah. She watched him playing cornhole against Mark; she studied his half-hearted turn holding the hose so the kids could run through the water. "Make a rainbow, Uncle Jonah!" Eva had kept pleading, and he finally did, using his thumb to fan the water and let the sunlight explode into a rainbow to dance in. Beth nodded to herself; that seemed un-depressed. The whole afternoon was punctuated with secretly trying to take Jonah's emotional temperature. Was that annoyance while Mark and Ozzy talked about kayaking? Boredom when the talk turned to whether it was better to get the kids involved in T-ball or soccer? Beth kept shaking her head at herself and refocusing on enjoying her friends.

Finally, around eight thirty, Jonah caught her eye and glanced toward the front of the house. She nodded; they said their good-byes, with a lot of hugs and handshakes and promises to get together soon.

"Remember, we want to have our neighbors over soon," Ozzy reminded Beth and Jonah. "Maybe I'll have Izzy set it up with you?"

"That sounds lovely," Beth said. "Looking forward to it." She turned to give Izzy a hug. Izzy squeezed a bit harder than usual and grinned as they pulled apart. Beth winked at her and then took Jonah's arm. "Let's go home before we end up going over for a late supper," she suggested, half teasing, and Jonah nodded.

Driving home, she sighed. "Well, that was nice."

"Not too bad, no." Jonah paused. "I wasn't in the mood but it turned out all right." Beth waited. There was another brief silence, then he continued, "Ozzy seems like he's all right, I guess. At least, he seems to really like Izzy. He's not my friend type." Beth thought, *Of course he's not.* "But," Jonah went on, "it's nice for Izzy."

"Get to catch up with Mark at all?" she asked.

"Yeah." Jonah pushed his hand through his hair. "We had a bit of a chat while Ozzy was playing with Izzy and Kitta and the kids." He glanced toward Beth. "Did you know he and Courtney had a bit of a rough spot a while back?"

"I guess she thought of it as maintenance, not a rough spot per se."

"Well, Mark was apparently one foot out the door in his head, anyhow. I guess maintenance is the nice word for it."

Beth nodded, pursing her lips. *Interesting to have a glimpse of the other side of Courtney's got-it-all-together casualness.* "Sounds serious."

"Yeah." Jonah paused. "I guess they did some counseling. And it helped."

"Really?"

"Yeah. Mark recommends it. He said he thought it was going to be a lot of psychobabble but instead it really was useful."

"Interesting." Beth guided the car into their driveway. "I guess you never know."

Chapter 17

Beth pulled into the parking lot at Dr. Garnette's office, parked, turned off the car, and sighed. She stretched the sun blockers across the windshield, pressed them into place with the visors, and sighed again. *Will Jonah show up?* she wondered. She'd mentioned the appointment only once this week, just this morning. He'd nodded and said, "Okay," but nothing more. The days were a blur of repetition, the evenings quiet except for some superficial chat about the workday and then the drone of whatever Jonah put on to watch.

Inside, however, Beth had been on eggshells, tense. Every time Jonah opened his mouth, she dreaded being accused of being "too quiet," or poked at about her intentions around seeing a therapist. Meanwhile, she'd navigated setting up another lunch with Alex in the next week, arranged a time to walk around the block to Ozzy's for a cookout on Sunday, and just today fielded a difficult call from Jonah's manager, Arthelle, who wondered how things were and if there was something going on that she should, you know, know about. Jonah had not quite been himself the past few weeks, missed a few deadlines and taken some half days off without much notice. Just asking as a friend, Arthelle explained. Beth had been stunned. Days off? Jonah certainly hadn't been at home, and he hadn't mentioned taking time to do anything. Beth sighed again and thought it was a good thing they, or she, was seeing Dr. Will Garnette today.

She jolted at the tap on the window; Jonah was standing at the door of her car. He gave her a little smile and wave as she recovered. She grabbed her bag and cup and got out. "You're here," she said.

"Yes." Jonah paused. "Just in there?" He gestured toward the building.

Beth nodded, heading toward the door. "Yes. A lot of businesses in here, so there's no huge sign outside. Very discreet. We could be going to see an accountant, or a realtor. Or maybe taking lie detector tests."

Jonah swiveled his head to look at her. "That's a weird one."

She shrugged. "It's an actual business in this building." She nodded toward the large sign with lists of businesses at the elevator bay. "There, on the third floor. Human Innovations and Solutions. I asked Dr. Garnette about it and he said it was mostly lie detecting, but they also do fingerprinting. You know, for volunteers and jobs and stuff."

Jonah shook his head. "What should I expect?"

Beth glanced at him. "Did you do the paperwork?"

"No. There was a lot of it. I didn't have time."

"You had enough time to take time off from work without even telling me."

"I needed to just get away. I was at the park. Well, a bunch of parks. And the diner. I needed space." He paused. "How did you find out?"

Beth shrugged. "I did. And you lied to me."

"I didn't lie."

"You did. You let me believe you were working and you were off, I don't know, staring at the grass or eating French fries. That's a lie."

"I just didn't mention taking time off. That's not the same as lying." Jonah's voice rose.

Beth felt the inside of her chest shaking but managed to say, only a little louder than usual, "Not telling is the same as lying," and so they burst into Dr. Will Garnette's waiting room, arguing about whether failing to mention a few half days off from work was the same as lying.

Dr. Garnette was standing at the reception desk. He appeared to be putting papers onto clipboards but had paused. He was grinning at them as they burst out of the elevator. Beth and Jonah stood gaping at him for a moment, and he said calmly, "I'm coming down on the side of, not telling is the same as lying. Lies of omission and all that. Obvious, right? But of course, I've interrupted your game. Hi, Beth. And you must be Jonah. Dr. Will Garnette. Good to meet you." He extended his hand to Jonah.

Please take it, please take it, Beth thought. Jonah hesitated, scowled just a bit, then shook Dr. Garnette's hand. "Nice to meet you, Will," he said. Beth groaned inside. *Here we go*, she thought, *Jonah the rude, disregarding the professional honorific*. Beth shook her head just a bit and realized, belatedly, that Dr. Will Garnette would take in every detail.

"Let's go back, shall we?" invited Dr. Garnette. Beth went in first; Jonah followed after a brief hesitation. The door closed softly and Dr. Garnette took his seat. He had a clipboard of papers with him. Beth sat on one side of the couch. Jonah took the other end. Dr. Garnette said, "So, Jonah, I didn't get your paperwork through the online portal. Any chance you brought copies today?"

"No." His voice was flat.

Dr. Garnette handed a clipboard to him; Jonah hesitated, but took it. Dr. Garnette said, calmly and matter-of-factly, "There are some things I absolutely have to have today, or else I have to ask you to leave. I've highlighted those in yellow. Then please have the remainder of the completed paperwork back to me via the portal, or drop it off in person, before we meet next. Thanks." He turned his gaze toward Beth. "We'll just chat a bit while we wait for Jonah. How's the week been?"

Beth nodded and shifted on the couch. *That was nicely handled,* she thought, *almost as if he was expecting Jonah's recalcitrance.* "The week's been fine. Busy, you know. Like everyone. The argument was ..." She glanced toward Jonah. "Well, I had a colleague let slip that Jonah's been not quite himself at work and that he had taken time off, some half days, on rather short notice. Which was news to me." She looked at her lap. "Which is why you heard us acting badly." She glanced up. Dr. Garnette nodded thoughtfully and glanced at Jonah, who was flipping through pages on the clipboard, trying to find all the highlighted spots.

"And you were angry and surprised," Dr. Garnette remarked. "Who are you angrier at, the colleague or Jonah?"

Beth jerked her head back in surprise. "At Ar—at my colleague? Why would I be mad at her?"

Jonah handed the clipboard to Dr. Garnette. "Oh, Arthelle. Of course," he grumbled.

Beth glared at him. "She *is* your boss."

"Interesting little dynamic around here." Dr. Garnette leaned back, arms folded. "Apparently Jonah's difficulty with authority flows everywhere. He's just a little disrespectful to me; his boss would rather deal with you." He turned toward Jonah. "Does this usually work for you? Being just rude enough to keep people at bay?"

Jonah's mouth hung open just for a moment and then snapped shut. *Uh, oh,* Beth thought. *Now he's done it; Dr. Garnette has blown any chance of Jonah talking.* The silence seemed endless but, glancing at the clock, Beth realized it was only a moment. Dr. Garnette looked calm and, she thought, just a little amused, as if Jonah's discomfort at having his game described had entertainment value.

Beth couldn't stand the silence. "And his mom used to hide from us sometimes. When they babysat the dogs while we traveled. She would be in her room and let his dad deal with us."

Dr. Garnette nodded thoughtfully. "And that's your mom, Jonah? A woman who hides from you?"

Jonah sank back against the couch, folding his arms across his chest. He stared at Beth and then at Dr. Garnette. "So, this is the big, helpful therapy? Jump on Jonah time? How does this help anything?"

Dr. Garnette nodded. "Well, you kind of set things up for us to get right down to the business of identifying patterns and reflecting on whether those patterns still serve a useful purpose. If there was ever a time when being ... rude? Maybe disrespectful and distant? If that was ever a useful strategy, maybe it's not now. Maybe not for your marriage." He paused. "No doubt Beth has some habits, some patterns, that aren't doing her any good and could be hurting the marriage. We look at those, we look at how each of you may be inadvertently reinforcing one another's unhelpful patterns. Then you decide how you want to change. Or not. Maybe this works for you." He shrugged.

"I'm fine. My wife," Jonah jerked his head in Beth's direction, "she wanted us to be here. So, this time I showed up. I think it's a waste of time and money. I'm fine."

"Okay. So, you're fine. Taking time off from work, lying to your wife, being just rude enough that your own supervisor what, doesn't want to deal with you? That is usually a precursor to career disaster, but, hey. You're fine." Dr. Garnette turned toward Beth. "Jonah is fine. He doesn't think these things are a problem. Maybe you could talk to Jonah about how these things affect you?" Dr. Garnette paused. "And

I want this to be how it affects you, Beth; share with your husband how his behavior impacts you. Don't tell him what he's doing wrong."

Beth nodded, blinked a few times, and half turned so she was almost facing Jonah. She glanced at Dr. Garnette, who nodded encouragingly, and then back to Jonah, whose face was flat and cold. "Jonah." She put a hand on his upper arm; he flinched but did not draw away. "Jonah," she repeated. "I felt ... scared and confused when Arthelle called me to ask if you were okay. I was afraid. Afraid something was really wrong with us, or for you at work. I was angry that you would keep secrets from me. I wondered what else you're not telling me. And I am worried that your job is in danger." Beth noticed, with a pang, that it was only this that seemed to get a glimmer of a reaction; Jonah's eyebrows raised in surprise. Beth steeled herself. "And here ... I was embarrassed that you didn't bother to do the paperwork, like I wasn't important enough to do this counseling for, and I was embarrassed that you were disrespectful about this whole thing: blowing off the first appointment, not doing the paperwork, being rude to the doctor." She nodded toward Dr. Garnette.

Dr. Garnette nodded. "Okay, good job, Beth, you talked about your feelings. Jonah, could you talk to your wife? About what she just said?"

Jonah stared at him, shrugged, and turned to Beth. His voice was tinged with sarcasm. "You're embarrassed because I made you look bad at work and here, and you're mad because I lied, according to you."

"It's not because you made me look bad," Beth retorted. "You're missing the point. I'm embarrassed that my husband doesn't think I'm worth doing things for. As far as work, I'm more scared. Afraid something's wrong, afraid you'll lose your job."

"Oh, please. I'm not going to lose my job." Jonah was almost sneering. "You're hysterical."

Before Beth could reply, Dr. Garnette interrupted. "Okay, thank you, both." He paused, looking at each of them. They both looked at him with stunned faces. "What I just observed, is that fairly typical? Of arguments?"

Beth nodded. "Except maybe I would push for a few more rounds, but it would be more of the same."

Jonah shrugged. "I wouldn't call this an argument. I'm just laying out the facts."

"Beth wasn't telling you *facts*; she was sharing her feelings and thoughts." Dr. Garnette paused a moment. "It can be hard, especially in an argument, to listen for feelings and respond to them, but it's essential to improve understanding. Beth." Dr. Garnette turned to her. "Beth, the two of you managed to fall in love and get married, so I imagine there are times when Jonah's better at responding to feelings."

It wasn't a question, per se, but Beth heard the invitation. She nodded slowly, her mind racing. She thought about how Jonah would sometimes just hold her and comfort her without words. Her eyes suddenly filled with tears and her voice went froggy. "Yes," she said, barely coherent, and saw Jonah turn toward her in surprise. "Yes," she repeated. "I mean ... well, for example, a few months ago, I thought maybe we were pregnant. But no. And I was in bed crying and Jonah just came over and held me and wiped my tears and was quiet. But I knew he cared about me."

"Beautiful. And very sad," Dr. Garnette said. "I'm sorry, this sounds like a painful disappointment. But Jonah, you are clearly able to be very sensitive to Beth, very warm and comforting for her. But when it goes verbal," and he gestured back and forth between them, "it gets a little rougher. And that's something we can work on, if the two of you agree."

"I want to," Beth said, sitting up a little straighter.

Jonah kept leaning back into the couch. He nodded once, slowly, and glanced at Beth, then looked at Dr. Garnette. "Okay. Me, too. I'm in." Beth noticed his voice was flat but felt relieved he didn't sound sarcastic.

The rest of the session felt more like psychology class than therapy; handouts on emotions and reflective listening skills; demonstrations; having them rehearse with silly, light topics, with Dr. Garnette acting out parts. Then he gave them homework.

"Okay, good work, you two. Thanks. So, homework. Here goes. Five times a week, I want you to go through reflective listening for one another." He held up the reflective listening handout. "Pick a positive or neutral topic, something of interest to you and something for the other person to practice good listening skills. Give reflection—not just paraphrasing, but the feeling, too—and ask salient questions. Build on the questions. Give this a good ten or fifteen minutes for each of you." He paused. "Questions?"

"I'm just impressed you used 'salient' in a sentence," Jonah said curtly.

Beth cringed, but Dr. Garnette half grinned. "And the purpose of that was ...? To make sure I know you're smart? I know you're bright, Jonah. Beth picked you and she doesn't seem to be a woman to pick someone who isn't at least close."

Jonah's eyebrows shot up. "Just joking," he mumbled. "Are we done?"

Beth counted to ten, trying to contain the shaking in her voice. "Can we set something up for a couple of weeks again?"

The appointment was set, payment was made by Beth, and they left. In the elevator, Jonah said, "Well, that was stupid. But if it makes you happy ..."

Beth turned to him, surprised at the heat that came rushing up from her belly. "Makes me happy? Is that what you think this is all about?"

Jonah shrugged. "What else?"

The elevator doors opened on the first floor. Beth stayed quiet until they passed the people waiting to board. As they stepped out into the Florida evening, she turned to face Jonah. "It's not about making me happy, Jonah. It's about convincing me you still want to be married."

"What's your problem, Beth? Is it PMS?"

Beth stared at him. Then she pivoted on her heel and strode to her car. When she pulled out, Jonah was still standing there in front of the office building, arms hanging flat at his sides, his face expressionless.

Beth came back from walking Apple and Mac to find Jonah at home. She took a deep breath before going inside, determined to act normal. She'd gotten home almost an hour earlier. "Hey there," she said, as normally as she could, as she stepped in. "Everyone's had their walk." Jonah glanced over from the couch but said nothing. Beth felt her chest tightening. She hung up the leashes and, stepping into the kitchen, added, "I'm going to put some dinner together. A salad with the leftover chicken sound good?"

"Um. Sure," Jonah said, and, after a pause, added, "Thanks."

Beth looked toward the back of his head. He was facing away, of course, toward the television. A documentary was on: It looked like it was footage from the Korean War this time. She pressed her lips together and then said cheerfully, "So, how'd you like Garnette?"

Jonah barely flinched. "Fine, for what he is."

"Meaning?"

Jonah half turned. "You know. I've got a flaky sister and her best friend, my 'cousin.'" He made finger quotes in the air. "So, I'm not impressed with psychology majors, generally speaking."

"Ah. So, what makes him fine for what he is?"

"Better questions. Just some teaching stuff. You know. Not flaky."

Beth shook her head. "Eventually you're going to have to give up this idea about Sandy being stupid, or silly, or whatever it is you have on your mind, Jonah." She arranged greens on two plates. "So, which questions or teaching did you like?"

"I didn't like any of it. I just thought it was fine for what it is."

"You don't see anything useful there?"

"No." He turned back to the television.

"No, and?"

"And what?" he sounded annoyed.

"Did you even listen to Garnette? Did you notice this was an entirely one-sided conversation?"

Jonah half turned again, frowning. "Meaning what?"

"Meaning, I showed interest in you. I asked you questions. I tried to build on what you said to make better questions. And you haven't offered any interest or concern. No, hey, it took me an extra hour to get home because ... why? Or asking what I liked about Garnette's approach. You just let me do all the work."

He stared at her, his mouth slightly open.

"Like now," she continued. "I walked all four dogs. I'm making dinner. And you," she pointed with a paring knife, "are just sitting there passively, being taken care of and having your opinion solicited." She went back to slicing radishes into paper-thin wafers.

"Since when do you need your opinion solicited?" Jonah asked finally.

"That's not the point, Jonah, and you know it. The point is dialogue. Back and forth. Two-sided. Interest and concern flowing in both directions. You know. *Conversation*."

Jonah shrugged. "Nothing to conversate about. We went. You like him. I don't. I went anyway. You win."

She put down the knife and tilted her head, brows drawn together. "Win? You think this is a win? It's not about winning, Jonah." She sighed and pushed the slices of radishes off the cutting board onto the plates. "I don't think you're happy. I don't know if you want to be married, or what the problem is. You're disappearing from work; you don't tell me what's going on. What am I supposed to think?"

"Why does that have anything to do with you?"

"Because we're married, you idiot." She slammed down the cutting board and knife. "How would you feel if I just disappeared for hours at a time, never said anything, and then you found out from someone else? Wouldn't you sort of wonder what was going on?"

He stared at her. "You're being hysterical. Is this about being embarrassed by my behavior at work?"

"Ugh! Jonah. You're missing the point. On purpose, probably." She turned to get the chicken out of the refrigerator. "Fine. You keep your little secrets and show no interest in me. We'll see how that works for you, shall we?"

"What's that supposed to mean?"

"It means what it means. Now I have to finish making dinner."

Dinner felt interminable. The television droned in the background, Jonah assiduously kept his eyes on his plate or in the general direction of the television, and Beth struggled to eat calmly and slowly, as if she were savoring the meal. She wrestled between the urge to make small talk, pretend everything was fine, and to just be quiet and see what happened. She opened her mouth to say some trivial thing about the upcoming cookout at Ozzy's and changed her mind when she saw Jonah staring at the television. *Never mind*, she thought. *Never mind.*

After dinner, Jonah put his dishes in the sink and went back to the couch. Beth wandered off to do chores: a load of wash, sorting the day's mail. The evening was clear and pleasant, so she went outside with Sol and sat, watching the sky change. Streamers of pink and purple flowed from the west, and the first stars were making their appearance. Cardinals sang their evening songs.

Beth took a deep breath, and then another. *Maybe tomorrow will be better*, she thought. *Maybe Jonah just needs some time to process the experience.* She wiped at her eyes and then stroked Sol's muzzle; he was nudging her arm, raising his eyebrow at her. "I know, Sol," she said softly. He made a soft grunt and rested his head on her lap, looking sideways up at her, eyebrow still cocked. She smiled, shaking her head gently, and petted his head as the night came over them.

Chapter 18

September in Florida meant summer temperatures, the threat of hurricanes, and the pretense, in stores, that it was already autumn, with Christmas just around the bend. Beth dutifully unpacked some autumn decor, replacing the seashore-themed wreath on the front door with a sunflower-laden one and putting out some small artificial gourds, but resisted the trend to start decorating for Halloween before October. She stood on the front lawn, facing the house, arms crossed, considering. Perhaps a couple of potted mums, she thought, something autumn-ish to brighten things up. Maybe she'd pick some up after the appointment with Dr. Garnette this evening. In the past two months, she'd gone back a couple of times, and both times Jonah had simply not shown up. Today she hadn't even told him; she figured she'd let him know when she left the house for the appointment.

She went back inside, petting Sol absent-mindedly as she closed the door. The last two months had been the worst of their marriage, with Jonah barely speaking. She'd been avoiding his family. Joe was off fishing; Alex had left for Georgia. Her parents had swooped through for a visit, but it was only a few days, and they were gone. For once, Beth was grateful for her parents' self-absorption, assuming they wouldn't notice the strain in their home. The four days had gone without a hitch; she'd invited Izzy and Ozzy over for dinner the second evening to entertain her parents and use up an evening. Her parents had been impressed with Ozzy and said so, almost before the door had closed behind Izzy and Ozzy as they left.

The night before they left, Beth's dad offered to come along on the walk with Sol and Anastasia. "I've heard they're more sedate that those other two," he remarked. "Maybe more my speed."

Beth was surprised. "Sure. Yes, when they're together, Anastasia sets the pace."

They strolled along under the late summer night. Her father made a few remarks about the visit. Mother had enjoyed seeing Isabelle. Oswald seems like a fine man and a good neighbor. An interesting guy; lots of diverse skills. Beth agreed.

"Beth," her dad said, and his tone was different. It was softer, a tone Beth dimly remembered from childhood.

She glanced up, feeling her chest tighten.

"Beth," he repeated. "Honey." A pause, and then, "Something's not right here. I mean, I know you know that. But I can tell." He shook his head. "Something is really not right. I'm not telling you what to do."

Good, Beth thought. *Don't try.*

"But I want you to take some time to sort things out. Figure out how to be happy. Because you are so very unhappy." He sighed. "And it hurts me to see you so sad."

"I'm not depressed."

"No, I imagine you're not. But you are so painfully unhappy." He stopped, and put a hand on her shoulder. Beth turned to look up at him; in the streetlight his face was lined with sorrow. "Just promise me you'll take some time to sort things out. To take care of yourself and not spend all your heart trying to appease Jonah."

She started to speak, and her dad shook his head. "Beth, please. I've been married to your mom for a long, long time. I know appeasement when I see it." He pressed his lips together briefly. "Don't do it, Beth. Don't build a life around appeasement." Her dad was silent for a few moments and then continued, "I won't say more about it unless you want to talk again sometime ... but I'm always here for you. Any time, Bethie, any time."

Beth burst into tears, trying to cover her face without letting go of the leashes. Her dad put one arm around her, stroking her hair, and gently took one of the leashes from her hand. She leaned into his chest, crying for what seemed a long time. Then she pulled back, looking up with a determined half smile, and he nodded, kissed her forehead, and they walked on silently. They came back to the house ten minutes later. She looked up and said, "Thanks, Dad," before they went in.

"Remember, Beth, any time." He winked and made a "shush" gesture with his finger in front of his mouth.

Neither her mom nor Jonah asked about the walk, or why both of their faces were streaked with tears.

Beth had revisited that conversation many times over the past six weeks, wondering what her dad saw. She decided that today would be a good day to break this open with Dr. Garnette. It also occurred to her, suddenly, that maybe Alex could use some company. Alex, it seemed to Beth, had spent way too many years being an expert in appeasing other people. Maybe Alex would have some answers.

Beth settled into her chair and logged back into work with a sigh. She glanced at the time—just a few moments before a team meeting with some of the other managers. A message came up: Arthelle, Jonah's manager.

Beth, how are you?

Odd, Beth thought.

Fine, she typed. *How are you?*

OK here, Arthelle responded. *Thought I'd check in and see how you were doing.*

Fine.

Beth paused. She pressed her lips together, worried. *Should I know something? Am I being laid off or something?* Beth wondered; it wasn't like Arthelle to be so solicitous.

I mean about Jonah, Arthelle replied.

What happened? Is Jonah okay? Beth typed furiously. Her mind raced. What could have happened? Was there an accident and no one told her? A random shooting? Workplace violence?

Her phone rang. It was Arthelle. Beth's heart pounded. "Arthelle? What's going on? Is Jonah hurt?"

Arthelle's voice sounded weary and sad. "Oh, Beth. Honey. You don't know." There was a pause, and then, "Jonah was let go two weeks ago. Didn't he tell you?"

Beth felt as if she had been punched in the stomach. "No ... no... he didn't say a word. He's been leaving every day to go ... somewhere. Arthelle—what happened?"

Arthelle sighed. "Okay, this conversation is off the record. That's why I called with my personal phone. He just ... stopped. Started cutting out of work, didn't perform, and well, you know how argumentative he is. The decision came down from on high. I'm so sorry."

"Thanks for letting me know." Beth sighed. "I appreciate it." She glanced at the computer. "Crap. We're supposed to be in the meeting. Arthelle, thanks. We'll talk more later."

Arthelle's voice was gentle. "Of course. See in you in the meeting."

Beth put the phone down, pushed her hair back from her face and shook her head, then unmuted, put on her camera, and smiled gamely. "Hey, everyone! Enjoying this beautiful day?"

The seemingly interminable meeting finally ended, and Beth could push herself back from the desk. She paced around the house, dogs following her with excitement. *How could this be?* Jonah had been fired. Fired. Their income had just been cut by about a third, and he hadn't said a word. She kept walking, picking things up and putting them back down, as if some small object would hold the key to an impossible situation. She picked up her phone, checking to see if somehow Jonah had texted her about this and she'd missed it, but even as she scrolled through messages, she knew that there was no message about this from Jonah. She felt ill, as if she were going to vomit. She went to the bathroom and stood there, leaning against the door frame, waiting for the queasy feeling to pass. When it did not, she resumed pacing. She glanced at the clock—an hour until it was time to leave for the therapy appointment.

I can't just pace around in circles for an hour, Beth told herself. *Get a grip. Do something.* She kept wandering around the house, touching items. She felt as if she were not quite attached to the ground and wondered if she was safe to drive. She pinched her sides, hard, like she did when she was a child and trying to assure herself that she'd awakened from a bad dream. She shook her head. *Awake all right*, she thought grimly. She wandered into the bedroom and stood in front of her chest of drawers. She glanced at her own reflection, disheveled and pallid. *How about you?* she asked herself. *Your husband got fired and didn't tell you, you look a mess, you're an object of pity to your work friends.* She shook her head again, harder, as if she could snap her thoughts into clarity.

She glanced at the closet, went over, pulled her duffel bag off the top shelf, threw it on the bed, and then started tossing clothes in the same general direction. She wondered, briefly, what Jonah would think when he came home and saw her duffel bag and a pile of clothes, shrugged, and decided to head to the therapy session early. At least she could sit in the waiting area and have time to think.

Beth seldom arrived someplace very early on purpose, and the strangeness of sitting quietly, alone, waiting, was oddly anchoring in the midst of confusion, fear, and sheer rage. She alternated between gripping the arms of the chair and clenching her fists to control the shaking in her chest. When Dr. Garnette stepped out to greet her, she was startled. He smiled quizzically, holding the door open. She stepped in and had barely sat down before she burst into tears.

Dr. Garnette sat down across from her, hands on his knees, leaning slightly forward, waiting. When she glanced up between her fingers he nodded encouragingly and said her name quietly. She snuffled, grabbing a handful of tissues and wiping her face, her breath shuddering for a few more moments. She sat straighter, took a deep breath and said, "Sorry about that."

Dr. Garnette shook his head, half smiling. "You come here with what seems like true heartbreak and you apologize? Why?"

"Why the heartbreak or why the apology?"

"Well, both, actually, but one at a time. Either. You choose."

"Because I'm an appeaser, just like my dad. And my mother-in-law." Beth clapped her hand over her mouth, eyes wide open.

"Surprised yourself?" Dr. Garnette commented. "Or just feeling particularly brutally honest today?"

"My dad said something about it when my parents visited. About not building a life on appeasement. And of course, I do. Appease Jonah. Or have. And then there's today."

"Today?"

"I found out today from a colleague that Jonah was fired two weeks ago. He hasn't said a word. In fact, he's been leaving the house every day to go ... somewhere. Who knows? Not a word. Obviously, this wrecks our finances. It would have been nice to have had a warning just for the income being sliced. But to not tell me! I'm his wife. What else is he not telling me?" She stared at Dr. Garnette as if he would have a reassuring answer. He shook his head sadly but was silent. Beth nodded. "Today's sort of a weird reality-ville. I was so upset I could barely fake my way through the longest, stupidest work meeting ever. And then I found myself putting a pile of clothes together with my duffel."

"And where are you going?"

Beth looked past Dr. Garnette's shoulder and then back at him. "I think to Georgia. To spend a few days in the mountains with Jonah's mom." Dr. Garnette tilted his head. Beth smiled and said, "She's on sabbatical. She's off hiking and drawing and painting. She has a pretty strict 'no company' rule but let me know I could be an exception. I think I need to give Alex a call."

"And then with a few hours' drive, you can be on a bit of sabbatical."

"Yes. Seriously, I need to talk to someone who understands Jonah and who did something I need to do."

"Which is?"

"Figure out how to be loving without appeasing." She shook her head. "Last year ... this past year, really ... Alex just, I don't know, she blossomed. I know that's a really weird thing to say about your fifty-six-year-old mother-in-law, but that's the best word for it. She went from seeming like she was old, sad, frumpy, and afraid of everything to being, well, like an older version of the Alex I saw in old pictures. When she was artsy and bold and happy." She sighed. "That was, of course, mostly before Jonah. Maybe Jonah sucks that out of people."

"Blaming Jonah for your own decisions won't help you make better decisions."

"Ouch," Beth said, trying to sound as if she were joking. It stung. "Am I doing that?"

"Well, you're an odd mix there, Beth. You apologize when you're genuine, like weeping because your husband has demonstrably lied to you, every waking moment, for two weeks. Then you get defensive when you're asked to take ownership for your own choices."

She nodded slowly. "I guess I own a piece of this marriage, this messy, messy marriage. I do appease Jonah. Everything rotates around him, his mood, his preferences. Once in a while I ask him to stretch and there's always a price."

"Is that okay?"

She shrugged. "I guess. I mean, every marriage has compromises."

"That wasn't the question, Beth. The question was, is it okay for you to perpetually compromise or roll over, except when you wheedle an exception and then tolerate Jonah's punishment, or 'price,' whatever that means."

"He's miserable, that's what. He goes nonverbal, or acts huffy, or superior, or some other, well, juvenile acting out, really."

"So, is that okay? Is that the marriage you signed up for?"

Beth sat back into the couch. Images from her life with Jonah flashed: their awkward courtship, the tedium of dragging him through marriage preparation, his intermittent engagement in household life. "Oh, crap." She paused. "Oh, holy crap."

"Is that a 'no'?"

Beth shook her head. "It's the marriage I signed up for, but I thought I was signing up for something else." She looked down at her hand, twisting her engagement and wedding ring around and around. "I really thought Jonah was a sensitive, misunderstood genius and that I, I, would rescue him. I could protect him from his half-wit sister, his dingbat, mousy mother, his absent-minded professor father and all the mean, vapid kids who didn't understand him. And now," she was interrupted by her voice cracking in a sob, "now I see that maybe I was the one misunderstanding."

"You misunderstood ...?"

"Everyone. His sister's a freaking genius. Super-high IQ, but we can't tell Jonah because he would feel bad. His mom, well, let's just say everyone underestimates her and then they find they're wrong. And yeah, his dad's an absent-minded professor but he doesn't hurt anyone, except maybe ignoring Alex, mostly, for a bunch of years. And everyone else who knows Jonah. Well, if someone has a problem with everyone maybe it's not everyone that's wrong." She sighed, less raggedly this time. "Maybe, I guess, it was me. Maybe he is an arrogant, selfish person. He has his good points—he can be so tender and kind—but it's so damned transient. And it mostly is a precursor to demanding sex. It's starvation rations for a marriage."

"A precursor to demanding sex," Dr. Garnette repeated quietly. The words seemed to resonate. "Did you hear yourself say that?"

Beth nodded.

"And does that sound like kindness to you?"

Beth covered her face. "No." Her fingers sank down her face, fell into her lap. "No, it sounds awful." She wrung her fingers and added, "And it feels awful to talk about him like this. I mean, I love Jonah."

Dr. Garnette nodded slowly. "So, Beth. You love your husband. You don't trust him, you don't particularly like him, and you're not too crazy about your own behavior lately. You're upset with the status quo and want to make a change. Sound about right?"

"Yes." She drew her eyebrows together. "That sounds very … curt. But yeah, that's the essence of the problem." She paused. "I do want to make a change."

"Well, who can you change?"

Beth snapped her gaze from her hands to Dr. Garnette's face. "Who can I change?" she repeated. "Well, me, I guess. I can change myself. But what do I do?"

Dr. Garnette tilted his head to one side. "Lots of possible answers there, Beth. The only piece of this puzzle you have significant influence over is yourself. So that's where to start. You'll have to do something differently. Or not do something. Or do something new." He paused. "Big changes start very small. Small changes accumulate. Don't think big, necessarily. Just figure out something true to yourself, small and real."

"True to me, small and real?" Beth squinted.

"Don't try to be someone else. Don't try to solve everything with one grand gesture. Be honest about what you're doing and what your intentions are, to yourself especially."

Beth nodded slowly. "Okay. I think I was on the right track after all." She sat up straighter. "I think I'm going to go spend a few days in the mountains with Alex. My mother-in-law," she clarified, not wanting Dr. Garnette to think she was visiting a man. "But I will of course let Jonah know and I'll make arrangements for the dogs to be visited by his sister. Which will annoy Jonah but at least I know they'll get good care while I'm away. And my intentions … well. Alex was a master appeaser, and somehow she broke out of it and never stopped being Alex. She just became … more herself. Kept being loving and kind. I want to talk to her. She knows Jonah. I think maybe she can help me sort things out."

"Does that feel true, small, and real? A few days in the mountains with your mother-in-law, getting some fresh air, hiking, resting, having some much-needed heart-to-hearts with someone who loves Jonah even more than you do?"

"Absolutely."

"That sounds like a plan, then," Dr. Garnette said. "So, do we set something up or do you want to do a wait-and-see?"

"No, we'd better set something up in ... a week or two? I need accountability."

The appointment was set, payment made, and Beth felt lighter as she left. She sat in the car for a few moments, and decided to text Alex.

Hi, Alex, how are the mountains?

Beth! Everything's beautiful here. How are you?

OK. Can we talk?

Call me when you can.

Beth called immediately. Her intentions to casually ask about a visit dissolved; she started crying when she heard Alex's voice.

"Beth ... are you okay? Is Jonah okay?"

"Yes, both okay. I just ... Alex, can I come visit? I mean, I know you're on sabbatical and everything, but I just thought—" Beth paused, trying to control the shaking in her voice. "I thought, maybe—"

"I would love to see you. No dogs. That's the landlord's rule. Not even Sol. When?"

"Well, it's Wednesday ... maybe Friday? I can leave super early."

"That would be great. I'll text you the address. It's pretty easy to find, but be rested. It's a good eight hours if traffic isn't too crazy around Atlanta. And traffic's always crazy around Atlanta."

"Thanks, Alex. This really means a lot."

"I'm looking forward to seeing you! It's supposed to be great weather; good daytime hiking and cool evenings. You'll love it."

"Thanks ... I'm in the parking lot. I'm going to head home."

"See you soon, Beth. Love you."

"I love you, Alex," Beth responded.

Beth took a deep breath and texted Sandy.

Sandy, weird favor to ask. I'm going to be out of town for a few days. Any chance you can stop in a couple times a day to take care of the dogs?

Sure. Should I just stay?

No, Jonah will probably be around but I want to be sure the dogs get their TLC.

No worries. When do you leave?

Friday early morning. Thanks, Sandy, this really helps.

It's nothing. Let's catch up for coffee when you get back! Or ice cream. It's been a while.

Sounds great!

Beth put her phone into her bag and put the bag on the back floorboard. She nodded at her reflection in the rearview mirror and headed for home.

Chapter 19

Walking into the house, Beth felt her heart starting to pound. Jonah was home. She fended off the dogs with head pats and murmured assurances of upcoming food and walks. She glanced over; the food dishes were empty, the water dishes dry. Jonah was slumped on the couch, the television playing a documentary about Mir.

"Hey there," she called as cheerily as possible.

There was no response. She rolled her eyes, and followed up with, "Have the dogs had their walks?"

Still no response. "Given their behavior, I'll take that as a no," she said, firmly, and snapped leashes on Apple and Mac. Her hands were sweaty; she wiped them on her clothes. She shook her head to herself as she took them for a brisk walk. The evening was still quite warm, with a soft breeze. Heading back, she changed the leashes to Sol and Anastasia, taking a slower pace, and then went on to feeding the dogs.

Jonah had seemingly not moved. She shrugged; she decided she was not going to play games. She pulled out ingredients for dinner. She started putting the salad onto two plates, as always, paused, and then decided to make a bowl. That way, if Jonah didn't want any, she could just cover it up and save it for tomorrow. She did the same thing with the leftover black beans and rice, heating a serving dish full and putting out the two places at the table. "Water or iced tea with dinner?" she called.

"Not hungry."

"Ah. Okay." She poured herself some water, sat down, and took a few slow, deep breaths. She folded her hands, said grace quietly, and raised her glass to the universe. "To true, small, and real," she toasted, and then ate.

She had expected to feel like she was force-feeding herself but after a few forkfuls realized she was hungry, more than usual, and that the food tasted unusually good. *I wonder what that's about*, she thought, and shrugged. *Just enjoy it*, she told herself. *Why shouldn't it taste delicious? I love beans and rice.*

After dinner, she cleaned up, covering the leftovers. "See you tomorrow, no doubt," she said quietly as she shut the refrigerator door. She washed the few dishes and went to the living room. Jonah was slumped with Anastasia in his lap and a half-eaten bag of chips next to him. She tried to act casual; in her imagination she was sauntering nonchalantly as if she hadn't a care in the world.

"What's going on?" Jonah asked. His voice was angry but his face seemed flat.

"Um, you're watching a documentary. I took care of the dogs and had dinner. The usual."

"You know what I mean."

Beth folded her arms and raised her eyebrows. "I know what I would mean if I said that, under the circumstances. But no, Jonah, I'm not playing mind reader today. So why don't you tell me what you mean?"

"Beth. Seriously. I'm not playing games."

"Oh, that's something, coming from you. You're nothing but games."

"What's that supposed to mean?"

"Ah. That's mine, so yeah, I'll interpret it. You got fired and you didn't tell me. You lied. You lied every moment of every day for two weeks, pretending you were going to work and coming home, and never saying a word. You sit here and make life miserable with your scowling and your supercilious attitude. You never ask how I am and so here's the update. I'm going to visit your mom for a few days at her sabbatical hermitage. I'm leaving early Friday. Sandy's going to stop by twice a day to tend to the dogs because it's been made manifestly clear that you either can't or won't do an adequate job. That's what's going on for me." Beth felt her heart pounding so hard against her ribs she felt certain it would show right through her blouse.

Jonah stayed slumped on the couch, but his mouth opened in surprise just briefly before he seemed to catch himself. His eyes narrowed, his lips pressed together, and he shrugged. "My mom? Seriously? That's your idea of a little getaway?"

"Why, yes, as a matter of fact. I'm looking forward to learning from her." And Beth turned and headed into the bedroom. She shook with anger. She had confronted him on the lying and his job, and all he did was criticize his mother? Beth looked at her duffel bag and the pile of clothes and started creating order, getting things put together for a few days in the slightly cooler Georgia mountains. She made a short list of the last-minute things to be gathered—her gratitude journal, her prayer books, a book to read, a notebook—clipped it to the duffel strap and put the bag against the wall. She nodded at it and then went to the chest of drawers to straighten out the mess she'd made rummaging blindly earlier that day.

She found the little yellow bear with its placid, sweet smile and embroidered flowers, clasped it to her chest and felt the tears start. She placed the bear in her duffel bag, not really understanding why, tucking it under the sweatshirts. Then she went to the kitchen to make a cup of herbal tea.

Heading out to the backyard, she let Sol out to romp a bit. She took out her phone, put it back in her pocket, pulled it out again, hesitated, and called Courtney.

"Hey, girl," came Courtney's cheery voice. "Perfect timing! We just got bath and bed wrapped up."

"Sure this is a good time?"

"Absolutely." Courtney's voice softened. "Is this a phone conversation? Or an ice cream emergency meeting?"

"Well ... would Mark mind if you slipped out for ice cream?"

"No, I'll just bring him home something." Beth heard Mark in the background, saying something about a banana split, and laughed.

"I'll let Jonah know. See you in a few."

Beth grabbed her purse and keys. "I'm meeting Courtney for ice cream. See you later." She left without waiting for a response.

Mr. Twisty is surprisingly busy for a September Wednesday night, Beth thought, and then realized she had no frame of reference. Who was to say what their usual Wednesdays were like? It seemed as if half the high school marching band had gone there after one of their hours-long practices, so she and Courtney had to wait.

Beth had planned to be calm and collected but Courtney's sweet, concerned face, like Alex's kind voice, triggered an outburst of tears. Courtney just wrapped her arms around Beth and waited. Beth pulled back after a few moments, nodding, and said, "It's just so great that you came out. I needed to talk."

Courtney nodded. "Jonah?"

"Yes." Beth sighed. "I'm ashamed to tell you." She paused. "Jonah was fired two weeks ago and didn't tell me. He's been leaving each morning and coming back every afternoon, not saying a word. Technically, he still hasn't. His boss let me know by accident, asking how I was about it. Naturally, she assumed I knew." She shook her head. "I confronted him today and he didn't even respond to that, just make a snarky remark about my plan to visit his mom this weekend."

"Isn't his mom off somewhere painting?"

"Yeah, she's in a cabin up in north Georgia for a few months as part of her sabbatical." Beth made a determined smile. "I have special permission to be a visitor."

"And that's what Jonah talked about when you told him you knew about him being fired ... two weeks ago, you said? My God, that's half a month. That's a half month of bills."

"Right. Maybe we'd be planning differently if I'd known our income was cut so much."

"You must be furious."

"Furious. And scared. I need some time. And I think Alex can help." Courtney tilted her head curiously. "My parents visited ... which you know. And my dad had a little chat with me." She recounted the dog walk and the appeasement conversation.

"Oh, gosh, Beth. That must been awful. For both of you."

"Exactly. I've been thinking about my parents' lives together entirely differently these past six weeks. And in the meantime, Jonah's been further and further away. And Alex, Jonah's mom, well, she was the master appeaser in that family. But last year, she sort of changed."

"Yeah, you said she kind of broke free."

Beth nodded. They were next in line; they paused to make their orders and then went to the pickup window. Once they had their ice creams, they headed off to a small table at the edge of the well-lit parking lot. Resuming, Beth said, "So Alex went from being the appeaser-in-chief to being her real self again, but she never got mean. Or super angry. She just ... I don't know. From out here it looked easy but I'm sure it wasn't. I want to spend some time with her."

Courtney nodded. "Alex is an interesting person, that's for sure. That whole science-and-art thing, for example. That's one complicated brain."

"Exactly. And Jonah keeps acting like she's an idiot."

Courtney shrugged. "Beth, seriously. Jonah treats everyone that way. Stop acting surprised."

Beth flinched, only half joking. "Hey!"

"I love you, Beth. But, really. Your husband is difficult. At first, I was trying to be generous, figured maybe he was depressed. Well, no. I'm not diagnosing him, but he's got narcissism written all over him. Any threat to his perceived superiority upsets him. Nothing new here. He was like this when we were in college." Courtney paused. "I'm worried about this secrecy. Any notion what he's been up to all day for two weeks? What's the phone show?"

"I don't know ... it never occurred to me to check on him. I guess I could look." She pulled out her phone and opened the app they used to keep in touch. It showed nothing. She looked up at Courtney. "It's been disabled on his phone. If I'd been trying to find him, I wouldn't have been able."

Courtney poked at her dish of ice cream. "Beth, this is weird. I don't know what to tell you, but I think a little time to figure out yourself in all this is important." She paused. "On the other hand ... any chance he's really depressed? Suicidal? Any signs of that?"

Beth shook her head. "Well, he seems really unhappy but that's been, well, months. Years? I don't know. He has moments of being wonderful."

"Do those moments have anything to do with anything besides sex?" Beth's mouth fell open, and Courtney gently reached over and patted her chin upward. "Is there any other time when Jonah is just tender and kind, apropos of nothing?"

"Well, yeah," Beth said. "Of course." She paused. "I just ... I just can't remember any off the top of my head." She paused. "Yes, sometimes he just ... knows what to do. I just can't think of any right now." Beth shook her head. "But we don't have fun anymore."

Courtney rubbed Beth's shoulder. "I think a long weekend in the mountains will do you a world of good, my friend."

Jonah was still on the couch with Anastasia half in his lap when Beth arrived home. He looked up when she greeted him. "Courtney sends her love," she said, as cheerily as she could.

Jonah nodded slightly. "How was ice cream?"

"Good. Chocolate with chocolate sprinkles. A waffle cone, dipped in chocolate." Beth poured herself a glass of water. "Do you want anything?"

"No." A pause, and then, "Thanks."

Interesting, she thought, *that little attempt at civility*. She glanced at the clock. It was almost her usual bedtime. She glanced at the back of Jonah's head and the television with its ever-present documentary footage. Now it seemed to be World War II, apparently the Russian front during winter. Hellish, she thought, just hellish. She wondered what the appeal was for this endless diet of misery. Instead, she stepped into the living room area and sat down on the loveseat, perpendicular to the couch. Jonah glanced at her sidelong and then reverted to the television. She leaned forward. "Jonah, we should talk."

"About?"

"About your job situation. About what we should be planning here. Maybe what happened? Why you didn't tell me. Where you have been going every day and why the family connection app is turned off on your phone. And yeah, I checked."

"Beth, it's late. I'm tired. You're tired. Let's talk tomorrow."

"Jonah, I think this is serious. I need at least something, something to help make this all make some sense."

"Well, apparently you know I was let go." Jonah shifted, eliciting a soft protest from Anastasia. "How much else do you know from ... Arthelle, I suppose? Your little comrade in arms."

"No, she asked how we both were and seemed to assume I would know." Beth paused. "Which was really embarrassing."

"So, it's about you being embarrassed?"

Beth nearly spilled her water. She set it on the coffee table firmly. "No, that's not 'it.' Maybe part of it, yeah. But who wouldn't be humiliated to find out their spouse was lying to them for two weeks?"

"Beth, stop being so dramatic. I wasn't lying."

"You were. Every moment you let me believe you were going to work, coming from work, that our financial situation was the same, was a lie. Jonah, didn't you think I'd notice when the payroll deposits came in, or in your case, didn't come in? How long did you intend to keep lying?"

"Not lying, Beth. I just didn't feel ready to talk about it."

"So where have you been?"

Jonah shrugged. "The library. The mall food court." He glanced at her face. "I was looking online for work, Beth. I wasn't just hanging out."

Beth shook her head. "Jonah ... what happened? People don't just get fired for no reason."

"Ask Arthelle."

"I can't ask Arthelle! She can't talk about that. It's confidential."

"Fine. It's confidential. And I don't feel like talking about it."

Beth folded her arms across her chest. She wondered if she could make her heart stop pounding by pushing her forearms into her ribs. "Jonah, I can't ask Arthelle. But you know damned well I can find out because people talk. I just have to ask my staff. I guess they had the good manners not to say anything." Beth suddenly flashed on the past two weeks of work, the way her staff looked uneasy in meetings, the quick sign-offs rather than lingering to chat. She'd hardly noticed, writing it off as post-summer funks. Now it seemed different; she realized they were avoiding having a conversation about their peer, her husband, being fired.

Jonah scowled. "Well, fine." He turned the television volume down but did not mute it; the narrator droned softly about the conditions on the eastern front. "I was sick of that job, sick of working there. You knew hat."

"Yeah, we talked months ago about you looking for something else."

"Well, nothing's shown up that looks interesting. And I guess I sort of tuned out on the job." Jonah shrugged. "I got tired of working with idiots."

Beth pressed her lips together and took a deep breath. "Jonah, there are no idiots at our company. They don't hire idiots." She paused. "All your peers have at least a bachelor's degree in engineering. Not idiots."

He shrugged. "Yeah, have it your way. I was tired of putting up with that place, with having my work kicked back for more details, to be sure it incorporated what clients requested ... doesn't anyone tell these clients their ideas are stupid? Anyway. I started refusing to do revisions that didn't make sense to me and apparently, they'd rather have the little sheep who do what they're told instead of someone who thinks for himself."

"Jonah." Beth paused. "Jonah. You just decided you knew better and you'd rather be fired than work with the team?"

He nodded. "Yeah, that's pretty much it. I've been looking online. So far nothing really appeals."

"I don't think appeal is the most important factor at present. Income is. Our lifestyle is based on two incomes, not one. And you're not even trying."

This time he pivoted to face her. "How would you know if I'm trying?"

Beth rolled her eyes. "Oh, please. You've been unemployed for two weeks. You haven't told me the truth. You haven't even pitched in more around the house to make my life a little easier. You've just been your usual lazy lump self while I've been naïvely working away, stupidly trusting you."

"Beth, I didn't lie to you."

She stood up, shaking her head. "Jonah, I just got done defending you to Courtney. I packed my bags to go visit your mom to have her help me figure out how to do better by you. And you won't even admit that going through this farce of dressing for work and coming home and never breathing a word to indicate you've been fired might have been wrong." Beth rubbed her temples. "I'm sorry, Jonah, I don't have anything else to say except, goodnight. Enjoy your little show." She left the room quickly, not wanting to look at him or say anything else. She stepped into their room. Sol was almost glued to her leg, looking up with eyebrows cocked. She bent over and pet him, rubbing his floppy ears and whispering his name. Her voice wobbled.

She straightened and looked around the room. She prepared for bed, then hesitated. She glanced at Sol, sitting attentively next to her side of the bed. "I can't do it, buddy," she said softly. "Not today." She sighed, gathering up her bedside books and her pillow. "Come on, Sol." She padded down the hall to the guest room. Sol whined softly. She petted his head and he seemed to settle down. Beth moved the trays of mosaic supplies to the work table and then slipped into the guest bed, with Sol curled up at the side of the bed. Before she'd read two pages, Sol was peeking over the side at her, one eyebrow raised. Then a big, yellow paw reached up and rested on the bed. Beth pretended to look at her book, watching sidelong as Sol, trying to be stealthy, crept one paw, then his head, then the other paw, then an entire foreleg, then the other foreleg, onto the bed. Soon the whole immensity of Sol was beside her, his head pressed up against her side.

Hours later, she woke up to Jonah repeating her name. She shook her head, confused, and then remembered she was in the guest room. Sol was snoring softly next to her. Jonah stood in the doorway in his T-shirt and shorts, his arms hanging limply at his sides. "Beth. Beth."

"Jonah. What?"

"What are you—why?" He gestured around the guest room. "What's going on?"

"Jonah." Beth sighed. She glanced at the clock; it was almost 2:00 a.m. "It's late. Go get some sleep. We can talk tomorrow."

"But you're not in bed." Jonah stepped into the room. "I can't sleep."

"Good night, Jonah." Beth slid under the covers and turned away. Sol shifted with a grunt to accommodate her. She heard Jonah walk away. She sighed, shuddering. Sol nudged her softly. "Good boy, Sol," she whispered, and Sol huffed with satisfaction.

Chapter 20

Beth woke up early, shaking her head before she was even out of bed. She dreaded the day, the conversation to be had with Jonah—if last night were any indication, it would be an infuriating waste of time. It was a regular workday, and she had to make arrangements to be out Friday and Monday. She had the time coming but usually didn't take time without considerable notice. Still, nothing huge was on the horizon and she could be reached. The morning was fairly typical, except Jonah did not emerge from the room at his usual time. She assumed that, with the ruse of employment blown, he felt free to just sleep in. She shrugged. *Fine, sleep in. That much less time I have to figure out how not to throw something at the back of your head.*

At lunchtime, Jonah was still not out. Sol was, as usual, under her feet at the desk. Apple, Mac, and Anastasia were in the hall, quieter than usual. They showed up for their walks and food but otherwise were subdued. Beth figured the family fight had them discombobulated. Finally, Beth could not resist checking; he was in bed. Anastasia ran in with her, and jumped on the bed, whining.

He did not respond to either her or Anastasia. She shook him. "Jonah. Jonah." She felt his face; he was pallid and damp. "Jonah," she shouted. "Wake up." He barely moved his head. He peered at her. "What?" His voice was slurred. She shook him again. "Jonah. Wake up." She glanced around. "Did you take something?"

"What are you talking about?" Jonah covered his eyes with one hand. "Crap, it's bright in here. What do you want? What's going on?"

"It's after noon, and you were unconscious. You don't look right. You're sweaty and pale and ... what the hell?" Beth's eyes fell on the nightstand. The bottles of ibuprofen and antihistamines were nearly empty. "How much of these did you take?"

"Huh?" Jonah rolled over onto his back. "Oh. Yeah. Headache. Wouldn't go away. Couldn't sleep. I don't know. Maybe three. Or four."

Beth rubbed her forehead. "All at once?"

"No. I took like, two or three when I went to bed. And then a few ibu and a few allergy pills this morning. Just wanted some sleep."

Beth picked up Anastasia with one arm and flipped the covers off Jonah with the other. "So, it wasn't three or four, it was more. My God, Jonah, what are you doing? Get up. Get up, start moving. Or I'm calling the paramedics."

Jonah turned away. "Get out of here. I don't need the paramedics."

"You get up or I'm calling an ambulance. I don't know what to think. Were you trying to kill yourself? Should you be in the hospital to be safe?"

Jonah whirled around and sat up, and then grabbed his head with one hand, steadying himself with the other. "Crap." He glared at her through his fingers. "So now you're a mental health expert, too, huh?"

"What the hell am I supposed to think? You're perpetually unhappy. You lose your job. You lie to me. And now this? Overdosing on pills?"

"Beth, stop being dramatic. I took a double dose a little too close together a few times. Killer headache. Fine. My bad. Can something happen here that's not about you?"

"It's not about me. Well, except I love you and yeah, I'm upset!"

He sneered. "Yeah, what would you tell your precious little friends then? Poor you, your loser husband got fired and then tried to off himself? Poor, poor, pitiful Bethie. Nobody loves her." He wobbled a bit and put both hands firmly on the edge of the mattress, feet on the floor. "Mommy doesn't love her, Daddy doesn't love her. Poor little Beth." He snorted. "Always all about you, Beth."

She stepped back from the bed, holding Anastasia tight against her chest. "Jonah." Her head spun. "You are seriously trying to pin this back on me?"

Jonah shrugged. "Wear it if it fits, Beth." He nodded toward the door. "Go ... take care of the dogs. Or work. Or whatever the hell it is you do all day."

Beth pressed her lips together and took a deep breath. "What the hell it is I do all day is support this family and take care of everyone, Jonah. That's what I do all day. And yeah, I think I'll just go get back to it." She whirled around and stomped out of the room. Anastasia whimpered at her; Beth put her down gently and the little dog ran back into the bedroom and leaped up on the bed to tend to Jonah. *Of course*, Beth thought. Mac and Apple were in the hall, quizzical. They didn't go into the bedroom but seemed to relax and go about their business now that the shouting had stopped. Sol pressed his head against her hip and then followed Beth back to her desk.

"Whatever the hell it is you do all day" kept ringing in her head. *Whatever I do all day?* Beth could barely see, she was so angry. *I'm transparent*, she thought. *Every moment of my workday is logged on and documented. Every walk with the dogs and trip to the store shows up as a map Jonah can see whenever he cares to. He probably saw my route to and from Mr. Twisty, watched my phone ping in the long line.* She imagined him sitting in the public library, watching her daily actions in their quiet predictability, like some sort of buzzard with its deathly gaze, circling overhead.

Jonah eventually made his way out of the bedroom, wearing sweats and a T-shirt. She assiduously focused on work, aware of his shuffling in the kitchen, the noise of the coffee maker, the smell of the toast. She heard the television and the crackle of a bag of junk food. She made a note to herself to stop buying junk food; it wasn't helping Jonah's overall well-being, and she didn't eat that stuff. A few times she heard him come to the doorway. She kept typing—what, she wasn't always quite sure—until he left and then revised the word salad that had served the appearance of diligent working.

She wrapped up her day with a sigh, set up her absence email response, and pushed back from the desk. Sol looked up expectantly. "Yep, time for our walk," she said. She leashed up Sol and Anastasia first; she wanted a slow start to the walk routine. Her mind reeled. All about you, Beth; all about poor Beth. Jonah's spiteful voice echoed in her head.

It is entirely unfair, she told herself. *He's the one who got fired. He's the one who lied to me every day for weeks.* She had to find him half unconscious and woozy. And he had the temerity to make it about her being dramatic, to say that it was all about her.

By the time she came back home to take Apple and Mac for their walk, she was feeling less physically agitated; the movement and fresh air had helped. Now she walked briskly, with an occasional trot tossed in to accommodate the greyhounds' pent-up energy. *All about me*, she thought. *Right. How dare he.* Mac paused and Apple obligingly waited while Mac investigated a fence post, then Apple took a turn. Beth waited patiently. A cardinal peeped insistently above her. She glanced up and thought fleetingly of Alex and her retreat. "I can't wait," she said aloud. "Can't wait." She sighed and gave a tug to the leashes. "Let's go, kiddos." They headed home. *Almost there*, she thought. *Just get through this evening and then leave. Maybe four-ish? Miss most of the traffic locally in the morning and near Atlanta before rush hour that way.*

Back at the house, Jonah was watching television. She announced she was home. He grunted a response, not turning his head. Then she got out the leftovers from yesterday and had dinner, not saying a word about it to Jonah. She could barely chew her food; the texture seemed wrong. It was hard to swallow. She left half of it uneaten. She cleaned up quietly, glancing at the back of his head. She felt shaky. Then she took a glass of water and stepped outside. Sol came out with her. She brushed the air in front of her face; the mosquitoes weren't too bad. She settled into one of the low Adirondack chairs, her face tilted toward the darkening sky.

She heard Izzy's giggle wafting over the fence. She and Ozzy were outside, too. Beth slunk lower in the chair, even though they couldn't see her through the fence. Still, she just wanted to be invisible. She heard Ozzy's voice—lower, not clear. Izzy's voice came through, with a running commentary on the events of the day. Beth smiled, shaking her head. Izzy was always bubbling with news. She watched the high clouds fade from bright pink to purple with rusty red bottoms and then seem to disappear into the night sky. She tuned out Izzy's voice until she heard, "Beth."

She shook her head. *Don't listen*, she thought, but she couldn't help herself. She heard Izzy say, "And Courtney said she saw Beth the other day for ice cream. I wish they'd let me know. I haven't seen Beth except for the monthly coffee in forever." Then Ozzy's lower voice, and Izzy's apparent response. "Well, she works all the time and the rest of the time it's the Jonah show." An Ozzy rumble and then Izzy. "Oh, crap, no, Jonah won't hear a thing. You can see the blue light from their family room; he's probably watching a show about rockets or wars or something." A pause. She assumed Ozzy was speaking, but then she heard his voice more clearly. "Izzy, that's Beth being Beth. She's your friend; you know how she is."

How am I? Beth wondered. She leaned forward, gripping the edge of the armrests.

"Yeah, she's a bit of a martyr, but I love her. She just worries about everyone else, that's all."

A bit of a martyr. Beth clapped her hand over her mouth to muffle a gasp.

"I don't know for martyring. She's a very kind person. If you're worried about her, why don't you reach out?" A pause and then, "Is that their dog digging at the fence?"

"Probably. Four guesses which one it is." Izzy laughed, and then called out, "Sol?"

Sol obligingly barked and Beth heard them both laugh. "Good boy," Ozzy said. "Maybe Beth's away. Jonah's the one who leaves the dogs outside for hours."

"Probably. I'll call her." She heard scuffling. "I want to go in. The no-see-ums are terrible."

Beth stayed still until she heard the door close, and then, bent over, tiptoed back to the house. She whispered for Sol, and stealthily closed the door. She turned and saw Jonah, arms folded, staring at her.

"What was the sneaky walk about?" he asked.

She shrugged. "I was outside and overheard a little conversation between Izzy and Ozzy and didn't want to let on I was out there."

He nodded. "Oh." Then he glanced at the kitchen. "What about dinner?"

"I ate leftovers earlier." Beth stepped into the kitchen. "Did you want something?"

He stared at her. "I can get my own food, thank you." He stepped past her to the cabinet. "Not super hungry. Just some chips and dip, I think."

She wondered if he was doing this to push her into offering him something more nutritious. She resisted. "Not much of a dinner," she commented.

"Well, I'm not much of a cook. Not much appetite." He shrugged. "I've just been sitting around all day."

"Well, the dogs could use a little walk before bed. Fee free," Beth offered.

"No, thanks." Jonah ambled back to the couch with his chips and dip. "Knock yourself out. I'll be on duty while you're in the mountains with Mom."

"Sandy's coming in twice a day for dog duty, remember? In case you're out."

"Oh, great. Miss save-the-world will be here twice a day. Maybe I will be out of the house."

"Well," Beth said. "Suit yourself. I'll miss walking the dogs." *But not enough to skip the trip*, she thought.

Beth was awake at three thirty, and decided it was smart to get up at that time. Sol whined at her but obligingly followed her to the kitchen. She gave him a small snack while she had breakfast and a cup of coffee.

She filled two travel mugs with coffee and slipped a protein bar and an apple into a bag for the trip. She let Sol have a quick outing into the backyard and then kissed him on the head. She left a short note for Jonah:

Off to see your mom's hermitage. Have a good weekend. Call if you need anything. Love you—Beth.

She hesitated and then drew a heart after her name, as she always did for Jonah. She sighed, left the note on the kitchen table, and glanced around the house. Then she packed up the car and drove away.

The ride was long. She listened to some music, then to the news, then music. She fretted about the time. What about rush hour around Atlanta? What if she ran late and had to navigate mountain roads in the dark? She stopped to fill the tank, used the restroom, and checked her phone. No word from Jonah. A *Looking forward to seeing you later!* from Alex, and a *Hey, how are you?* from Izzy. Beth felt her shoulders slump. *A bit of a martyr*, she thought, but texted, *Hey! All good. On the way to see J's mom in the mountains for a girls' weekend. How are you?*

We're good. The weekend sounds fun! Looking forward to hearing about it.

Thanks.

We should catch up when you get back! Just us girls, or maybe all four of us?

Ha, fat chance, Beth thought. *I can't possibly impose Jonah on anyone in his current state.*

She texted, *Just us girls first. Miss you!*

Miss you! Let me know when you're back!

Will do.

Beth sighed, tucked her phone back into her bag, and placed the bag on the back floorboard. She pushed her hair back from her face, adjusted her sunglasses, and headed back on the road toward Alex and the mountains.

The trip seemed interminable. Finally, she was off the interstate and then off the highway, onto country roads that wrapped themselves around the landscape. It was late afternoon; warm sunlight streaked the faded macadam and glowed on orange lilies that crowded, impossibly thick, along the roadside. Beth opened her window and breathed deeply, settling into the slower speed after highway travel. Mountain air, the smell of different forests than Florida, a touch of late afternoon coolness. Her GPS intoned instructions: turn here; turn there. She made what seemed certain to be a wrong turn, an almost 120-degree angle to the right onto gravel, steep up a hillside. Impossibly, it wasn't a driveway; it was a road. Long driveways into tree-filled lots, houses barely visible, punctuated the clusters of red, gold, green, and orange, with splatters of daisies on the roadside. The road dead-ended ahead. The driveway to Alex's friend's home was the last right. She pulled in and parked next to Alex's car. Stepping out, she looked past the house toward the back of the property. It sat on a steep hill and the view encompassed miles of trees, hills, and a distant town.

The door opened. Beth turned to see Alex hurrying toward her, smiling happily, arms outstretched. Beth had time to extend her own arms before she was enveloped in a hug that seemed too big to come from Alex's smaller frame.

And much to her own surprise, Beth burst into tears. She leaned her head into Alex's shoulder and sobbed. Alex just hugged her and gently stroked Beth's hair. Finally, she said, "Let's grab your things and get you inside, Beth." Beth nodded silently. Alex sighed. "Jonah?" Beth nodded again. They gathered Beth's few things and went inside.

Chapter 21

"And so that's it. He got fired, he lied about it, he's been doing God knows what, and he practically overdosed on medicine. He refuses to come to counseling and now he's blaming me, that I'm the narcissist who has to have everything perfect for 'poor me.'" Beth sighed and leaned back on the huge couch, her hands wrapped around a mug of cocoa. She wiggled her shoulders into the cushion. *The furniture here was made for lumberjacks*, she thought. Everything seemed large, and by comparison, Alex, comfortably folded up in the armchair beside the couch, seemed too small for her surroundings. Alex nodded silently, took a sip of her cocoa, placed it on the coffee table, and half turned so she could face Beth directly.

"Beth, Jonah's my son, and I love him. But we both know he's always been ... challenging. Surely you noticed this before. I mean, the negative attitude about other people."

Beth shrugged. "Well, yeah, but. I mean, he would be different with me." She paused. "At least, sometimes, he used to be." She looked up defensively. "Sometimes he would seem so soft." She thought of how he had gently reproached her for buying the flowery bear and how he just held her when it became clear that, once again, she was not pregnant. "But most of the time, yeah. He's pretty negative, and it's gotten worse. He never wants to go anywhere. He used to complain about work all the time. And, of course, now he doesn't have a job."

"That sounds depressing."

Beth pressed her lips together and raised her eyebrows. "For both of us."

"How long has it been worse? I mean, you said he refused to go to counseling. That means you did ask him about it."

"I did. He went once. It was awful. He insulted the therapist and refused to go back." Beth paused. "I went back. I've been going back. I think I have my own work to do." She looked straight at Alex. "And I guess that's why I'm here. To sort of kickstart that, past talking with the therapist. And I wondered ... I wondered how you did ..." Beth waved vaguely around the cabin. "How you did this. Just decided to do something that was right for you."

Alex nodded slowly. "Well, that's a long story. And it's late. Late for a girl who's been driving all day, stressed out, and usually has her schedule managed by four dogs, a job, and Jonah. So why don't we just have a little something to eat, watch the night settle over the hills, and pick this up with a long walk tomorrow?"

The evening was relaxing. Alex heated up some black bean soup and made two plates of salad. She spoke enthusiastically about Joe's sabbatical. He was having a great time fishing, talking to locals and investigating the regional historical societies' information on fishing as he explored the Eastern Seaboard. She also spoke about her work on this sabbatical: the long hikes and photography for future reference, the hours spent sketching and painting, the careful journaling about her observations, the process of painting, and her thoughts and feelings.

"It's been amazing," Alex smiled. "I can't believe I had doubts about doing this."

Beth shook her head and gazed up at the bright stars, glowing in the clear sky between the trees ringing the cabin. "This is incredible." She grinned, turning to Alex. "What's it like, really? Being up here by yourself? Do you ever, you know, get into town?"

Alex nodded. "Of course. There's Helen, fairly close to here, so I hit the grocery—there are a few on the outskirts, regular groceries, but I've been enjoying Betty's Country Store in town. I usually go there on the way home from church Saturday night. We can do that if you like, maybe get a bite to eat. Occasionally I go into town in the early morning on a weekday and just sit and enjoy a fancy coffee and watch the tourists and the regulars go by. And then that's enough."

"And you're not lonely?"

"No. I miss Joe, and Sandy and Cody, the twins, Gloria, you two." Beth smiled inside; she knew that Alex had rarely seen the two of them because of Jonah's avoidance and belief that his mother and sister were fools. "But missing people isn't the same as lonely. Frankly, I'm more worried about dealing with going back to it all."

"How so?"

"Well, I can't go back to how it was, precisely. Times have changed and so must I. Or I have changed and so the circumstances around me will have to, too. But in any event, I will be doing more art, more research, and a lot less catering to everyone else. Except the twins, I suspect."

"Sandy and Cody are pretty serious?"

"It certainly seems so. I don't ask questions, much, but they seem very much at ease with one another and Cody and the twins bring out the best in Sandy. I didn't see this coming. When they were little, and I was imagining joining our families, I thought, well, maybe Matt. And by middle school it was pretty clear it wasn't going to be Matt. Then I thought, well, maybe Kevin. But Cody was a surprise, and yet, once I saw them together, it made perfect sense."

Beth shook her head. "Jonah doesn't know what to make of that match."

"I'm not surprised." Alex laughed. "Poor Jonah is under the impression that Sandy is as dumb as a box of recycling, so Cody being head over heels for her just isn't going to make sense to Jonah."

Beth hesitated. "It's more than that. I don't think … I don't think Jonah understands relationships. Which doesn't make sense. I mean, we've been married five years, and … but yet, no. He doesn't seem to get it." She took a deep breath. "I don't think it occurs to Jonah that part of the deal is bringing out the best in each other. I don't think Jonah thinks about what *is* the best in me. And then Izzy told Ozzy that I'm a bit of a martyr. I mean, I overheard it. They were in Ozzy's backyard and I was in our backyard and … oh, Alex. Alex, am I a martyr?"

Alex reached over and rubbed Beth's shoulder. "I think you're trying to think too much after a too-long day. You're not crazy, or bad, or sick in the head, or whatever you're thinking. But you are, as usual, working too hard." She stood up, stretching, her face blurred by starlight. "Let's go inside and call it a night, shall we? I think this conversation will go much better with morning sunshine and a long walk in the woods."

Beth nodded, rising. "You're right. I didn't mean to get this serious."

"But you needed to talk a little bit to just set things out. And I appreciate it, Beth. I appreciate your willingness to be frank about all this, because it sounds very scary and painful." She wrapped an arm around Beth's shoulders as they headed inside. "Now. I have your room made up for you. I hope you'll like it. There's a kettle and some teas and a few goodies, in case you want to just get cozy and relax a bit before sleep. See you in the morning." She kissed Beth's cheek and sent her off to bed.

As she went up the stairs, Beth heard Alex sigh quietly. She glanced back and saw Alex turning into the kitchen, shaking her head.

Beth had barely glanced at the room when they'd put her things in. In the soft lamplight, the slanted ceilings were cozy. Instead of a window, a double sliding door led to a small balcony with two camp chairs and a small table. There was a skylight over the bed; stars shone above through branches. A patchwork quilt, a lot of pillows, a small table with a softly glowing lamp by the bedside. A chest of drawers with an electric kettle, mug, tray, teabags, sweetener, and a spoon. The bathroom adjacent. The only mirror was in the bathroom. Beth prepared for bed, made some chamomile tea, slipped between the sheets. She wondered if it was all right to leave the balcony doors ajar. She was upstairs, so no one should be able to get in. Or would a bear get in? She found herself worrying about things and decided that, for tonight, she'd leave the doors shut. She stood on the bed and cranked open the skylight so fresh air came in and got back under the covers.

She thought about Jonah. She thought she should text him, let him know she was here and okay. He hadn't checked in on her. She texted, *At your mom's. Drive OK. How are you?*

It was early by Jonah standards, only ten, but to Beth it felt like the middle of the night. She waited, thinking he'd respond fairly quickly. She was sure he was in his usual spot, watching the big screen, barking out his criticisms of scientists, generals, or Mother Nature.

She picked up her book and glanced over at her bag, frowned, and got out of bed once again. She pulled out the little yellow bear and looked at its placid, vaguely smiling face. She imagined it was hopeful looking, with its gentle expression and embroidered blossoms. She held it against her side and once more slipped into bed.

She looked at her phone. She checked to see if her alerts were silent—no, and there was still no reply from Jonah. Beth grimaced. She started worrying. Perhaps he was hurt. Perhaps he'd taken too many pills or had too much to drink. What if he was with someone? Her mind started to reel, and she whispered to herself, "Stop it. You know what he's doing; he's punishing you." Beth sighed and put the phone aside.

She sipped her tea, read until the words stopped making sense, turned off the lamp, and slipped down under the covers, the blossomy bear tucked against her chest.

Chapter 22

Sunlight streamed in and glowed on the slanting ceiling across from the bed as Beth opened her eyes. She looked around, momentarily confused, and then remembered. She was visiting Jonah's mother, not at home. She sat up. In the morning light, the room was bright, simply decorated and peaceful. She glanced at her phone on the bedside table. No word from Jonah. Beth shook her head, sighing, and got up to prepare for the day.

Ten minutes later she headed downstairs. Alex was at her easel. She turned to smile at Beth. "Good morning! Sleep well?"

"Yes, thanks. The room is cozy." She glanced toward the kitchen. "Coffee?"

"Help yourself," Alex said. "We're in a cabin but we have all the comforts of home. Well, my home, anyway."

The floor plan was open; the living room and dining area, with Alex's easel and art supplies, were all in view. Alex was standing a few feet back, arms folded, head tilted, gazing at the painting in progress.

Beth poured herself a cup of coffee and loaded it with cream and sugar. "Working already?"

"Hmm? Oh, the painting. No, just having a fresh look. It's helpful to step back."

Beth came to stand next to Alex. "It's really pretty. It's around here, I guess, right?"

Alex nodded. "I did a few plein air sketches and took a couple of photos, and this is my first attempt at a studio piece on this scene .It's so hard to resist the urge to put in every stupid leaf." She rolled her eyes, grinning. "That's one reason stepping back is important."

"Oh," Beth said politely. She didn't know quite what to say; she'd taken one obligatory art class as an elective, stumbled through, and hadn't looked back.

"Any time we're looking at two-dimensional art—print, photo, painting, drawing—the optimal viewing distance is about two to two and a half times the diagonal. The smaller the piece, the closer the viewing; the larger the piece, the further away we need to be to appreciate it. Which always makes me wonder about people who hang huge paintings over their sofas in small spaces. They can't possibly view the piece properly unless they stand outside their house and peek in. Which would be weird," she added.

"Oh, okay, that makes a lot of things make sense," Beth replied. "I always wondered about the people in museums zooming in and then backing way up to look at the same thing."

"Right. Well, that's your art lesson for the day. You're here for a little R&R and a bit of quiet time, right?" Alex nodded toward the kitchen. "How about some food and a nice, long, easy walk? The leaves are turning and it's just glorious here."

They had a bit of breakfast, chatting about the drive and Beth's work. Alex wasn't prying about Jonah. *That must take some effort,*

Beth thought gratefully. Beth's phone vibrated. It was Sandy, checking in. The dogs were all okay and had enjoyed a long walk. She was thinking about taking them to a dog park with Cody and the twins that afternoon, if that was okay with Beth. Beth frowned.

"Anything wrong, Beth?"

Beth shrugged. "Sandy checking in. The dogs are all okay. The weird thing is she's asking me if it's okay for her and Cody and the twins to take them to the park later. Which of course it is, but it's weird that she didn't just ask Jonah."

"Maybe Jonah's not there."

Beth texted back. *That would be great. How's Jonah?*

Grouchy. Watching TV. Didn't want to ask him anything.

Thanks! Let me know how the park goes.

Will do! Give Mom a hug.

Beth gave a halfhearted smile. "Sandy sends a hug. Jonah's grouchy and watching television. I guess I don't have to worry." Alex's eyebrows went up, and Beth grimaced. "Well, he has a lot going on and then there was the taking too many ibuprofen and allergy medicine, and when he didn't text back I was a little worried." She looked at Alex and then said, "Well, a lot worried. To tell the truth, I mostly thought he was punishing me by not responding last night, but there was that little nagging fear."

Alex frowned. "It's been that bad, then? That you're worried about his safety? Oh, Beth," she said sadly.

"No, no, he hasn't been saying or doing anything else even remotely suicidal. But the job, and the not wanting to do anything, and the ripping into me that I'm the narcissist who has to have all the attention and wants a pity party, it's been so awful."

"Of course." Alex sighed. "Let's go for a walk. You've got good hikers, right?"

"Absolutely," Beth said. They geared up—a light pack with a bottle of water each, hats, and a walking stick—and headed out.

"There's a trailhead just up the road, next to the property at the dead end, off to the left," Alex told Beth. "We'll take that. It's sort of winding and mostly uphill to the top of the mountain, and then we'll kill our quads going back downhill." She gestured with her walking stick. "This will help in a few spots." She winked. "And you can always use it to push away snakes."

"Snakes?" Beth almost squeaked, and Alex laughed.

"It's not so bad here, Beth. Mostly friendly creatures everywhere. Including the two-legged ones and the no-legged ones. Come on, let's go." They headed into the woods.

They walked in silence. Beth felt anxious and kept glancing at Alex, who seemed to be enjoying the walk. Nothing seemed to make sense. Here was Alex, looking like she belonged out here, with her hiking shorts, tanned legs, and thick socks pushed down to the tops of her hiking boots, floppy hat sliding down the back of her head, a small backpack smudged with paint against her back. She kept hearing Jonah's endless criticism of his mousy, boring mother. She recalled, guiltily, how easily she'd bought Jonah's story and had, in fact, discounted Alex and Sandy for years.

Beth shook her head. *Jonah*, she thought. *What is going on with him?*

"Maybe you should spend more time thinking about what's going on with you," Alex suggested.

Beth stopped in her tracks, mouth hanging open. "Oh my gosh. Did I just say something out loud?"

Alex grinned. "You said, 'Jonah,' and then, 'What's going on with him?'"

"Anything else?"

"No. Was there anything I should have overheard?" Alex smiled gently. "Beth. Seriously. I love Jonah, more than you do. But I think you need to take a big step back and use this time to enjoy the days and think a little bit about you. Who are you, Beth, besides the girl in charge of forcing Jonah, who has never been happy, to be content?"

"Ouch," Beth said, trying to be light. "That's a little harsh."

"Well, maybe. But you're the one here. If Jonah were here, I'd be encouraging him to start sorting out what's going on with him." Alex paused to gently touch some bright golden leaves drooping down from a tree. "Beautiful," she said quietly, and then, conversationally, "I mean, it's not a criticism. Heck, that's one reason I'm here, if you recall."

"Right."

They strolled on in silence. Occasionally, Alex would stop to point something out—a tree that looked like lots of other trees to Beth, or a view that allowed someone's cabin to barely peek through a riot of foliage. Alex had stopped and sketched here, found some wild grapes over there, picked a bunch of daisies for her table just over there. Beth tried to pay attention but kept coming back to the recommendation to focus on herself.

After an hour or so, they reached the top of the mountain. *It was a gentle walk the whole time, no rocky, scary parts, no cliffs to fall off,* Beth thought with relief. She had wondered just how rough it would be. Sure, Alex had said it was a "walk," but who knew? Reaching the apex, there was a marker, and the view stretched out around them in every direction.

Alex gestured broadly around them. "Isn't this glorious?" She pointed off into the distance. "There, you can see that little town? That's Helen. We can go into town this weekend if you like." She pointed out various scenes and then took out her water for a long drink.

"It's beautiful," Beth said quietly. It seemed very large, so much bigger than her small office, small yard, small neighborhood to walk the dogs. She felt a little lightheaded.

"Beth? Why don't you look down and just take a few deep breaths? Here." Alex took her arm. "Let's just walk in a bit of a circle. You look like you're having a bit of altitude plus open-space overwhelm there."

They walked slowly and Beth felt herself becoming clearer. She shook her head. "Wow. Is that a thing? That happens?"

"Oh, sure." Alex nodded toward the mountains around them. "It's pretty humbling, isn't it? Just stunning."

"Absolutely. It makes you think ... differently."

"Yes." Alex paused. "Want to have a seat and stay and take it in? Or would you rather wind back to the cabin?"

"Truthfully, I'd love to just sit and relax."

And so they did, finding a place in the grass without any blossoms and bees. Beth took a long drink of water, carefully closed her bottle, and looked squarely at Alex. "So. My therapist. My friends. You. Jonah. My friends behind my back. Everyone seems to think I need work."

"I don't recall saying that," Alex said mildly.

"Well, okay. But you did ask me about where I am in all this. And that thing about being in charge of making Jonah happy."

"Right. Isn't there more to you than that, Beth? Being Jonah's caregiver?"

"Well, yeah."

Alex looked off into the distance, silent for a moment, and then nodded. "You know, Beth, I spent a lot of time, years, I guess, doing what other people told me was a good idea." She grinned, shaking her head. "I never wanted to be a librarian, but other people said it was a good idea because of the kids' schedules and Joe's job. I don't like working Christmas pageants, I don't like having purple hair, I don't like adapting my schedule perpetually around your dogs. No offense," she added.

"None taken," Beth said lightly. "Even Jonah doesn't like adapting the schedule to our dogs."

Alex raised her eyebrows. "Well. It got to a place where I realized, with a little help, that all this was my problem, not anyone else's. And that meant I had to do something different and not wait around like Rapunzel in my little prison for someone to rescue me."

"And that's why this ... adventure?"

"Well, this adventure is part of who I really am. I like all this." She gestured around. "I could live here full-time, frankly. And maybe someday we will. But reclaiming the activities I love, and stopping saying, 'Oh, yes,' to things I really don't want to do as the automatic doormat response, that's the important thing." Alex turned to Beth. "You know I trained as a scientist as well as an artist? Two degrees, lots of field experience. The library is not my natural habitat." She sighed. "Well, actually, it is. I love the library! I love books, the quiet, the chance to pick up a book and learn something new ... which is not what I do at work."

Beth nodded slowly. "So, when you ask where I am ..."

"I'm not being critical. I'm being curious. The way YOU should be curious. For yourself." Alex stood up, stretching. "One thing has changed for me, for sure—sitting in one position requires a bit of stretching now." She grinned. "Let's head back."

"Okay," Beth agreed, rising. She felt a little stiff, too, and wondered again how many ways she might have been wrong about Alex. *What else am I wrong about?* She shook out her legs and started following her surefooted mother-in-law down the mountainside.

They walked back, the silence punctuated by conversation and commentary about the scenery, Beth's surprise at how hard hiking downhill was, and when Beth might like to go into town to have a bite to eat and see the Alpine architecture, impossibly perched in the Georgia mountains. They reached the cabin and Alex suggested they have a bit of a break; she had some work to do and perhaps Beth needed a little time for herself?

"Sounds good," Beth said gratefully.

"I sort of graze during the day, rather than lunch properly," Alex said. "I hope you don't mind just having at whatever you like in the fridge and cabinets. I was thinking soup and grilled cheese for supper, unless you want to go into town this evening?"

"I'd kind of like to do town in daylight, tomorrow?"

"Sure, sounds good. Maybe late afternoon, so you can see it by daylight and when it's evening. It's worth seeing both."

"It's a plan." Beth rolled her shoulders and twisted her neck back and forth. "I'm going check out that balcony off my room and rest a bit." Beth paused. "Enjoy your work."

"Will do. Enjoy your break."

Beth went up to her room and rummaged in her bag. She found her notebook and pen. She liked to write things down sometimes, or at least she could doodle. She glanced at the sliding doors. The balcony was in the warm sun. She stepped out, settled into a chair, and put her feet up on the railing. She looked out over the treetops—green, gold, bright red, burgundy. She wondered what Jonah was doing; her fingers itched to send him a message.

Maybe I should just text him just to show him I'm not going to behave like he does, she thought. *On the other hand, what if that's caving in? But he's my husband. I should care how he's doing. Besides, I owe it to him to let him know I'm okay. As if he cares. If he cared, he'd call. But he hasn't, he hasn't responded to my texts.*

She glanced at her phone. Sandy had sent a photo from the dog park—Cody, the twins, and all four dogs. Marta had Sol in a bear hug; Sol was grinning affably. Sean was pretending to be dragged away by Apple and Mac. Cody was grinning and holding Anastasia in his arms like a baby. She smiled. Anastasia usually only tolerated that level of affection from Jonah, and then only briefly. *Funny*, she thought. And no, not a peep from Jonah. She sent back a smiley face and put the phone down with a sigh.

Then she picked it up, frowning with determination, and send Jonah a text.

Hey, hope you're having a good day. Looks like the pups are having fun at the park. Just climbed a mountain with your mom. All good here. Love you.

She put her phone down again, folded her arms, leaned her head back, and closed her eyes. The sunshine was warm through her eyelids. She rolled her shoulders, trying to ease the stress that suddenly seemed unbearably obvious.

Thoughts rolled around in her head. Izzy confiding in Ozzy, behind the fence. "Well, she works all the time and the rest of the time it's the Jonah show. Yeah, she's a bit of a martyr, but I love her. She just worries about everyone else, that's all."

Courtney, gently nudging her. "Beth, it won't get better by itself. Jonah will be more and more ... Jonah, and you'll be more and more bitter, and then you'll be miserable. And feel stuck."

Dr. Garnette, kindly asking, "What makes it so hard to talk to your husband?"

Her father's sorrowful face and tender request. "Just promise me you'll take some time to sort things out. To take care of yourself and not spend all your heart trying to appease Jonah."

Jonah, sneering at her. "Poor little Beth. Always all about you, Beth."

Her mother, laughing humorlessly to the neighbor. "Such a little disappointment. Always not quite good enough. She has, what? One or two friends? She can't even make friends well."

Alex, soft-spoken and certain, suggesting, "Maybe you should spend more time thinking about what's going on with you."

What is going on with me? Why can't I even think straight? Beth sat up straight and took her notebook in hand. Maybe writing things would clear her thinking; just listing thoughts and feelings sometimes helped sort things out.

Beth wrote down what she'd heard from Izzy, from Courtney, from Alex. She wrote down the gentle questioning from Dr. Garnette and the mean things her mother had said. She wrote her father's words and started to cry. She couldn't tell, really, if she was crying for herself or for her father, so weary and sad, who she had misunderstood for all these lonely years.

She wrote about Jonah. She wrote about how much she loved him and how gentle and kind and creative he could be, and then she felt her chest tighten and she felt hot, shaky, and realized she was angry. She wrote *angry, angry, angry* in letters so hard they dented the paper. She scribbled an angry face, she slapped the notebook down on the table and cried harder.

What if he isn't? Gentle and kind and creative? What if those are just little slivers and mostly he is the way he usually is? Beth felt horrified. *Did I marry a monster?* She looked at her left hand and twisted the rings on her third finger. *What if Jonah is really like everyone says, and I'm the one who's wrong?*

She cried some more, and realized she had a headache. *Of course you have a headache*, she scolded herself. *You've been blubbering like a baby and you haven't had enough liquids.* She went into the room to make a cup of tea. She heard Alex downstairs, puttering: the sound of water running, the murmur of the tea kettle downstairs. She smiled. Maybe it was time to go down for a snack and see about having a cup of tea with her mother-in-law.

Alex looked up, smiling, as Beth came down the stairs. Beth appreciated that Alex didn't say anything about her puffy eyes. Instead, she just said, "Perfect timing. I'm having a break for tea and a snack! Can I make you a cup?"

Beth nodded gratefully. "That would be great, thanks." She leaned against the counter, arms folded, watching Alex set up two mugs for tea. "Alex."

"Hmm?" Alex glanced up, and then straightened up to turn to Beth directly. "Yes?" She nodded encouragingly.

Beth grimaced, rubbing the side of her neck. "You said earlier that Jonah's never been happy. Like, never, never? Or just when he grew up?"

Alex sighed gently and raised her eyes briefly to the ceiling before looking straight at Beth, gentle and calm. "Jonah was difficult from the day he was born. He was fussy and demanding, and once he could talk it got worse. Usually, when kids start talking, you understand them more, and they're less frustrated. But Jonah kept raising the bar." Alex reached for the kettle and poured the hot water for tea. "He drove us crazy and he was so hard on Sandy. But frankly, Sandy handled him better than Joe and I did. She would either ignore him or call him out so bluntly that he would usually just shut up, at least for a few minutes."

Beth shook her head. "I don't know. When I met him, he seemed... well, I don't know. I mean, I know the other students didn't seem to like him. He wasn't welcome in group projects, that sort of thing."

"I can imagine," Alex said, dunking the tea bags up and down. "Sweetener?"

"A little stevia, please," Beth said. "But, you know, I just figured it was jealousy."

"So you bought his story about being so smart and misunderstood and you just took pity on him and took on the job of Jonah's defender." She said it matter-of-factly with a nod and handed Beth a mug of sweetened tea.

"Well, yes." Beth sighed, her shoulders sagging. She looked at Alex, frowning. "You tried to tell me, didn't you?" She recalled the week after the engagement—an engagement, she began to see, she had pretty much engineered with Jonah as a passive participant. Alex had invited her for lunch. Beth had been anxious, thinking it was going to be a protective mother making sure Beth was good enough for Jonah. But Alex had asked rather odd, circumspect questions, about how they met, and how they resolved differences, and whether they had discussed children. She asked whether Beth felt that Jonah respected and valued her the way a wife should be respected and valued. Beth had felt uncomfortable with this line of conversation. She remembered thinking it was pretty ironic, Jonah's mousy mother trying to give her, the engineer, advice. She remembered telling Alex, "Of course Jonah appreciates me! I think I'm the only person who's ever understood him." She cringed, now, thinking about it.

"Cut yourself some slack, Beth." Alex interrupted her thoughts. "You couldn't possibly have known. But yeah, I did try to talk to you about it. Before the wedding." Alex smiled gently.

Beth shook her head. "So did my parents. I guess I'm glad now I caved into them, and to Jonah, and signed a pre-nup." She half smiled, remembering. "Jonah was afraid I'd be foolish and irresponsible and ruin him, and my parents were afraid Jonah would take advantage of my naïveté. Two different reasons, one big, iron-clad pre-nup."

"I wondered about that," Alex said. "It being sort of outside Catholic tradition and all."

Beth was appreciative that Alex didn't ask the obvious question: Beth could only be thinking about their pre-nup if she were thinking it was going to come in handy. *Happy couples don't look at their prenuptial agreements after the fact. They laugh about how foolish and unnecessary such things were*, Beth thought.

They moved into the living room area and settled into the lumberjack-sized furniture. "So I was thinking," Beth began tentatively. "Like, how did you decide to just do stuff? I mean, you know. The real-you stuff."

Alex nodded. "I waited until I was miserable—constantly at Cody's office complaining about needing a root canal because I was grinding my teeth so badly. Long story short—good teeth but bad fit. Life, that is. I started seeing a therapist, doing the homework, clearing my head. And I stopped complaining about the things I did to myself and stopped trying to blame them on other people."

Beth sat up straight. "Okay, that sounds significant."

Alex tilted her head with a one-sided smile. "Oh, it was. Is, actually. I was tolerating all sorts of demands and expectations and acting like I was a martyr."

Whoa, Beth thought. *Martyr.*

"And it was really on me. Like, I'm the one who agreed to walk the dogs on my lunch hour and took forever to say I had to stop. Nothing personal."

"Of course not," Beth agreed.

"And I'm the one who went along with the last Christmas pageant fiasco. And letting Joe talk over me whenever I wanted to discuss my own plans. And I'm the one who agreed to go to grad school for library science even though I didn't want to, don't like it, and can't wait to retire. I let Sandy dye my hair with beet juice and push me around with her latest wacky save-the-planet agenda." Alex put down her tea and stretched her arms over her head. "And it turns out that I did all those things to myself. So, I stopped."

Beth stared into her mug. "Just ... stopped? That easy?"

"Hell, no." Alex laughed. "Not easy! It took months. Absolute misery, terror, tears, and a bunch of money at the therapist. But worth it."

"What would I do?" Beth wondered. "I mean, what do I complain about?"

"Not having fun." Alex reached for her mug. "You complain about it. You say Jonah complains about it. But nothing happens. It's not my business, but I would say, to start with, for God's sake, Beth, go have fun." Beth stared at her. Alex smiled. "Have your friends over for dinner! Go paddleboarding! Go kayaking with Izzy and—what's her boyfriend's name—Ozzy? Have Sandy and Cody and the twins over for a cookout so the kids can play with the dogs. If Jonah wants to participate, he will. If he doesn't, live your life anyway. Stop doing what Jonah wants to do—which is very little—and then complaining."

"I can't have people over without Jonah being okay with it." She imagined Jonah's explosion if Sandy, Cody, and the twins invaded for a weekend afternoon.

"Yes, as it turns out, you can. Just do it." Alex leaned back into the chair. "I know how miserable he can be. Trust me. And so do all your friends. But have your life, Beth, and then see how you feel. Who knows, maybe that's what it will take for Jonah to finally wake up and smell the coffee. To realize that life isn't miserable just because it's not up to his impossible expectations."

"I just can't imagine putting up with the aggravation he's going to cause."

"Is it going to be worse than what you have now? Where he does what he wants, complains about you, and you're miserable? Because that seems pretty awful."

Beth nodded and took a sip of tea. It was pretty awful. It did make her sound like some sort of martyr on the altar of Jonah the Miserable. She wondered what Jonah would do, if she just went ahead and started having the fun life around her work that she wanted for both of them. Would he just meld with the couch and pretend to ignore them all? Would he punish her with his sarcasm and put-downs?

"Jonah can be pretty mean, and I'm sorry about that." Alex's voice cut through Beth's worried whirl of thoughts. "Joe and I probably should have come down harder on that behavior from day one. Especially the lying."

Beth put down her cup and leaned forward. "What?"

Alex frowned. "The lying. Jonah was ... sneaky. He usually didn't tell active fibs, he just left stuff out. Like he'd get kicked out of a group for the science fair and neglect to say he'd called the other students morons and refused to share his data because they were too dumb to understand. Or that he'd quit the debate team because the rules were 'stupid' and didn't mention it until we asked about the countywide competition in the newspaper. That sort of stuff."

"Oh." Beth felt her mind reeling. "That leaving stuff out … he still does that."

"Well, to be fair, a lot of people have a hard time admitting they've been fired."

"No, it's not just that."

"No one ever only lies about one thing," Alex said sadly. "There's never just one thing."

"There's other stuff, but it was between us and kept other people out." Beth looked down quickly. When she looked up, Alex was just gazing at her calmly. "He had good reasons, privacy and not wanting to upset other people, so I went along with it."

Alex just said, "Ah."

"And he gets really upset when I talk about just talking about it and so … so I don't."

"Well, any time you want to talk, I'm available, Beth." Alex smiled. "Marriage has its own rules about privacy. But still, I'm sad to hear how much Jonah's childish behavior has continued. Joe and I should have done more than reason with him." She grimaced and added, as an afterthought, "He was probably having a running critique of our ideas behind that stony face."

"I don't think you get to be responsible for Jonah's behavior at this point in time," Beth replied.

"Neither do you, Beth."

"Fair enough." Beth paused. "Thanks for listening. And for the encouragement. It's easier said than done, then, to just stop complaining about what I do to myself and start living again. But you're right. It beats the status quo."

Alex nodded. "And one thing about the status quo, Beth. It isn't static. It won't stay the same."

"Right," Beth said, and imagined, bleakly, how it could get worse if she failed to make any changes.

Chapter 23

The rest of the weekend whirled by: an afternoon trip into Helen to sightsee, pick up groceries, and have a meal; a walk in the mountains; more time sitting with their feet up on the railing, taking in the view and enjoying one another's company. Monday morning rolled around all too quickly.

Beth hugged Alex tight. Alex hugged her back, hard, and thanked her for coming. She held Beth at arm's length, hands on her cheeks. "It's all going to be okay, Beth, whatever happens. We love both of you. Just drive home safe and start living again. And see that Dr. Garnette. He sounds good."

"I will," Beth promised, and hugged Alex again. "I love you," she whispered tearfully into Alex's neck.

"And I love you, Bethie. Drive safe. Let me know when you get home," Alex said.

Beth glanced into the rearview mirror as she drove off. Alex was standing in the gravel road, hat askew, waving and smiling. Beth smiled, shaking her head. She wondered what Jonah would think of the woman she just spent the weekend with.

The drive home was long and uneventful. She stopped about two-thirds of the way to have lunch, enjoying the break and the experience of savoring a big salad in a roomy booth and half listening to the conversations of other diners. Two middle-aged women compared notes on their disappointing adult children. Four men were arguing about football statistics. A group of about eight older people, five women and three men, were eating at a booth meant for four with two small tables pushed up against it to provide enough seating; they were laughing and telling stories. She listened closer, picking up bits of their conversation. Straining to listen, she heard fragments.

"My wife, she wouldn't want me to sit around doing nothing. She'd kick my butt if I let myself stay stuck."

"After fifty years of marriage, I don't think I'll ever stop missing my husband. But I know God has something else for me, some purpose now that I'm not caring for Will anymore."

"This grief support group has been the best thing to happen to me since my husband died."

They're all widows and widowers, Beth thought, stunned. It's some kind of church grief support group having lunch together. And they're laughing and crying and talking about their *purpose. Their spouses died*, she thought, *and they're more determined to have a real life than I am. I'm a loser; I can't even rally more hope than a bunch of old widows and widowers.* Then it occurred to her that was unfair. They were clearly working at it but also bold, and willing to encourage one another.

Like my friends, Sandy, and Alex all support me. Like my dad supports me, Beth thought. *It's not like I'm all alone in this, either. I just pretend it's that way.* She smiled at the grief group. *Help comes from the weirdest places,* she thought.

The rest of the drive felt lighter, until she was almost home. She dreaded going into the house. Would it be a mess? Would the dogs be okay? *Of course the dogs will be okay. Sandy will have seen to that.* She sighed and got out, grabbing her bags and heading in. Sol nearly tackled her. She put down her bags and knelt on the floor, hugging him and letting him lick her face. She looked past Sol; Apple and Mac were right behind him, waiting their turn, and Anastasia peeked over the edge of the sofa. She straightened, petting Apple and Mac, and went to the living room area. "Jonah! I'm home," she said, thinking he was in the other room. He was awake, on the couch, stretched out. He looked at her lazily as she leaned over the back of the couch.

"I heard you," he said. "Kind of hard to miss the rumpus." He sat up, rubbing his head. "How was the drive?"

"Smooth. How are things here?" She glanced at the kitchen. There were dishes stacked past the top of the sink. *He's been eating but not cleaning up after himself.*

"Fine. Sandy's been by twice a day. I wish you wouldn't have asked her to take care of the dogs. Now we owe her."

"That's between me and Sandy." Beth folded her arms, leaning her hip against the sofa. "What have you been up to while I've been hiking the mountains with your mom?"

Jonah shrugged. "The usual."

Beth nodded slowly. "The usual?"

Jonah shrugged. "Just hanging out, I guess. I mean, it's the weekend."

"Yeah, well. You've sort of been on weekend mode for weeks."

"I've been looking for work, Beth. Sorry not to meet your timetable."

"My timetable isn't the thing." Beth shifted her weight and uncrossed her arms, reaching one hand to scruff Sol's head, which was shoved, hard, against the side of her leg. "Just missing out on communication. You know, where are you looking? What sort of feedback are you getting? What you're learning about the company culture at these places ... that sort of stuff."

Jonah stared at her. "I've been looking, okay?"

Beth nodded her head toward the kitchen. "And staying on top of everything else, too, right? Cleaning up the house? Tending to the yard? Bathing the dogs? Or the usual vegging out and complaining that your life sucks?"

Jonah scowled at her. "Ha, ha. Nice to see you, too."

Beth went to the kitchen. She texted Alex to let her know she was home and safe. *Here safe and sound. All good. Thanks so much for the retreat.*

Alex texted back promptly. *Wonderful to see you. I hope it was what you needed. See you guys before you know it.*

Beth tilted her head and then remembered: Alex would be home before Thanksgiving. It really wasn't too far away. Beth gave the dogs fresh water and food, cleaned up the dishes, emptied the trash, opened the refrigerator, and took a quick inventory. She'd have to go to the store tomorrow, either early, before work, or after work. She jotted down a quick list for the supermarket, checked the supply of dog food—good so far. She grinned. Sandy had left a sticky note on the big bag of kibble, suggesting they use a better container to keep it fresh and recommending a brand with recyclable packaging. She crumpled the note and threw it away. There was no use trying to engage Jonah with a shared laugh at Sandy's environmental enthusiasm.

Beth took the dogs for their walks, had a small salad and a half can of soup for supper, cleaned up, and glanced, over and over, at the back of Jonah's head, barely visible over the top of the sofa. The television droned on, documentary after documentary, punctuated by his annoyed criticism of the idiocy of a general or a president.

"I'm going to bed," she announced, finally deciding to intrude again on Jonah's invisible cocoon. He glanced up.

"Oh. It's early, isn't it? Good night."

Beth shrugged. "It's almost ten, and I might run out to the supermarket when it opens at seven, so I don't have to at the end of the workday." She paused, wondering if Jonah would say, "Oh, I'm not doing anything tomorrow—let me get that for you." The moment passed. He just nodded and turned back to the television. Beth pressed her lips together, took a deep breath, and said, "Okay. Good night." And then, "Come on, Sol."

She readied for bed. She hadn't unpacked yet; she left the bag against the wall. Sol nosed her side after she lay down. She stroked his ears and told him what a good boy he was. For the first time in a long time, he decided to climb up on their bed, stretching out between her and Jonah's side of the bed, one big front paw on her shoulder and his forehead shoved up against the side of her head. Beth squeezed her eyes shut hard and waited for sleep, but her brain would not stop whirling with thoughts about what she needed to do. She sat up, apologized to Sol, put on the bedside lamp, got her notebook out of her bag, and wrote down some of the chaotic, fractured ideas that spun through her mind. She tucked the notebook into her bedside table, turned off the light, and lay down again. Sol gave a huffing outbreath of satisfaction and began to snore quietly. Beth closed her eyes and wondered if she would ever sleep.

She must have fallen asleep at some point. When she awoke, before her alarm, Sol was curled up near her feet. Jonah was on his side of the bed, snoring, still wearing the clothes he was wearing when she came home. She wrinkled her nose, wondering if he'd showered since she left to visit Alex. Beth shook her head and got out of bed to begin the day.

By the time she started her workday at 8:00 a.m., the dogs were walked and fed, groceries were bought and put away, chicken was defrosting in the refrigerator, and her laundry was in the dryer. Jonah was asleep. She put herself off camera during one long, boring training so she could revisit her list from the night before. *It's horrible*, she thought, *that I'm actually contemplating all this. Still, it's necessary.* She looked at her calendar. She could stretch her lunch break on Wednesday. She had an appointment with Dr. Garnette on Thursday. She texted Sandy to see about coffee or lunch on Friday, and sent a check-in text to Izzy, Courtney, and Kitta to confirm Saturday. It was going to be a busy week.

Wednesday evening, after work, she stepped out of the home office to find Jonah on the couch, as usual. She glanced over and, as always, said, "Hey there! It's five o'clock ... how was your day?"

And as was almost always the case, he grunted, "Okay."

She hesitated, waiting; he was silent. She nodded, more to herself than to Jonah. "Anything interesting going on?"

He gestured toward the television. "More riots out west. And the rocket launch tonight's been canceled due to weather."

"I meant with you. Anything interesting for you?"

Jonah half turned, looking at her sideways. "You mean like, did I find a job, huh?"

Beth made a concerted effort to not roll her eyes. "I meant, anything interesting? Did you hear from your dad about his sabbatical? Go for a walk? Read something intriguing? Yeah, I'd like to know how job hunting is going, too. Obviously."

"Yeah, I know, money, money."

She headed into the kitchen to tend to the dogs and prepare for their walks. "Yeah, money does make a difference." She paused and went back into the living room, walking around to stand between Jonah and the television. "Speaking of which, I went to the bank today."

Jonah looked annoyed and shifted slightly to one side to look around her at the screen. She stepped to that side.

"So, I opened a new account in my name, and my pay will be direct deposited there. Our old checking account will have just enough for you to have some spending money. Clearly, I can't have you spending as if you're still pulling a good salary and keep the bills covered. And I canceled all but one of the streaming services today. So when the next billing period comes up, they'll be gone. Unless you start a subscription with your money. Oh, and I canceled all the credit cards with your name on them where I'm the primary accountholder. And to be fair, I canceled my card on your gas card account. Since that's the only account that had you as primary."

Jonah stared at her, his mouth slightly open. "What the ...?"

Beth tried to have a serene face. *Yoga face, Beth*, she told herself silently. Aloud she said, "Jonah, it's been weeks. You have not been forthcoming about your job-hunting process. You have refused to sit and have a meal with me and engage in the basic business of running a household. Fine. If you want to check out and act like an adolescent home on probation from college, then that's what I have to deal with. So, I am." She felt her voice just starting to quiver. "I look forward to when it can be different. Oh, and I have an appointment with Dr. Garnette tomorrow. Five thirty p.m. You're welcome to meet me there if you like."

Jonah rolled his eyes. "Oooh, the assistant principal is going to scold me! Did he put you up to all this?" He paused, and then, narrowing his eyes, said, "It wasn't my mom, was it?" He shook his head. "Nah. She's not smart enough to figure that out."

Beth burst out laughing. "Oh, Jonah. I am *so* not going to take the bait on that one. But no, neither Garnette nor Alex have any idea what I've been doing this week. Except for the banks, you're the first to know." She stepped out of the way of his television viewing. "And now I'm going to walk the dogs, and then have dinner, and then arrange with Sandy for her and Cody and the kids to come over for a thank-you pizza party for taking such good care of the dogs for us. I'm hoping this weekend."

She took just a bit of satisfaction at watching Jonah's mouth drop open as she pivoted on her heel to go back to the kitchen. He collected himself enough to begin protesting, and Beth just said, "Jonah. She helped us out, I'm grateful, and the dogs will love having the kids over to play. Who knows, maybe I'll invite Izzy and Ozzy, too, since they'll be hearing the ruckus from their yard." She snapped Sol's leash on, ruffled his head, and added, "You're free to go somewhere else for the duration if you can't stand company." And she walked out the door, letting it close firmly—but not too loudly—behind her

Chapter 24

"Oh. My. Gosh. How did he take it?" Izzy leaned forward, eyes gleaming.

Courtney gave her a stern look. "Izzy. No gloating."

Izzy pretended to flinch with indignation. "Me? Gloat? Over that bloviating, arrogant slug getting his just desserts?" She placed a hand over her heart and rolled her eyes toward the sky. "Far be it!"

Kitta sighed. "I'm sorry, Beth. This sounds miserable." She sat leaning slightly back, one hand resting lazily on the slight slope of her belly.

Beth shook her head, smiling as well as she could. "It was hard. It felt awful, actually. And good. Both." She stirred her coffee, watching the gently swirling cream. She looked back up. "You know, I think I might have felt like a real adult for the first time in my life. I know that sounds dumb, but ..." She shrugged. "It just felt like I was doing something because I decided it was right and fair, not just based on feeling sad or feeling guilty or feeling bad for someone else."

Courtney rubbed Beth's shoulder. "Sounds rough, Beth. But necessary."

"Maybe Jonah will get it now," Izzy offered. "You know, actually try to get a job. Help out around the house."

"Well, not so far, so I'm not hopeful. He's just angrier." Beth rolled her eyes. "You should have seen his face when I told him Sandy, Cody, and the kids are coming for a pizza party tonight as a thank-you." She paused. "Nothing personal against you guys." She looked from Courtney to Kitta. "But, Izzy, since you and Ozzy will be stuck listening to the ruckus, feel free to come over. You'll hear the twins with the dogs."

"We just might," Izzy said. "Interesting to see how he does. Plus, I'm looking forward to seeing Sandy and Cody and company."

"I feel guilty talking about my husband like he's a recalcitrant child." Beth sighed. "But there you have it. You should have seen the pile of dishes. He didn't seem to have washed one dish the whole time I was gone. Or even put anything in the dishwasher. I don't think he took a shower or changed his clothes." She sighed. "Thank God I thought to have Sandy come for the dogs twice a day."

"Beth, stop." Courtney hesitated. "Why don't you focus on you? Take some of that advice Alex gave you. Have fun. Let Jonah come along if he likes but stop making it the Jonah show." She turned to Beth directly. "You're doing the same thing you've done along, making it all about Jonah, except, it's in reverse. Or at least sideways."

Beth shook her head, paused, nodded. "You're right. Of course," she added with a wink.

Kitta was watching all this. "You know, you all really helped me with figuring out the whole Hunter thing." She paused. "I let things go too long. I used to, anyway," she said quickly. "So, just kind of returning the favor ... Beth, what's the time frame here? You guys have been married what, five years? How long do you wait for a turnaround? Five more?"

Izzy shook her head violently, hair whipping around her. "No, definitely not that long. That makes ten years. That means you might have to pay him alimony, especially if he's been a slug the whole last five years." The others all looked at her in surprise, and she shrugged sheepishly. "Not that I ever discussed this with an attorney or anything."

Beth nodded slowly. "Did Ozzy mention ten years and then alimony's a possibility?"

"Well, not specifically." Izzy shrugged. "But it's worth a thought."

"I couldn't possibly take this for five years," Beth muttered.

"Well, Beth, you already have." Courtney paused, sipped her coffee, and placed it down carefully. She reached under the table to scratch Sol's head, then put both hands back around her coffee cup. She tilted her head. "Beth, it's already been five years. If you think Jonah's acting any different, except for being unemployed, then that's not what we've been seeing. And hearing. This is just Act Two, not something new."

"Act Three," Beth said grimly. "I've talked to his mom. And sister. Apparently, Jonah's being Jonah. I just kept focusing on the small, bright pieces."

"Easily done," Kitta said, stroking her belly. "Oh, brother, is it easily done."

"But the lazy thing. And the hygiene thing, that sounds kind of gross. Maybe there's something wrong with him. Like he's really depressed." Izzy made an earnest face.

Beth shook her head. "I hate to say it, but the sitting around wearing the same boxers or sweats and T-shirts all weekend ... yeah, that's not new. Unless we have to go someplace, he can pull that stunt from when he gets home Friday until he goes back to work. And when I've gone on work trips, the kitchen is a train wreck. Every time. While I'd like to think, oh, he's depressed, he needs help, I'm feeling that maybe he just feels entitled to me catering to him."

"So …?" Izzy prompted.

"So, pizza tonight with the crew. I'm seeing a therapist, regularly now. Jonah's mom comes home from Georgia to have most of the rest of her sabbatical at home in a week or so, and then it's Thanksgiving, practically. So … let's say until January." Beth nodded and sat up straighter. "Right. January second. We'll see where things are then."

"Too squishy," Courtney opined. "What's that mean? We'll see where things are? What things?"

Izzy nodded. "Yeah, kind of unclear, Beth. What has to be different?"

Courtney gave an emphatic slap to the tabletop. "You need clear objectives. Is Jonah seeing a counselor, exercising, and cooperating at home? Eating dinner with you and providing updates on his job search, or gainfully employed, by January second? Is he acting like a good teenager instead of a spoiled, lazy one? What's that look like?"

"You sound like a therapist," Beth remarked. Courtney shrugged.

"And you should let him know what your expectations are," Izzy added. "You know. Nicely, of course. But let him know." Izzy smiled mischievously. "But I do like that you stepped up and took care of protecting yourself financially."

"I'm glad I did, too," Beth agreed. She hesitated. *These are my best friends*, she thought. *I can tell them.* "It turns out Jonah was spending money as if he were still employed, except not helping with any bills. More than when he was working. He was burning through our money. Fastfood, drinks at a sports bar, all that time he was pretending to be employed he was just wasting time away from home and spending money. It would have been bad enough to be lied to if he'd been at the library reading, or online looking for work, but he was just living the good life on my dime and lying to me." She pressed her lips together. "Actually, he lied about that, too. When I found out he'd been fired he claimed he'd been spending a lot of time at the library and parks."

"Alone at these bars?" Izzy wondered. Courtney shot her a look. Izzy held her hands palms up and shrugged. Beth pressed her lips together tightly.

"Maybe he was at the parks. Sometimes," Kitta offered.

Beth felt her stomach turn. She thought of the other lies. "Maybe. But, yes, January second it is."

"Usually the holiday season whirls by," Courtney observed. "At least for you people without little kids. It'll be interesting to see how it goes."

"Interesting," Beth repeated flatly. "I guess that's a word for it."

Sandy, Cody, Marta, and Sean were there promptly at five. Beth stepped out to greet them each with a hug. The twins were first; they gave sincere hugs but were quickly in the door to greet the dogs.

"Sorry about the brush-off." Cody laughed. "But the dogs ..."

"I totally get it." Beth smiled and hugged Cody. He hugged back warmly. "Believe me," Beth added, "there are definitely people who are lower on the ladder than the dogs." She rolled her eyes toward the house.

Sandy laughed and caught Beth in a bear hug. She whispered, "How are you? Everything okay?" Her sincerity triggered a surprising burning of tears. Beth blinked them back and smiled as well as she could. "Oh, all is well. As to Jonah, well, it remains to be seen if he's going to participate."

"Ah. That's how it is." Cody frowned. "I'm sorry."

Beth shook her head. "Don't be, or I'll cry more. And Izzy and Ozzy might wander over. I'm sure they can hear the noise already." The twins were laughing and Sol, Apple, and Mac were already romping with them, barking playfully in the backyard. "Those characters sure have fun together."

Sandy grinned. "I bet you didn't know Sol could play hide-and-seek."

"Get out of here."

"Seriously. At least he plays along with it. You know he has to be able to tell right where the kids are by scent but he pretends to be looking at other hiding places first. It's hilarious."

Beth shook her head, smiling. "Sounds like dog sitting was a family affair."

"Absolutely!"

They stepped into the house. Jonah was in his usual spot.

"Hey, big brother," Sandy called over. Jonah grunted.

"Jonah, how are you?" Cody strode into the living room and plopped down on a chair, leaning forward conversationally. "What's on?"

Jonah stared at him for a moment and then gestured toward the television. "Documentary. It's part of a series on the Korean War." He grimaced at the television. "You can't believe the strategic errors these idiots made. It's maddening."

Beth and Sandy were in the kitchen, watching the conversation while getting out ingredients for pizzas. They glanced at each other and shrugged.

Cody was not easily put off. "Jonah, sometimes it seems like you're more of a history expert than your dad. I mean, he has his thing, colonial and early U.S. history, but you seem to be a real twentieth century expert."

Beth watched Jonah barely turn his head toward Cody. "Nah. Not really."

Sandy leaned toward her and whispered, "That counts as two sentences. A miracle!"

Beth shook her head, placing a finger over her lips in the universal librarian "hush" sign. Aloud, she said, "So are you thinking we should slice up olives and peppers and onions and have those ready for the putting on pizzas now? Or wait until the dough is rising?"

"How about if I do dough and you slice? Or would you rather knead the dough?"

"How'd you end up in technology, anyway?" Cody wondered. "I mean, you have the appetite for history."

"Teaching history doesn't pay much," Jonah said.

"Another sentence!" Sandy whispered, clattering a cutting board to cover the remark.

"That's what my sister's boyfriend says. He teaches high school history." Cody paused. "Still, he was able to go to Ireland for a month, and not just visiting family. And he'll be able to travel up to spend his spring break with your dad fishing, so I guess he's got some money to burn."

"Huh." Jonah barely elevated his response above a grunt.

"Not a sentence," Beth whispered to Sandy, stirring flour into the water, yeast, sugar, and salt.

Sandy held up a green pepper. "This looks perfect." She tilted her head and turned to Beth. "Is this organic?"

"Oh, I'm not sure," Beth said. "The bins are right beside each other. I probably screwed up."

"What? Saint Beth the Holy Martyr screwed up?" Jonah's voice cut across the room.

"Yeah, I'll just pretend I didn't hear that," Beth offered, stirring more flour into the dough. "But yes, Jonah, I may have bought a regular pepper instead of organic."

"My, my," Jonah said mockingly, turning his head to glance at the kitchen. "Big of you to admit it."

"Don't start, Jonah."

"Start what? Poor Bethie with her miserable husband." Jonah's voice was sharp. Cody sat up straight, looked down at his hands, and stood up. Jonah didn't even glance at him.

"I'm going to step outside and check on the kids and the pups," Cody offered. He glanced at Jonah. "We're just trying to have a nice visit, Jonah."

Jonah ignored him. "So, Beth, are you going to go cry tonight? Pull out your little stuffed animal and whimper about your mean husband? Or just go tell your shrink and my mom how awful I am?"

Beth's mouth dropped open and tears sprung to her eyes. Before she could speak, Sandy whirled around, paring knife still in hand. "Okay, Jonah, that's enough." As it had since early childhood, there was something about Sandy when she was angry that could stun even Jonah into silence. She pointed at him, seemingly unaware that her pointing included the glint of a blade. "You're the one sitting around having a pity party. Not Beth. Beth's trying to have a nice, family dinner for all of us. Including you. And you're just sitting around being critical and snarky."

"Sandy," Beth tried to interrupt.

"And I don't know anything about St. Beth the Martyr, but I'm sick of it. Sick of it. Jonah, you're a spoiled brat. Don't think I don't see what's going on, big brother. I'm on to you. I've been on to you since I was four and figured out I had to pretend not to read better than you did so you wouldn't have one of your famous meltdowns."

Jonah had turned and was kneeling on the sofa, facing them across the expanse. Now his mouth gaped.

The door swung open, and Izzy and Ozzy stepped in, just in time to hear Sandy continue. "And I was on to you when you started picking on Mom, pretending she was dumb when she was just trying to make a better life for all of us."

"She's a freaking librarian," Jonah managed to squeak.

Sandy's gesturing was not slower for the paring knife flashing in her hand. "Which is more education than you have, big brother. And she was a scientist and an artist and damned good at both and she set it all aside for Dad's career, and for us. And all she got for her sacrifices was you being demeaning and imagining you're superior."

"Sandy, seriously." Beth was afraid Sandy was going to wade into dangerous turf.

"So let me set you straight, once and for all. Mom's the smarter of the two of them. Mom and Dad, that is." Sandy pointed back at herself, knife flashing. "And I'm the smarter one of us kids."

"That's a laugh." Jonah turned back to the television, snorting.

Sandy marched into the living room and stood in front of the television. "Okay, Jonah. Listen up." Jonah tried to see around her. Sandy seemed to bachata back and forth as she spoke, blocking his view, still gesturing with a paring knife. "Guess where Cody and I went for Labor Day weekend?"

Jonah shrugged, sat back, and folded his arms. "Of course. We *all* know. Some wacko environmental thing."

Sandy smirked and Beth cringed. "No, Jonah. That was the story to coddle you. We went to the Triple Nine Society annual gathering. High IQ. Top one tenth of one percent. Just to clarify, Cody was my guest and I'm the member. And I was a presenter." She paused. "And you, dear brother, are not. If I recall your IQ test results, which you bragged about for a month during high school, you don't qualify. As a member, that is. Mom belongs, too, but she didn't go." Sandy paused. "So how about letting off with the 'Mom is dumb and Sandy is dumber' routine, huh? Because it's getting old." Then Sandy marched into the kitchen, flipped her hair behind her shoulder, and resumed cutting peppers into small pieces. She held one up to the light. "I can never get over how beautiful these are, with the light shining through them," she remarked, as if nothing unusual had just happened.

Beth managed to find some oxygen. "Yes, yes they are," she said quietly. She glanced over; Jonah's head was barely visible over the back of the sofa. She went over to greet Izzy and Ozzy, and called in Cody and the twins for introductions all around. She kept shaking her head in a small, tight "no" to Izzy's raised eyebrows and head jerks toward the back of Jonah's head.

Sandy had moved on to other topics. "How was Mom? You guys have fun?"

They talked about the trip. Beth took great pleasure in pounding the pizza dough to the point where Sandy gave her a questioning look and Beth just smiled. The kitchen was crowded. Ozzy made his way toward Jonah to say hello, ask how he was. Beth kept an eye on things; Ozzy put up a good fight in the effort to have a conversation with Jonah before wandering back to the kitchen.

Beth tried to focus everyone on pizza. "Okay ... there are choices. We can each make our own pizza, or whoever wants to can make their own and I can make a bigger one for the rest of us to share."

"Make our own!" Sean called out. "That's what we do sometimes at Aunt Alex's house."

"Yes, make our own, please," Marta seconded, nudging her brother. She leaned over and whispered, "Manners!" and he rolled his eyes, nodded, and nudged her back.

"I can go either way," Cody chimed in.

Beth glanced at Sandy, who was serenely chopping vegetables. "How about if Sandy and I set out the rest of the ingredients, I pound out circles of dough, and everyone can just have at it?" She paused. "Jonah? Would you like to build your own pizza or do you want to share mine?"

Jonah was silent. The twins and Sandy turned toward him. Cody, Izzy, and Ozzy looked assiduously in other directions, avoiding one another's gaze.

Beth waited a few heartbeats. "Jonah?"

"Not hungry," he announced, paused, and then added, "You all go ahead without me."

"Will do!" Sandy said, a little too cheerily. Cody shook his head at her slightly. She leaned forward and kissed his nose. "Just a little brother and sister sport," she whispered, and winked. Beth watched as Cody smiled, kissed Sandy's forehead, then kept his gaze on her as she turned her attention to putting the dishes of cut-up peppers, onions, and olives neatly in a row on the breakfast bar.

Beth blinked, hard, and pounded dough into small circles, winked at Sean, and stretched one out a little bigger. He nodded, grinning. Beth grinned back. It was going to be a good evening after all; she was sure of it.

Thursday afternoon; another appointment with Dr. Garnette. He didn't have any late openings, so she moved her lunch break for an early afternoon slot. As usual, she let Jonah know; as usual, he grunted. This time, she let him know where she was going as she headed out, since he was home, on the couch. He looked up lazily; he was lounging in boxers and a stained T-shirt. The same ones, she noticed, he'd worn all day yesterday and to bed. Beth controlled her facial expression and asked, "Need anything while I'm out?"

"No. Have fun."

No, thank you, she thought. Aloud, she said, "Okay, see you in bit," and left, whispering to Sol she would be back soon and giving him a quick kiss between the ears. Sol made a grateful huffing sound and went off to lie down, probably under her work desk.

This was her first daytime appointment, and Beth was surprised at the activity in the office building; she had to wait for the elevator and there was a receptionist on duty on Dr. Garnette's floor. The receptionist smiled and said, "Welcome! Who should I call for you?"

"Um. Usually, I just show up. I guess I've never been here during the day, so ..." Beth hesitated. She glanced around at the people waiting. She didn't want any of them to think she was crazy. Or mentally ill, or something. Fortunately, Dr. Garnette appeared just down the hallway, saying, "Hello! Come on down," and she escaped the eyes in the lobby. After they sat down, she said, "Sorry, it was a little weird seeing all those people and the receptionist. Usually I'm here after hours, I guess."

Dr. Garnette nodded. "Yes, I forgot that was the case, or I'd have told you to have her call Will. And not to give her your name. You notice I didn't greet you by name this time."

"Ah. Nice. Thanks, I didn't notice. Too freaked out."

Dr. Garnette leaned forward just a bit. "Beth. There's a lot going on, isn't there? Barely cracked the ice last time."

She nodded, looking at her lap. "Yeah. Cracking is a good word for it. Cracking up." She looked up at him. His patient eyes waited, gazing calmly. She took a deep breath. "I really am thinking about giving Jonah an ultimatum. I don't think I can do this much longer."

"What's the 'this,' specifically?"

"Specifically. Wow. Well. It's like ... Jonah's mask is off. But it's not so much his mask. I think I'm starting to see the Jonah other people warned me about. The one they saw."

"Meaning, what?"

"Like what a jerk he was the time he did show up here. Like him lying about losing his job and then when he was caught lying about what he was doing while he was lying. Which he kept insisting he didn't do, by the way, even though I would say, 'Have a good day' and 'How was work?' and he never said, 'Well, actually, work wasn't.' You know?"

Dr. Garnette nodded. "Yes, you said he's been pretty consistent about denying he's dishonest."

Beth threw up her hands. "And then I started thinking ... about how he insisted we lie to his parents about me seeing fertility specialists. And how his mom tells me he's always been a liar, especially the lies of omission, just leaving important things out." She put her hands over her eyes. "I'm afraid to find out what else he's lying about. What else he isn't telling me."

"And so, you cover your eyes."

"Huh?" Beth lowered her hands, looked at them in surprise. *My gosh, I was. I was covering my eyes. I was literally trying not to see.* "Oh, crap."

"Yeah."

There was a long silence. Beth struggled to find words. She had a moment of panic, that there would be something, something big and horrible that Jonah hadn't told her. *What will I do? What will I do if I find something so terrible it can't be borne?* She looked at Will Garnette. He sat, looking gently sad and calm, and he nodded encouragingly. "Scary, isn't it?" he asked softly.

She nodded, fighting back tears. She lost the fight. "I'm so afraid now. I thought—I thought everything was fine and if I could just be kind and encouraging enough, Jonah would shine like the diamond I knew he was. Thought he was. Who knows? And now everything seems crazy and confusing. Like I'm in a tornado."

Dr. Garnette nodded slowly. "Yes, yes, that makes sense. A terrifying way to feel. And yet, like Dorothy—you know, in the book—you actually have the power to straighten all this out, Beth."

"I don't think I can try much longer."

"Try what, exactly?"

She felt a twinge of impatience. Couldn't he see?

"Yeah, that sounded harsh, didn't it? But what exactly are you asking yourself to do? Keep lying to yourself as much, if not more, than Jonah does?" Dr. Garnette watched Beth slowly sit up straight, arms going from folded across her chest to gripping the arm of the sofa with one hand, the other bracing against the cushion beside her. He waited. "Seriously, Beth. I know you're upset with me, but I'm trying to be helpful. Think about it, Beth. Have you been lying to yourself?"

"Everyone lies to themselves! About how much they eat or whether their jeans are too tight or whether they've done enough work for the day or whatever." Beth realized she sounded like a teenager. "Yeah, I'm close to sounding like Jonah right now." She grimaced. "Dr. Garnette ... how do I do this? Deal with lying to myself?"

"I can tell you, but you're not going to like it."

"Oh, great." She paused. She looked around the office: the peaceful greens and blues; the nature photographs; wiry, energetic and yet peaceful Dr. Will Garnette, eyes twinkling. "Go for it, then."

"Okay, two things. Both critical, so the order is irrelevant; both happen concurrently. Ideally, anyway. One, you get a journal, and every day, you sit down for five or ten minutes—no longer—and write about this: 'If I were honest with myself, I would admit.' Six times a week. Just do it quickly, without editing. After two weeks, we should have some serious grist for the mill."

"If I were honest with myself, I would admit ... what?"

"Whatever comes to mind in five or ten minutes of just writing. No editing. Whatever it is. That the little dog is mean, that you get annoyed with your staff, that you're sick of your clothes, that you're disappointed in someone—just the things that bubble up."

"That sounds okay." Beth wondered what writing about the same thing over and over would do for her. "What if I can't think of any-thing?"

"Oh, trust me, most people can." He sat silent for a moment. "You may write pretty much the same things every day. Maybe, though, your unconscious, knowing the homework looms, will more easily bring things to mind as the days pass. We'll see."

"Okay, that makes more sense. And the other thing?"

"Ah, that's harder." He made a little grimace. "You must decide to be honest. Tactful is okay. Gentle is okay. But honest. Ruthlessly but tactfully honest. Across situations, unless it is truly dangerous. And dangerous doesn't mean, 'Ugh, I don't want to have that conversa-tion.' You must begin being honest. And, frankly, we all have work to do in that area. So don't feel badly about it."

"I don't lie." She felt heat coming up in her chest.

Dr. Garnette shook his head. "Not lying, per se, Beth. But, for example, have you told Jonah that you are five minutes away from moving to the guest bedroom because he smells bad most of the time? That you expect him to pitch in, instead of imagining that he'll pop up off the couch and clean up, make dinner, take out the trash, and thank you for working so hard to cover for him while he's unemployed? Have you been up front with your mother-in-law about where you really were on those fertility doctor trips, instead of letting her think you were a jet-setting brat?"

Beth's jaw dropped open. "I can't tell him he stinks."

"Interesting one to pick first. Well, you could. But no, I'd recommend being tactful. You know, 'Jonah, I much prefer sharing a bed with you when you've showered,' or 'I'd appreciate you giving me a hand with chores. Do you want to cook dinner or clean up? You pick.'"

"And if he doesn't? Shower? Or pick? Or do anything?"

Dr. Garnette shrugged. "Natural consequences work. Move to the guest bedroom. Take your nighttime stuff. Set it up nicely, make it homey. Make and clean up from your dinner and let him figure it out. Go out to eat with a friend. I don't know. Just be honest and then act on it."

Beth nodded slowly. "Okay. That's going to be really hard."

"Yes. I'm sorry. But being authentic will save you, Beth. There's no other happy way to live."

Chapter 25

The honesty journal turned out to be less burdensome than Beth had expected. After a few days, she looked over what she'd written. Some of it was pretty superficial.

I seriously need a makeover. I used to blame it on the webcam but, yeah, it's not the webcam.

I really enjoy hanging out with Sandy and Cody more than with Jonah. I think I like mosquitoes better than Jonah.

I really need to update my playlist. I'm not in high school anymore.

But some of it was painful to read, and those kept cropping up.

I should have seen the warning flag when Jonah insisted that we lie to his parents.

I was too proud to listen to other people's input.

I wish I had half the courage of Sandy.

I envy the way Cody looks at Sandy. Not for Cody but for how it would feel.

Beth looked at the time. Three o'clock; just two hours and she could be off the clock. She wondered what Alex was up to. The days were getting shorter; certainly she wouldn't be up on some mountaintop a couple of hours from now. *When was Alex due home anyway?* she wondered. She decided she would call Alex after work. *Jonah will probably interfere,* she thought and then thought, *So? So what? I have a yard. The guest bedroom. Our room. He won't follow me to see what I'm doing.*

The time dragged and yet she felt herself becoming anxious. *Ruthless, Beth, be ruthless,* she told herself. *You can do this. The way to a happier life lies with being authentic. Alex is safe. She's a lot of things—a painting, researching librarian with the ends of her hair still purple. She is good, and kind, and wise, and safe. Breathe, Beth.*

Five o'clock finally came: time for dog walks and feeding, a few chores. Then the sun had set, but the sky was still streaked with warm light on the edges of the higher clouds. The first stars were showing. She kept a sweatshirt on and took her phone and a mug of hot tea out to the backyard. She stared at her phone for a while and finally dialed Alex. *Please go to voicemail, please, please, please.* But, no, Alex answered. "Beth! How are you?"

"I'm okay," Beth said, realizing she sounded anything but okay.

Alex must have heard it, too. Her voice was quiet. "So, what's going on?"

"Oh, everything's fine. Really. When are you due back?"

"Next weekend. This one coming. I promised I'd be out of here by the Friday before Thanksgiving, so I figure, leave early, give the place some breathing time before the family comes in for the holiday break."

"So ... Saturday? Sunday?"

"Saturday, driving home all day." There was a pause. "Care to come over Sunday for a visit?"

"I'd love to. But Jonah never wants to, you know, go anywhere ..."

"I didn't ask Jonah. I'm asking you. Do you want to come over Sunday for a visit? Joe isn't due back until the Wednesday before Thanksgiving week, assuming he doesn't end up distracted and staying someplace an extra day to talk to local historians."

"Ha! You mean fishermen," Beth joked. "So, it would be just us. That would be great. What time?"

"Oh, let's say eleven? I'm going to church early. And bring Naughty Sol if you'd like."

"Sure, and, and, Alex." Beth's voice went ragged. "Um, I have a homework assignment, which sounds really dumb, but it's for therapy. Which I know you understand about. But one part is a journal which isn't this, and this part is, is—" Beth paused. *God, I sound like an idiot. Just talk, just talk normally.* She took a deep breath and said, "I'm supposed to be honest, just ruthlessly honest, but tactful and gentle if I want to be, and so I have to tell you that those trips, three of those trips or whatever when you kept the dogs, were not vacations. They were doctor trips, they were trips to fertility specialists because there's something wrong with me and we can't figure out what it is, and the doctors say I'm fine, but I can't be because Jonah's fine and we're still not pregnant and there. There it is. I didn't tell you the truth because Jonah said you were super Catholic and you'd be judgmental if we weren't all natural and, and, well, there." Beth was shaking.

The phone was silent.

"Alex?" Beth asked. "Are you mad?"

"No, Beth, I am definitely not mad at you. I appreciate you letting me know. And Jonah was wrong about me judging you. I'm sorry you've been going through this, and I can't wait to see you on Sunday."

"Thank you, Alex. Me, too." Beth heard Alex's breathing.

Alex's voice was ragged as she said, "Bye, sweetheart. Sleep well. Everything's going to be okay."

Beth smiled at the phone and said, "Thanks, Mom." She sat quietly, looking up at the stars, and felt her heartbeat gradually become slow and regular. Sol came from his fence investigation and rested his big head in her lap, gazing at her in the light from the kitchen window. She smiled at him, stroking his head.

Chapter 26

Beth opened her eyes, stretched a bit, and waited a couple of breaths. Sure enough, Sol lifted his head off her shoulder and made his soft huffing sound. "Good boy," she whispered, and then caught herself. *I don't have to whisper. I won't wake Jonah talking normally.* She sat up and glanced around the guest bedroom. It seemed strange to wake up here, and not in her own bed, but Jonah had just rolled his eyes and said, "Fine, got it," when she explained that she'd rather share a bed with him when he'd showered. Then he came to bed with what seemed to be three days of body odor, and she spent her lunch break the next day quietly moving her nightstand contents, pillows, and lamp into the guest bedroom and carefully moving the large table with his mosaic supplies up against one wall. It wasn't exactly roomy, but she was able to sleep without wanting to gag. Jonah had grumbled at her, insisting he couldn't sleep with her in the other room, but she reminded him she'd been gone for a weekend and he'd managed to sleep.

Today was Sunday, and she would be going to spend some much-needed time with Alex. She went through the morning routine, hoping Alex wasn't angry with her. She'd said nice words, but she'd sounded so upset on the phone. What if Alex was angry at her for lying all this time? Then she corrected herself. Of course, Alex would be understanding. And then, *Well, Alex knows Jonah, probably better than me.*

Just before eleven, she stuck her head into the bedroom. Jonah was still asleep. Beth shrugged and, in a normal speaking voice, announced, "I'm heading off to your folks' house. Spend some time with Alex, help her get things sorted out after being away. Sol's coming with me. I'll leave a note." Then she left a note by the coffee machine and headed for the door. In the doorway, she stopped and turned, went back to the coffee machine, and sighed. *No, let him make his own coffee. I don't have to set it up for him; he's an adult.* Beth shook her head at herself and headed off with Sol. She hummed along to the music in the car on the short drive.

She knocked and waited, looking around. Alex already had a fall wreath on the door. *That was fast,* Beth thought, and then Alex swung the door open and immediately hugged Beth. "Beth! Sol!" Alex leaned over to take Sol's face in both hands. "Sweet, naughty Sol! Come in, come in." Alex gestured around. "Everything's a mess! So much dust! And I'm doing laundry. I did get groceries and get the clothes unpacked. But, still, it's a mess."

"It looks good to me." Beth followed Alex back to the kitchen. A few dishes were in the drainer, recently washed.

"Coffee?" Alex asked. "I'm having some. And food. I had a little snack a couple of hours before church, so I'm starved. Toast? A bagel? Yogurt?"

"Oh, a yogurt and coffee would be good. Maybe wake me up, I guess."

They chatted companionably while the coffee brewed and then moved to the dining room. The sliding glass door was open, so birdsong drifted in clearly. Sol was lying along the screen, reveling in a sunbeam, glinting gold. They both looked at him. "Do you think he knows how gorgeous he looks with the sun on him?" Alex wondered.

"I'm sure." Sol lifted his head to look at Beth, one eyebrow raised. "See that?" she added. "Dead giveaway. He knows."

Alex smiled. "I know we're not supposed to have favorites, but ..."

"Oh, don't feel bad. He's my boy. Anastasia is Jonah's girl, and Apple and Mac ... well, I love them but frankly they could have a better home than ours. Maybe that's a good idea."

Alex looked up with a concerned face. Beth shook her head. "I mean, nothing bad, but ... oh, crap." She looked down, blinking back tears. *Ruthlessly, tactfully honest. Be ruthlessly, tactfully honest.* Looking up, she said, "Alex, I'm sorry, but things are really bad between Jonah and me. And I am going to be giving him an ultimatum that things change, demonstrably, and soon, or we're separating." Beth looked out the window, avoiding Alex's gaze. "I wouldn't tell you this, of course, but, well, trying to be honest. With myself, too. Because I'm not sure it's that things are so much worse as much as I've finally realized things are awful." She turned back to Alex, who was pressing her lips together, eyebrows drawn, looking worried. "Alex, he's actually not doing anything different than he did on weekends when he could get away with it—vegging on the couch, not showering or putting on real clothes, letting me do most of the work. Now it's just all the time, and if I ask for help or try to engage him in any conversation at all, he acts annoyed and tries to hurt my feelings."

"Which he can be good at," Alex interjected. "In my experience, anyway."

Beth nodded. "So, I've decided to give him until January second to start shaping up, to really job hunt and be accountable, to start helping at home, you know. Be a partner. He's going to absolutely freak out. I guess I'm telling you partly so I have accountability, because it won't be a fun conversation."

"Ruthlessly, tactfully honest. Hmm." It was Alex's turn to gaze out the window, frowning. She turned to Beth, sighed, and put her coffee mug down. She reached across the table to rest one hand on Beth's forearm. Beth looked down at the small hand and felt a twinge of pleasure; Alex still had traces of paint under her nails, little marks of freedom. Beth looked up and saw Alex's sad face.

"Alex?" Beth felt her stomach begin to tighten.

Alex's eyes had tears in them. "Oh, Beth. I do not want to tell you this, but I have to. Beth, there's a reason Jonah didn't want you to tell us about the fertility problems. And it's not because I'm some kind of religious freak or that Joe and I would reject you or see you as defective and unworthy of our family name, or whatever kind of story he told you."

Beth frowned. "So, it was just Jonah and his weird privacy fixation."

Alex shook her head. "No, Beth. Jonah," her voice wobbled, "Jonah knows you're not getting pregnant because Jonah knows he might be the one with the medical problem."

"No," Beth said. "No, that's not right. He told me. He said the urologist said he was fine. Fine."

"Did you see the reports? The actual test results? Anything but Jonah's word?"

Beth looked down at her coffee. "No. I trusted him." She whipped her face up to Alex. "But what?"

"Beth, you know Jonah had a hernia operation when he was a teenager, right?"

"Yeah, he has that little scar. He told me about that."

"But not about the problem. There's a slight—very slight—risk of damage that will make a man infertile. Not impotent, but not able to father children. Jonah's known he might not be able to have children since he was fourteen." Alex wiped her eyes. "Oh, Beth, he was supposed to tell you. Obviously, this discussion is supposed to be part of marriage prep. And he kept you away from us."

And sold me on keeping away from you, Beth thought. She began shaking; the room was suddenly ice cold. The pit of her stomach ached. She pushed away from the table, half stood and dropped back into the chair. "But it might not be Jonah. I'll look at the urologist reports. He wouldn't lie about that." Beth hugged her arms around herself. It felt as if her bones were vibrating. "Five years," she said slowly. "Five years. He's been happy to let me go on these crazy, expensive trips just to appease me and keep me on eggshells and defensive and distracted. Oh, Alex." She burst into tears. Alex took a deep breath, went around the table, and, placing her hands on Beth's shoulders, said quietly, "Beth. Beth, let's go sit on the couch." Beth let herself be guided to the couch. Alex gently sat her down and pulled over a blanket, draping it over Beth and then stroking her hair. Beth drooped over onto Alex's shoulder, crying and shaking, and then just rested, quietly whimpering, before settling into shuddered breathing. After what seemed a long time, she sat up, wiping her face with the back of her hand. Alex handed her a tissue and Beth blew her nose, noisily. Sol whimpered. His head was resting on her leg and his eyebrows were drawn up in concern. Beth gave him a weak smile and petted his face.

Alex looked down at Sol. "He came in with us. Well, about five minutes later. Such a good boy. Well, mostly."

Beth nodded and tried to laugh. "Yeah, Naughty Sol. Remember that time he ate your Sunday roast?" Then her voice wobbled. "That was one of our fake vacations."

Alex shook her head. "No. Stop blaming yourself."

"But I lied. I lied for him."

"Yes. And on the other hand, you had made a commitment to God and to Jonah—not to me and Joe. I understand. And given that Jonah sort of... misrepresented his family, it makes sense that you went along. I'm not angry. Joe's not angry. With you, anyway." She pressed her lips together. "I could just about wring Jonah's neck. Not that I would, of course. But I am angry and ashamed of his behavior."

Beth shrugged off the blanket to her lap. She had stopped shivering. "I'm trying to figure it all out. It doesn't make sense. Why marry me, without telling me the risk, knowing I wanted children? Why? Why not just pick a girl who wanted to just play house with dogs?"

"And who else was waiting in line for my son?" Alex asked. Beth looked uncomfortable. "Beth, I know Jonah's difficult. When you showed interest in him, I'm sure it surprised him as much as anyone else, if he were honest about it. But he's simultaneously so arrogant and insecure that he acted entitled and, well, you sort of fell for it. That he was a real prize." Alex looked at the ceiling and then at Beth. "I wish I had known from the beginning that he was lying to you, because I never would have covered for him."

Beth thought about that. "But the grandchildren remarks ..."

Alex nodded. "Yes, we did hint around about that. And, of course, none of us knew for sure. Anyone can have fertility problems—between environmental toxins and infections and endometriosis, so much can go wrong. As far as we knew, there was a good chance he could have children. And those comments weren't just aimed at you. God knows Sandy is taking her sweet time growing up. Although that seems to be changing. And then, from our perspective, the two of you were living the jet-set life with all these last-minute jaunts. We started figuring, well, they're going to wait to adopt, or maybe we're going to have to get those 'My grandchild is a golden retriever' bumper stickers."

"I feel like an idiot."

"Well, don't. Seriously. Just stop it. That's the trick, isn't it? He pulls a fast one and you get to feel stupid. You're the brains of the outfit, Beth. Be angry at being deceived. Fine. But don't feel stupid."

Beth nodded. "Yeah. I am angry. But now I'm really hungry. My yogurt is probably nice and warm in there."

"If Sol didn't eat it." Alex paused. "Beth, if you haven't, you need to look at all the medical reports yourself. For your own peace of mind."

Beth laughed weakly. "Peace would be ... a change." She stood up. "How about I have something to eat, and we get this house vacuumed and dusted and ready for Thanksgiving? I need to do something practical. That will help clear my head."

The next few hours passed quickly. Between them they dusted and vacuumed in every room, then remade Alex's bed with fresh sheets and blankets. "Sandy was here the whole time, wasn't she?" Beth asked casually.

"Oh, she was officially here, sure," Alex agreed. "But I'm not naïve. I'm sure she spent a majority of her time with Cody and the kids and that this was just the place to crash at night. Her room, as you can see, looks plenty lived in. Sandy wouldn't sleep over at Cody's with the kids there unless she was babysitting for Cody. If that happens, she and Rachel will be over there together having some sort of big four-kid pajama party. Those two are as bad as the twins. And as far as Cody having a night off, well, Jenna just about never sees the twins. Sandy just slept here." Alex rolled her eyes. "The refrigerator was down to her breakfast foods and snacks for nighttime. I came in from driving for hours and had a withered apple and an outdated yogurt."

Beth smiled. "As long as it was organic ..." They were unpacking a box of autumn decorations. She paused, an autumn-themed toss pillow in her hands. "Alex. Mom, I'm just not sure what to do. Do I go home and just tell Jonah I know? What happens next?"

Alex shook her head. "I don't know, Beth. You probably need time to think, to digest all this. If it were me ... I'd take a few days to think. And then I'd talk to people I trust and figure it out." Alex pulled out plastic turkey salt-and-pepper shakers and held them at arm's length. "Do you ever find yourself surprised you even own something? Like, what made me think these were a good idea?"

"Right now, it seems like all the time." Beth placed the pillow on the sofa and refolded the blanket. "You're right. Time to think. Because until I know how I feel and what I want, I hardly know what to even say to Jonah. I think I'll just go home and try to act normal. See if I can get together with the girls. Maybe talk to my dad. Check back in with you. Talk to the therapist."

"But no one can make decisions for you," Alex warned. "It's got to be true to you, Beth, whatever you decide."

Beth nodded. "I know. This one's all on me."

Chapter 27

Beth went home late Sunday afternoon. Jonah was on the couch; he stirred to greet her and wave lazily. "How was my mom?"

"She's great. Had a good time just hanging out and helping her get things cleaned up after being away. Some fall decor out, that sort of thing." Beth went into the living room and sat on the loveseat. "How about here?" she asked casually. "Anything going on?"

Jonah shrugged. He was in the same T-shirt as yesterday. "Not too much. Took the dogs for a walk. Had some breakfast a few hours ago." Beth nodded. *A few hours ago*, she thought. *That means around lunchtime.*

"Anything interesting going on?"

Jonah rolled his eyes. "Beth. Seriously. No, nothing interesting. I've applied for three jobs in the past week. No one returns texts or emails on Sunday."

"Jonah. I mean besides that. You know ... see anything interesting on the dog walks? Work on your mosaic? You know, life." She paused.

"Nice to know about the job applications, though. Anything look interesting?"

"Well, there's one out in Texas. Austin area. I'm not sure how they feel about remote work; it wasn't clear."

Well, that would make things easy, Beth thought. *You just go move to Austin.* Aloud, she said, "The job itself?"

"Sounds better than the local ones. Opportunity for advancement, better pay, good benefits package. The company seems to be trending up."

"Nice. The particular job? Sounds good to start?"

He shrugged. "Well, it's kind of simple. Probably boring. But I figure I can put my stamp on things and move forward."

Beth nodded. The usual Jonah, she realized, thinking like a teenager: that he, the new person, would come in with all the answers to improve things before he really understood how things worked. "Well, let's keep our fingers crossed! Any ideas for dinner?" She stood up.

He shook his head, eyes back to the television screen. "Nah. Not too hungry."

"Okay," Beth said briskly but not harshly. "I'll just fend for myself."

She made herself a salad and threw some extra cheese on it, fed the dogs, and started the evening walk routine. She figured a couple of nice, long dog walks would be just the thing to start clearing her head. Jonah had grunted when she told him she was taking Sol and Anastasia for their walk. They didn't get far before they ran into Izzy and Ozzy, holding hands and strolling the neighborhood.

They chatted about the pleasant weather, the upcoming holiday season—Thanksgiving was just around the corner, and they were still working out plans. Ozzy's parents were traveling to Nebraska to visit his sister and her family—the grandchildren were quite the draw—and Izzy's parents were going on a cruise. "My mom announced she's not cooking Thanksgiving dinner again until there's a grandchild." Izzy shrugged.

"I'm sure we can accommodate her, just not this year," Ozzy remarked, and Izzy giggled and elbowed his side.

Beth raised her eyebrows. "Oh," she said, leaving a pause for either of them to fill.

"Sort of a first sight thing. Or at least a first talk-half-the-night thing," Ozzy explained sheepishly.

"It was the cooking breakfast after talking half the night that reeled me in," Izzy teased.

"Beautiful," Beth said, feeling just a little sad. Then she added, "If you're going to be on your own, I'm guessing Alex and Joe ... Jonah's parents ... will be happy to have you. They're both on sabbatical, so there will be lots of stories to share."

"I wouldn't want to impose," Ozzy said, "but a family dinner would be nice, and you're basically Izzy's extended family, so it will be good to get the inside scoop on my girl here." He squeezed Izzy's shoulders.

Izzy gave him a sidelong look. "It does mean you'll have to endure dinner with Jonah. Nothing personal, Beth."

"Not at all," Beth sighed. "I guess I'll have to endure dinner with Jonah, too."

"We should talk," Izzy said.

"Any time." Beth stood a bit straighter. "Seriously. Right this minute is fine by me. Maybe I need some male input on this."

Ozzy nodded slowly. "How 'bout you get the pups home and come on over? We'll put on some decaf."

Jonah didn't say anything when Beth came in, announced she'd be heading over to visit with Izzy and Ozzy, and left again. She knocked, and Izzy called, "Beth, just come on in." She went in, taking a quick look around. The layout was much like her home, a sort of mirror image. There was artwork on the wall over the fireplace—no television in sight—and the furniture was simple and vaguely Scandinavian. The colors were soft—different tones of wood, greens, quiet blues. The entire place felt peaceful. The kitchen was warmly lit and she smelled coffee. "The place looks great," she commented.

"Thanks," Ozzy said. "I'm happy with it. This is a great neighborhood you've got."

Beth nodded and sighed. They filled their mugs and settled into the living room—chairs and a loveseat around a table strewn with books and a precariously balanced tray of cookies with some napkins next to it. "In case we need fortification," Izzy explained, and promptly took one.

There was a brief silence, and Beth took a deep breath. She looked at Izzy, her dear friend, so enthusiastic about everything and now glowing with love; at Ozzy, smart, kind, serious when it mattered, and absolutely at ease, a faded surf shop T-shirt hanging off his lean frame, his sun-bleached hair disheveled so that she could not imagine him practicing law. But his eyes were so kind, so much like Izzy's eyes, that she nodded and began to speak.

She went over how she learned Jonah had been fired; his deception for two weeks, his prolific spending of money that was no longer coming in, and his angry attacks on her for being upset with him. She told them about her seeing a therapist and trying to make things better and Jonah being so awful to the therapist. She described her weekend with Alex and her intention to try to set some boundaries, and how angry Jonah had been when she separated her funds from his. Izzy and Ozzy made reassuring sounds—soft comments of encouragement, gentle, "Go on," and "It's okay," when she paused for a breath. Then Beth began to cry and said, "But this last thing, this last thing," and covered her face, shaking her head. Izzy moved over beside her, sitting on the edge of the same chair and hugging her.

"Beth, whatever it is, we're here for you."

Beth managed to quiet herself, to catch her breath. She leaned her head on Izzy's shoulder, looked over at Ozzy. "So, this … this takes the prize. It turns out that Jonah's been lying to me for all these years, making me believe—letting me believe—that our infertility must be due to me. And it turns out that no, he had a hernia operation as a kid and maybe, maybe it went wrong, it's a possibility, and I never looked at the urologist report so maybe it's not me, not me at all and he's just been letting me blame myself. His mom let on. I've been pouring money into appointments and tests with specialists who keep telling me I'm fine." She hiccupped. "And of course Jonah told me his doctor told him he was fine, and I never asked for proof." She looked down at her lap. "So, there you go. That's the story of my marriage, one big ugly lie after another."

"Oh, Beth." Izzy began to cry.

"Maybe you could get the urology report?" Ozzy wondered. "I mean, we're jumping to conclusions that he is lying about that."

"Too," Izzy said emphatically. "Lying about that, too."

Beth sighed, her shoulders sinking. She shook her head and looked at them both. "We have it. It's in the files. I never even looked at it."

"You never even looked?"

"I just believed him." Beth covered her face and then, thinking of Dr. Garnette, pulled her hands down to her lap quickly. "I chose to just take his word. Which was a really stupid idea."

Ozzy rubbed his temples. "Jeez, what a nightmare. Beth, I haven't known you two long but, wow, if it's really been him all along … I can't fathom that degree of cruelty."

Beth drew in her breath sharply at the word. Yet she couldn't argue with herself: Jonah had been cruel, and she had been foolish. What a perfect setup.

"Dump his sorry ass," Izzy said firmly, wiping her cheeks. "Just throw the bastard out. You have a pre-nup, right? I remember that your parents were sort of insistent."

"Insistent is an understatement," Beth replied, trying to stay on one thing at a time. "Yes, a good pre-nup. I can buy him out easily, send him off with Anastasia. She's small enough to live in a condo or whatever he'll be able to afford with his share of the equity in the house."

"Sounds like you've been thinking," Ozzy said quietly. "That's serious stuff. No chance of reconciliation, then?"

Beth shrugged, shaking her head. "Yes. No. I can't imagine it, actually ... I mean, can I really live with a man who lies about important things? Things like babies and money and work? What else don't I know?"

Ozzy nodded. "As a guy, I could imagine the job situation. You know, being so ashamed that you'd try to hide it while you got another job so you could present it as a done deal—no harm, no foul, so to speak, but of course it would be harmful. It's lying, day after day." He paused. "But to know from before you were married that you wanted children and that he did not want them and there was a risk he couldn't father children, well, that's leaving you high and dry. If he'd told you and you'd accepted the risk, or adoption or a donor, then that would be different. But he didn't give you that option."

"No," Beth agreed, shaking her head. "No, he set things up for me to become resigned and despairing, and never the wiser. And he could be good, loyal Jonah, sticking by me, spending my money trying to figure out what's wrong with me." She sighed, turning her coffee cup slowly between her hands.

It was quiet for a few moments. Izzy rested her head on Beth's shoulder. Beth put down her coffee and hugged her. "We're all here for you, no matter what," Izzy said quietly. "You know that."

Beth leaned her head down on Izzy's. "Thanks, Izzy." She smiled weakly at Ozzy. "Thanks, Ozzy ... sorry you've been dragged into the wild vortex here."

Ozzy shrugged. "I'm okay. I'm sorry for you both. Sorry for your heartache, sorry for Jonah." He looked at their incredulous faces and added, "Sorry for him, that he doesn't even understand what the problem could be. Like he's missing a piece of humanity in there. He's a pizza, short of a slice."

A pizza short of a slice. Beth nodded slowly. "Thanks, Ozzy. That really helps." He looked confused. "The pizza metaphor. I can see it. I can see it and it's not just me not being nice enough or patient enough or generous enough or smart enough." She paused, staring at her coffee cup as if it were a crystal ball. "But I get to own some of this. I see that. I let Jonah believe it was okay to be rude, to be selfish, that his sporadic moments of play and kindness were enough for me. Crumbs."

Izzy stayed sitting against Beth, rubbing Beth's back as if Beth were a distressed preschooler. "You kinda do put up with a lot before you bark back," she said gently. "All our Saturday coffees ... how much time did you take center stage with all your difficulties?" She paused. "I'll tell you. Like, three times? Maybe? Over all these years." She gave Beth's shoulder a playful punch. "Game's over, kiddo. It's catch-up time."

Beth looked sidelong at her. "I have a therapist. I can't bother everyone ..."

Izzy got up, walked over to the kitchen and came back, phone in hand. "Here she goes," Ozzy said to Beth. "You know better than me. Stay out of her way." He grinned, jerking his head toward Izzy.

Izzy, meanwhile, typed furiously and then looked up at Beth. "Okay, waiting to hear from the girls but we're on for coffee. Tomorrow. Flex the time. It's an emergency ... you need to have people who love you listen to you think out loud so you can start sorting things out."

"Wait a minute," Beth protested.

"No waiting," Izzy said briskly. "You're in a tornado, spinning around. Maybe a centrifuge? I don't know. But you're not organized. Your head is all over the place. Trust me, talking with other people can be the best way to straighten out your thinking." Izzy paused and then shrugged. "Ask Ozzy. He's been helping me get straightened out." She smiled at him and blew a kiss. "And he's fabulous at it." Ozzy beamed at her.

"Okay," Beth sighed. "What time?"

Izzy glanced at her phone. "Courtney and Kitta can both do nine thirty."

"Okay," Beth replied, wondering if she was capable of saying anything else.

Beth let her team know she'd be away for a couple of hours and signed off at nine. She wondered what good it would do, having Courtney, Kitta, and Izzy meet with her. She grabbed her bag and put the leash on Solar. She glanced toward the bedroom; Jonah was still in bed. She thought, briefly, of letting him know she was going out and then of leaving a note by the coffeemaker, shook her head violently, and left.

For possibly the first time, her three friends were at a table outside the coffee shop, with a cup waiting for her and a bowl of water for Sol slipped under the table. Everyone hugged her, she sat down, looked around at their faces, and felt her throat tightening. She opened her mouth, intending to thank them, but instead she just burst into tears, put her head in her hands, and sobbed. Izzy reached across the table to rest a hand on her arm; Kitta and Courtney each rested a hand on her shoulders and all sat quietly, waiting. When Beth collected herself, sitting straight and wiping her eyes, they all smiled gently, waiting with a strangely serene and respectful silence. "Okay," Beth said. She glanced at all of their faces, one by one, nodding and receiving a smile from each in turn. "Okay. So, you all know, I guess."

"I didn't share anything," Izzy said quietly. "Just that this is an emergency. Practically. Because it is."

Beth nodded. This time she was able to recount Jonah's last, and worst, betrayal—a betrayal now years old. Kitta and Courtney both became tearful; Izzy was past tearful and into the raging phase.

After a silence, Courtney spoke up first. "Beth, I'm so sorry. If it turns out he can't have children and knew it and lied to you ... how absolutely hideous."

Kitta nodded. "Awful. But at least—" She paused. Courtney and Izzy turned their heads toward her, frowning. Kitta shrugged, rubbing her belly. "But at least," she repeated, sitting up straighter and looking at Beth, her gaze direct and honest. "At least you're young. Young enough to start over and maybe have that family you want."

"Well, that was blunt force." Courtney sighed. "Seriously? Right to the kill, Kitta?"

Kitta shrugged. "I wasted way too much time investing in Hunter. It turns out Jonah's a bad investment, too. Maybe worse, because with Hunter, all the lying was by me, to me." Her shoulders dropped. "I am trying really, really hard to not lie. Not to myself, not to anyone. So," she turned her wide, earnest eyes to Beth, "divorce him, Beth. Get out and get free. You can do better. In like, five minutes."

Courtney rubbed her temples. "Can we just let Beth talk, everyone? Beth ... maybe you want to think out loud and just have us here for you. Whatever you decide to do, we're behind you all the way."

"Except capital crimes, maybe," Izzy added quickly. Three faces whipped around to stare at her. She shrugged. "Kidding. Right?"

Courtney was still rubbing her temples. She turned back to Beth. "Seriously. Just think out loud."

Beth glanced around; the outside tables were otherwise deserted, so she started talking. She talked about the lying about the job, the spending money, the verbal attacks and the disdain. She talked about the years of believing she just wasn't trying hard enough.

"I always felt like Jonah was some poor, misunderstood genius," Beth said. Izzy snorted. Beth raised her eyebrows at her and went on. "I know now that wasn't the case, that he's just always been kind of narcissistic. I mean, the way he treats his mom, his sister. The weird way he just hates other people. Like Matt, for example."

"See, that's red flags all over the place. What sort of person can hate Matt?" Izzy interjected. "Next you'll be saying he hates Tim, too, which is just as ridiculous."

"Shh," Courtney scolded.

Beth paused, shuddered, reached down to pet Sol, who was pushing his nose against her thigh in concern. "I kind of shut everyone out who tried to tell me about Jonah. Until he got fired and didn't tell me. And I learned ... a lot. A real lot. That's how I found out he probably can't have children, and that he knew it all along. He didn't tell me, let me go on thinking I was broken."

There was silence, and then Courtney said, gently, "And?"

Beth nodded with a weak smile. *Shades of Dr. Garnette*, she thought. "And ... I can't go on being married to someone who is that deeply dishonest." She looked around the table. "So, that's it. That's the decision. The questions are how. When."

Izzy leaned forward, elbows on the table, cup in one hand. "How? First, get a lawyer and have papers drawn up that go with your pre-nup. Second, be sure you've protected anything he can mess up—family jewelry, money, whatever. I can hold onto anything you need. Ozzy has a safe. Third, let Jonah know—tell him yourself or let him find out when the papers are served. Assuming he ever gets out of bed to be served." Izzy took a sip. "One, two, three."

"Someone's dating an attorney," Kitta remarked. She turned to Beth. "What do you want to do?"

"Buy him out. Get the divorce. Get an annulment." She looked around. "A church annulment. So that I'm free to marry again." They nodded. "Move on. Move forward. Whatever that means." She stroked Sol's head. "I want Sol. I don't want Anastasia. I don't know about Apple and Mac." She paused. "This sounds crazy, but I was kind of thinking that Sandy and Cody and the twins would like the greyhounds."

"You've been thinking a lot," Kitta remarked.

Courtney nodded slowly. "Yup, a lot of thinking. Interesting about Sandy and Cody. Official news?"

Beth shook her head. "No, but it's practically a given." She winked at Izzy. "I think they're as magical as Izzy and Ozzy, just a little weird, given they're practically related."

Kitta smiled. "Nice for Sandy to find someone smart enough for her." She drew her eyebrows together at their puzzled faces. "Oh, come on," she said, mildly impatient. "Seriously? You can't tell in five minutes who has the brains in that sibling dyad? For all her flakiness, which I suspect is partly a ruse."

"Fair enough. And true," Beth added. "That's another weird thing. The girls in that family—Alex and Sandy—had some strange little high-IQ secret that they leave the boys out of. Apparently neither wanted to deal with Jonah finding out he wasn't so special."

"I think I was there when Sandy blew that system out of the water," Izzy remarked dryly. "I did manage to pay attention to what she was saying, even if she was doing a lot of pointing with a knife."

"It wasn't what it sounds like," Beth protested, glancing at Courtney and Kitta.

"Yeah, it kind of was," Izzy shot back. "Is Jonah still sulking?"

"He never said a word about the whole thing," Beth said, wondering now at that aspect. "I would have expected some sort of argument."

"Jonah doesn't argue. He just asserts and puts people down," Courtney said.

"I'd love to hear more about the knife business," Kitta added, rubbing her belly. "Maybe I could get some tips from your-soon-to-be-ex-sister-in-law."

"Oooh," Beth breathed out. "I didn't think about that. About losing Sandy and Alex and Joe."

"Do you seriously think you're going to lose them?" Courtney shook her head with impatience. "Don't you think it's more than coincidence that they've made a point of building up their connection with you, absent Jonah, in the past few months?" Courtney pressed her lips together firmly before continuing. "I don't believe in coincidences. I think they sensed things were unwinding, and you're not losing anything except being shackled to Jonah."

Beth took a sip of coffee. "Okay." She sighed and repeated, "Okay." She looked around at her friends. "So here goes ... you're my accountability team. And support system. It's two weeks until Thanksgiving.

My goal is to have everything done before Thanksgiving. Well, not everything, but the divorce papers. Valuables from my family in Izzy's care. A chat with Sandy about Apple and Mac. And a meeting in advance with Alex and Joe. Then they can decide whether or not I should go. To their place for Thanksgiving, I mean." She glanced at Izzy. "If they don't want me there, you and Ozzy can come over to our house."

"Okay," Izzy said cheerfully. "But if I were Alex and Joe, I'd pick you over that fungus."

"Izzy." Courtney sighed.

"What?" Izzy asked. "You haven't seen him lately. Or smelled him." She rolled her eyes and Beth couldn't help giggling, and then laughing, surprising herself at the waves of laughter that came burbling out. Izzy joined her, then Kitta, and then, finally, shaking her head, Courtney.

When they'd caught their breath, Beth continued. "Then I want to tell Jonah. A little afraid about that, but I think it needs to come from me and not someone from the court system."

"The house?" Courtney asked.

"I can buy him out of his share. The house is mostly mine—all in the pre-nup. I can set him up with enough to put down on a small condo and have a little cushion or maybe move away for a job. Whatever. I can't imagine what he'll decide. But I'd like him out by the end of the year."

"Well," Kitta said, "you'd better get going."

Beth nodded. "Yes. I have an appointment with an attorney this afternoon. Thank Ozzy again for the referral," she said to Izzy. "The phone conversation made it sound pretty straight forward. Quick and easy. We could be finalized in a couple of months." She shook her head. "Who am I fooling? It's going to be hard."

Courtney rubbed Beth's shoulder. "Just one step at a time, Beth, baby. Just one step at a time. Keep moving."

"And, Beth," Izzy said slowly. "You still haven't looked at the medical files." Beth cringed and looked away. "If it helps ... I'll be with you while you do."

"Thanks, but I think I have to take that on first, by myself." She looked around at them. "I promise to keep you all in the loop."

"We promise to keep up with you. You won't be able to go radio silent," Courtney said firmly, and Kitta and Izzy echoed her.

"Not to worry," Beth said quietly. "I can't do this solo. It's going to be a hard ride."

Chapter 28

Beth got into her car, feeling her body shaking with a post-adrenaline reaction. Tara Mallory had been as pleasant as Ozzy had said, a warm, red-haired woman of about fifty, a suit jacket draped over her chair, flipflops on her feet, a pair of painful-looking pumps poking out from under her desk. She had asked for the prenuptial agreement and tax returns in advance and was ready to give her professional opinion and answer questions. She had raised her eyebrows at the financial offer Beth suggested for Jonah. "That's very generous," she said mildly. "Can I suggest dialing that back twenty percent? In case he pushes back?" Beth had nodded agreement. The paperwork would be ready in a couple of days; a date was set for Beth to come back and review everything and sign off, and then the paperwork would be filed. That gave her two days to put other plans into place.

When the shaking stopped, Beth texted Izzy, Courtney, and Kitta.

Atty step 1 done.

Three quick affirmations came in short order.

She put her phone away and drove home. Jonah was lying on the couch and barely grunted a response to her. She was going to offer an excuse for her absence but decided against it. *Let him ask if he cares.* Instead, she went into the bedroom they had shared until so recently. She wrinkled her nose; it stunk. She moved a few more of her things into the guest room, her movements quiet and deliberate. Then she carefully packed her grandmother's jewelry, old family photos, and her grandfather's glasses before sending a text to Izzy.

Stuff boxed up. Can I drop off at Ozzy's tonight?

The response came quickly. *Absolutely.*

Beth sat on the guest bed, looking around the room. The table with Jonah's rarely touched mosaic was still sitting there; she wondered what Jonah would do about that. *Have fun packing*, she thought, and then frowned at herself for being unkind. She took Apple and Mac for a walk, needing the fresh air and the quicker pace to burn off another surge of adrenalized shaking. She had to connect with Alex and Joe, and soon; that would be hard.

What are you thinking? Alex knew the whole story. What Joe was aware of so far, who knew? She went through the conversation with them in her head, over and over. It occurred to her, briefly, that this ought to be Jonah's problem, but then she considered how Alex and Joe were her family, too, and odds are, she thought grimly, she'd be the one closer to them as time went by. She'd tell them and then her parents. *My parents will be relieved*, she thought. She wondered what to tell them, how much to share. She thought maybe she'd go visit them for a quick weekend and have a nice, long walk with Dad first and then, depending on his guidance, decide what to share with her mother. She shivered, thinking of how cold her mother would probably be. *Well, Beth, of course, we're very disappointed. Not surprised, I'm sad to say.* Beth sighed and shook her head, hard.

Back at the house, she switched to Anastasia and Sol, taking them for their slower walk. Jonah did not respond to her greeting or her good-bye. She left, shaking her head. What could he be thinking? She kept rehearsing conversations with Alex and Joe. She wondered how it would go. Alex she could predict. Would Joe stare at her and then launch into some sort of pedagogical soliloquy, working up into an arm-waving enthusiasm about ... something? What? His son's mystifying character defects? The history of annulments due to deceit? She surprised herself by chuckling at the image of Joe spiraling off into one of his talks and imagining Alex's wry sidelong glance and the new Alex's willingness to cut him off when necessary. The mental movie of Alex rolling her eyes and interrupting Joe's imaginary speech lightened her mood. Back at the house, she started putting her dinner together and texted Alex.

I'd like to see you and Joe. Sooner is better.

Of course. Tomorrow? Any time.

How about lunchtime?

Perfect. We'll be here. Everything OK?

Yes—everything is OK.

Beth sighed and put down her phone. Of course, nothing was okay. *But it will be*, she told herself. She had her dinner, grabbed the box out of her bedroom, and took Sol for another walk. Jonah, meanwhile, barely glanced up. He was still wearing the same flannel pants and misshapen T-shirt he'd seemingly had on for two days. She promised herself to check in with him when she came back from Ozzy's house.

Ozzy's garage door was open, so she went in, knocking at the interior door. Izzy swung the door open, hugged her, and led her in. Sol began exploring, and Beth told him to be good; he looked up with his golden retriever grin, wagged his tail, and headed promptly toward the kitchen.

"Don't worry about him," Ozzy called from the living room. "Come in, come in."

Beth handed the box to Izzy. "Grandma's jewelry, Grandpa's eyeglasses, some old photos." She sighed. "The money's already taken care of. Met Tara today," she said to Ozzy. "Thanks; you were right. She's great. Very efficient. I see her again day after tomorrow to sign the paperwork."

"Good work," Izzy said, as if she were a proud parent. "And?"

"And tomorrow at lunch I'm going to see Alex and Joe at their house. Nice and private."

"How are you?" Ozzy asked quietly. "This feels very ... quick."

Izzy glared at him and Beth smiled. "It probably does feel quick from the outside. And in some ways to me, too. And on the other hand, well ... it feels very natural. Like I've been pretending things are okay, just lying to myself about some things."

"That's not fair." Izzy was indignant.

"No, it is," Beth said firmly. "I never did verify the urologist's report. I didn't check the bank regularly. I just trusted. I made excuses for Jonah's rude behavior, I put up with things I should never have tolerated. So, yeah, Jonah's a jerk. And I've been a willing fool." She paused and added, "Up until now."

Ozzy nodded slowly. "Expecting any problems with Jonah's parents?"

Beth smiled. "I drove myself crazy about that, and then I had this image in my mind—a movie, really—imagining Joe spiraling into professor mode and Alex either rolling her eyes or just cutting him off at the knees. And that seems more realistic than all the scary, critical movies I conjured up at first." She shook her head. "Besides, Alex knows the whole story and Joe may by now, too." She glanced at Izzy. "Or Alex is filling him in tonight. You know how couples are."

Izzy sighed and hugged Beth again. "Oh, Beth. I'm sorry." She made a determined smile. "Kitta was right, you know."

"And that is not something I hear very often," Ozzy commented.

"Me, neither." Beth smiled.

"I mean it," Izzy said, nodding hard once. "At least you're young. You can find someone right for you. Someone who wants a family and all that normal stuff. Maybe not right away, but still. Beth, it's out there for you. I know it."

"Izzy—no," Beth interrupted. *Please, Lord*, she thought, *don't let Izzy have any ideas.*

"I don't have any ideas to set you up with anyone. Not yet, anyway." Izzy paused. "And, yeah, Beth, you really do have a habit of saying the quiet part out loud. Do you do that at work? Like during online meetings?"

Beth grimaced. "A few times. Mostly I keep my mic off. But one of my colleagues is a really, really good lipreader and sends me little side messages if I get out of hand."

"Not a good plan," Izzy said disapprovingly.

"Interesting commentary from the woman with barely a filter," Ozzy said, but he was gazing up at Izzy with such affection and admiration that the words had no sting. Izzy laughed at him and sank onto the loveseat, more on his lap than the cushion, and kissed his cheek.

"Like you mind at all, you crazy surfer," she teased.

"I'd better be going," Beth said, figuring it was time for an exit. "Besides, Sol needs to go home before he does anything wrong."

"Oh, he's fine," Ozzy said, still naïve about Sol's appetite for destruction.

"His real nickname is Naughty Sol," Izzy warned him. "You have no idea."

"He will," Beth said, half grim and half joking. There were hugs and warm words all around, and she headed back home.

Jonah was still on the couch. She greeted him, hanging up Sol's leash and stepping into the living room. He glanced at her, sat up a bit. Her heart turned at the sight of him; pale, hair disheveled, glasses smudged. "How was your day?" she asked, trying to keep her voice normal, as if she were asking him the question after a long workday.

He sat up a bit, glanced at the television, muted it, and turned back to her. "Actually, pretty good." He paused. She waited, counting her breaths. *Let him do some work*, she told herself. He looked quizzical. She remained quiet, nodding and trying to look only mildly interested. He frowned and then continued, "I heard from that job. In Austin. Third interview tomorrow."

"Congratulations," she said. "That's good."

"Well, maybe," he said, sounding surprisingly neutral. "We'll see. I'm hoping they make an offer with this one."

"And then what?" Beth asked.

"Then we'll see what they offer." Jonah shrugged and turned back to the television. "Maybe we'll be celebrating my new job tomorrow. I'll let you know."

"Good luck," Beth said warmly. "I hope you get an offer you like." Jonah glanced sharply at her before turning back to the documentary.

He must be in a good mood, Beth thought, because he began tossing out comments about the documentary. "Why does Rommel have such a reputation for being a genius in desert warfare?" he complained at one point, and then, "The Germans totally hosed up that operation."

Beth nodded to herself as she made some tea. *Make it easy*, she thought. *Get that job, move to Austin—make the fresh start easy for us all*. She stood staring out at the dark sky, frowning. *Since when*, she wondered, *has Jonah made anything easier for anyone?*

She turned back to pour her tea, and, as it brewed, she went into the bedroom closet, where the filing cabinet with financial and medical records were. She flipped through files until she found what she was looking for. Her hands were shaking as she read the report summary. *Right here in plain sight*, she thought. *He didn't even bother to try to hide it from me; he just took for granted I'd believe whatever he said.*

She heard a sound; Jonah was in the doorway. She held the file up to her chest.

"Beth, what are you up to?"

"Nothing."

"Beth." Jonah rolled his eyes, folding his arms and leaning again the door jamb. "Are you going over the fertility doc stuff again?"

She nodded wordlessly, hugging the files. She felt as if she couldn't speak. Jonah stepped closer. He spoke quietly. "Beth, just let it go. Just be happy with what you have. We have. Let it go."

Beth blinked, staring at him. He gave a half smile, turned and left the room. She put the file in her work papers, closed up the filing cabinet, and went back to the kitchen. Jonah was back on the couch, slumped and silent except for occasional rebukes to the Germans on television.

Chapter 29

Alex was in the open doorway before Beth was out of her car, pushing wavy hair off her forehead. She hugged Beth silently and then, slowly letting go, whispered, "It's all going to be okay."

Beth nodded, blinking back tears. *Great, already falling apart,* she thought, stepping into the home she'd been to, it suddenly seemed, not nearly often enough. She followed Alex. "Joe's in the backyard," Alex tossed over her shoulder. "It's such a beautiful fall day, it's a pity to waste it. If that's okay, we'll visit there." In the kitchen, Alex stopped. "I just put together a plate of cheese, crackers, and fruit. Coffee?"

"Sounds great and yes to coffee," Beth said. "Alex, I appreciate you and Joe making time ..."

"Oh, Beth, we're happy to see you. Nice that you work from home and can flex a bit around your lunch break." Alex looked at her sideways. "We're glad to be here for you," she added mildly. Beth pressed her lips together and nodded. They made their way out the back sliding doors. Joe was sitting quietly, face tilted up to the sun, eyes closed. He straightened and smiled, rising to hug Beth.

"Joe! How has sabbatical been?" Beth asked.

"Glorious," Joe said, sitting back down. "I can't believe how wonderful." He tapped a book on the table beside him. "I actually spent time each evening making notes—a travel journal plus notes when I interviewed people along the way." He glanced at Alex and added, pointedly, "I was, after all, doing research."

"Right." Alex nodded, putting out small plates for each of them.

Joe picked up his coffee and added, "I'm going to enjoy being home for the holiday season and then back on the road again."

"Beth? Something to eat?" Alex gave the platter of food a slight push toward Beth.

Beth placed a few crackers and a couple chunks of cheese on a small plate, took two slices of apples. She wondered how she would choke any of it down. "Thanks, Alex." She glanced up at Alex, and then at Joe. Alex nodded slightly. Beth opened her mouth but only a weird croaking sound came out.

Alex put her coffee cup down and rested a hand on Beth's arm. "I told Joe about the lying, Beth. I know it's yours to tell, but I figured it would be hard."

Joe shook his head, his face fallen. "Beth, I'm sorry." Beth drew her eyebrows together, but before she could protest Joe continued. "I'm his father, and I've failed."

"No," Beth began, but Joe put up a hand.

"I know I tend to do a lot of ... lecturing." He looked sideways at Alex, who gave a small shrug and smile. "But I didn't do enough of the right kind. I let Jonah think it was okay to treat his mother, his sister—really, just about everyone—with disdain. It was my job, above everyone, to put a stop to that behavior when he was a child. I failed,

Beth, and in doing so I have failed my wife, my daughter, and you." He fidgeted, suddenly no longer the confident professor. "I owe each of you an apology, and I'll be apologizing to Sandy separately." He gave Alex a nod.

"Thank you," Beth said softly. "But ... And ... And I have more to say." She paused. "I did look at the medical report on Jonah. The one he filed away and then told me the doctor said he was fine." She shook her head. "He could argue himself off on a technicality ... his chance of fatherhood was slim, but not none. In other words, possible but highly unlikely. Like a sperm count—"She paused, glancing sidelong at Alex, who nodded. "A sperm count," Beth continued, "that was low for low. Like if fifteen million is low, his was under three million."

"Oooh." Alex breathed out. "So, you're right. He could pretend he's okay—he was producing sperm, so he wasn't 'lying,'" she said, making air quotes. Joe just kept hanging his head, shaking it back and forth slowly, a pendulum of self-recrimination.

"There's more," Beth said quietly. Alex and Joe both leaned in just a bit. Beth paused and suddenly Kitta, sitting up straight and speaking firmly, popped into mind. Beth sat up straighter and said, almost firmly, "Alex, Joe ... I've decided to divorce Jonah." She looked fearfully from one face to the other; they did not look surprised, just sad. She blinked, hard, feeling burning tears beginning. "I don't see another way. He won't work with me on this marriage. But, but—" She put her hands over her face and began crying.

Alex rubbed Beth's shoulder, letting her cry for a few moments, and then, as Beth quieted, said, "Well, of course, you're not divorcing any of us, so you are still our family. Every day, the holidays ... Thanksgiving and Christmas, too. I suspect this year that will be a particularly rocky time, so yes, this year, too." Alex grinned and added, "Matt and Tim will be here for breakfast."

"Nice," Beth managed to say. "Not going to Gloria and Bob's?"

"They'll be over Thanksgiving morning with us and then going to Gloria and Bob's in the afternoon. Same for Sandy and Cody and the twins. So, for the full family experience, I'd definitely recommend coming for Thanksgiving breakfast, whatever your plans for the day. Of course, you're welcome to stay here all day."

"The boys were with me for a couple of weeks this fall. It was great," Joe remarked, drawn back to his fishing sabbatical. "It was nice to have them to myself. Well, sort of." He rolled his eyes. "You can't go anywhere with them without people wanting to talk to you. Well, them. It's like being with Alex in that regard."

"Being around them is an emotional intelligence test," Alex commented, pretending to ignore the backhanded compliment. "Do you like Matt? Do you like Tim? If so, you're a nice person." She sighed. "And, of course, Jonah hates Matt and is dismissive of Tim." She turned to Beth. "So, do you have a plan?"

Beth nodded. "This sounds really awful but I'm glad we have that pre-nup. I meet with the attorney to finalize the papers on my end tomorrow. So tomorrow I'll tell Jonah." She took a deep breath. "I'm going to buy him out of the house and keep Sol. He can keep Anastasia." She smiled mischievously and added, "I thought about offering Apple and Mac to the twins and Cody. And Sandy ... but not at your house."

Alex nodded thoughtfully. "That would work, all around. I recall the house was mostly your investment, right?"

"Yes. Jonah should be walking away with more than enough to start fresh with a good down payment on a condo where Anastasia is permitted. And he has a third interview today. For a job in Austin."

"Texas?" Joe clarified.

Beth nodded. Alex asked, "Did he even ask you about this? About your willingness to relocate?"

Beth gave a small laugh and said, "No."

"Figures," Alex said, frowning.

Beth went on. "I intend to stay in the house. To stay here,"she added, looking from Alex to Joe.

"We're glad," Alex said quietly. "We don't want to lose you."

"It will be awkward." Joe shook his head. "Especially this year."

Alex snorted. "Thanksgiving was going to be awkward anyway, because if Jonah bothers to come, he hates Matt, dislikes Tim, is perpetually annoyed with Sandy, and now believes Cody's gone insane. He thinks I'm stupid and that you're boring." Alex was facing Joe, who looked surprised, and then resigned, at that last bit. "That Beth is cutting him loose with his favorite dog and a chunk of money is, well, just one more slice of awkward." She turned to Beth. "So, seriously. However things go, you are always our family. Always."

"Thank you," Beth said, wiping her eyes. "This means a lot. I mean, you know. I wanted to tell you first. I still haven't told my parents. I'm thinking of flying up to visit and talking to my dad and letting him handle Mom. She can be pretty awful." She paused. "Do you mind ... how do you think I should let the rest of the family know? I mean, Sandy. Gloria and Bob's family."

"Well, once Sandy knows, Cody and Rachel will know." Alex paused. "I can talk to Gloria and Bob, but as far as Gloria and Bob's other boys... maybe let them know yourself. It might be good for you. Therapeutically speaking, I mean."

"Okay. I'll get in touch with Sandy first."

"Here I am." Sandy was suddenly in the doorway, coming out, glass of water in hand. "What's going on?" She picked up a wedge of apple and gave her mother a sidelong look. "Organic? Or will you just say so to shut me up?"

"I love you, too, sweetheart." Alex grinned. Sandy laughed, bent to kiss her mom's cheek and then plopped into an empty chair. She turned her eyes on Beth.

"What's my brother up to?"

Beth shook her head. "Well, it's more what I'm up to." She twisted her face, blinked hard, and continued. "Jonah finds out tomorrow night, so until then ... it's a secret." Sandy made a zipping gesture across her mouth, and Beth went on. "I'm filing for divorce. Tomorrow."

"Well, that's sad. Or it would be, except it's Jonah," Sandy said philosophically.

"Sandy," Joe began.

"Dad," Sandy shot back. "Let's face it. Everyone knows Jonah's a lying, arrogant, lazy jerk. He always has been." She rolled her eyes. "Look how he treats people! Look how he's been behaving since he got fired! He should be waiting on Beth hand and foot."

"Yuck." Beth shuddered.

"Yeah, well," Sandy said. "But seriously. You should be wondering, wow, do I want him to *ever* get a job? Having all these chores done, and done well, is great! Look at the flowers in the yard! I never fold laundry or go grocery shopping anymore! The dogs are in their best shape ever with all that walking! But I bet that isn't how it is. *At all*. Right?"

Beth nodded, shrugging. "You are right. It's been a wallow for months."

"Will you get an annulment?" Sandy asked. All three looked at her, surprised. Except for volunteering with the youth group, since when was Sandy concerned about the nuances of Catholicism? Sandy caught the look, and, twirling a lock of hair with a clumsy attempt at nonchalance, said, "Cody's been working on an annulment from the marriage to Jenna. I've been hearing about the process. A little. That's all."

Alex leaned forward, catching Joe's eye and raising her eyebrows a bit. He gave a barely perceivable nod. Beth saw it and was caught off guard at how much the casual display of marital connection moved her; it felt like an exhibit of just how dysfunctional her marriage with Jonah was. Was there any context in which she and Jonah could communicate with such infinitesimal expressions?

"And don't jump to conclusions," Sandy added. "Well ... hop, if you like. No leaping, though."

"Fair enough," Alex replied.

"I guess I'll know what's going on when Cody calls and asks to meet with me," Joe sighed. "Things are certainly lively around here. I'm afraid of what will happen by the time I'm done with sabbatical."

"Daddy," Sandy said with exaggerated patience. "Jonah might move to Texas. Beth will be here. I'll be here. Aunt Gloria will still try to boss Mom around and Uncle Bob is basically all better, and you'll go fishing. I promise to keep nagging you about your terrible environmental and dietary decisions."

Joe shook his head. The conversation moved on; they wondered about the job Jonah was interviewing for, about the third interview today. They discussed Sandy's job, the upcoming holiday season, and how the twins were doing in school.

Beth got up reluctantly; she had some work that afternoon. There were hugs all around. "Let me know how it goes," Alex said. "Be in touch whenever."

"Same here," Sandy echoed. "I'll be right there."

"Of course," Joe said and then, pausing, reached into his pocket. He drew out his phone, raised his eyebrows, and nodded slowly. "And

I think I'll wander into my den and return this text. From Cody." He patted Beth's shoulder one last time and headed indoors.

Outside on the deck, the three women spent a few moments in a group hug. Beth pulled away, thanking each of them, and added, "I'll see myself off ... no doubt you have some talking to do."

When she glanced at the house as she pulled out of the driveway, Alex and Sandy were waving good-bye from the front window.

Back at home, Jonah seemed to have not moved, but his hair was brushed, he was clean-shaven, and he was wearing a shirt and tie with his sweatpants. He barely glanced up when she came in.

Petting the dogs, she asked, "How are things here?"

"Interview went great." Jonah sat up straighter. "They made me an offer."

"Congratulations." Beth went into the living room and sat down on the loveseat. "What do you think?"

"I didn't say yes immediately, of course. I asked for a day. The salary is good—more than I was making before. It's a mix of on-site and remote." He looked straight at Beth. "It requires relocation."

She nodded but said nothing. She felt her heart pounding against her ribs and wondered if Jonah could see it from where he sat.

He waited, seeming surprised at her silence, and then continued. "I think it has real potential. Room for creativity. Advancement. The benefits are good."

"Sounds good," Beth offered. *Wait*, she told herself, *just wait for him. Let him talk.*

Jonah sat up, swinging his feet from the couch to the floor; he leaned his elbows on his knees, hands pulled into loose fists and then half turned to face Beth. "Oh, hell, Beth. You don't want to move. And I don't want to be married. Let's just call it done."

Beth nodded slowly. For a brief moment, she wondered if Jonah was going to actually make something easy for the first time. "You mean you're leaving?"

Jonah nodded. "If I say yes tomorrow, I start in two weeks. They have a corporate condo I can use for a couple of months while I find a place." His eyes darted sideways. "Anastasia is under the weight limit."

Beth was silent, eyes riveted on Jonah.

He looked past her, out the window. His jaw muscles clenched and unclenched, and he shifted slightly to meet her gaze. "I'm leaving, Beth. I can't do this. This," his hand gestured toward the kitchen, "this domestic thing. I feel stifled."

That's a hell of a word choice, Beth thought. "Stifled."

Jonah shrugged. "You're never happy, Beth. Ever. Always wanting more. The babies and friends and doing more stuff. So go get more."

I'm never happy. Never fun. Never enough. Beth nodded, breathing slowly. *Enough*, she told herself firmly. *Enough*. She breathed out slowly. "Okay. So, will it help that I already met with a lawyer? That the papers will be ready tomorrow?"

Jonah stared at her.

She continued. "In the papers, I buy you out and settle you with more than your share of the house." She rolled her eyes. "And yeah, you can have Anastasia."

Jonah shook his head. "That's it? No ... drama?"

Beth sighed. "Jonah, I've had drama for years. I've been crying for years. I'm mostly cried out." She stood up, shaking her head. "I meet with the attorney tomorrow at three. Feel free to go with me, we can just sign everything and have her file it and take care of all the paperwork. And you can pack, and we'll order a storage unit to have sent out to you when you settle someplace."

"I don't need anything much," Jonah said. "Just my personal stuff."

"Well, figure out what you're doing with the mosaic."

"I'll put it in storage, then, with some of my other stuff. And, yeah, let's just get it over with tomorrow." Jonah turned back to the television, unmuting it as he added, almost as if to himself, "Well, that went better than I expected."

Beth nodded slowly to herself. *Better than* he *expected*, she thought. *Thank you, Lord.* So far, it felt like a miracle had occurred. "I'm going back to work," she called, and went into the small home office, Sol at her side. Before she signed in, she let Tara Mallory know that Jonah would be accompanying her to finalize all the paperwork, and sent a quick text to Courtney, Izzy, Kitta, Alex, and Sandy.

Jonah suggested a divorce and is relieved I have made plans to oblige him.

Chapter 30

The visit with Tara Mallory went smoothly. Beth felt as if she were drunk; everything seemed a bit off, sort of as if the entire world were swaying. It all seemed very crisp and businesslike, which, she supposed, it was. Jonah had started out being himself, interrogating Tara on her experience and education. When he found out she had several Ivy League degrees and had clerked for his favorite Supreme Court justice, he quieted down and then just nodded, asked a few questions, mostly just confirming how things would go. He took his copy of the papers, and the letter from Tara's office confirming that she was holding, in escrow, his settlement, awaiting the legal completion of the dissolution of the marriage of Jonah Bonhall and Elizabeth Corcoran Bonhall, and tucked them into his inside pocket; he had put on a jacket for the occasion. Beth put her copies into her tote. They all stood up and Tara shook hands with both of them. She had her shoes on this time; she was taller than Jonah, and in her spike heels she was over six feet tall.

Tara had recommended, strongly, that Jonah consult with one or two other attorneys and then, if the agreement was acceptable, they wrap up the signatures and then the papers would be filed. Jonah had said, to Beth's surprise, that he had one appointment set for the following week and would get another opinion, too.

The ride home was more of the same oddness for Beth; Jonah was chatting about the weather and about whether she thought it would hold for a trip to the dog park on Saturday. Beth said she supposed it would. Jonah wondered if maybe they should have pizza for dinner, something sort of celebratory, or would that be weird? Beth replied they were having a weird day anyway. Did he want to go out, order in, or make it at home? To her surprise, he suggested they stop on the way.

Beth slid into the booth and looked at Jonah. He looked bored, as usual, but not angry. They ordered and, when their waters with lemon had been served, Beth played with her straw wrapper and then looked up at Jonah. "I don't understand."

"Don't understand what?"

She rolled her eyes. "This," she said, drawing a circle with her finger to include both of them. "What happened? What just happened?"

Jonah sighed and for a moment he looked as if the Jonah she'd seen almost exclusively for the past year or more would emerge. He nodded and said, "Fair enough. Maybe it seems sudden to you. But, Beth, I haven't been happy for a long time."

"As in, never?"

He frowned. "That's not fair. I think we were happy. Or we thought we were."

"So, when did you turn unhappy?"

He sighed. "Beth. When were you ever happy?"

"You go first."

He turned to gaze out the window at the parking lot. She watched his eyes narrow. She glanced out. A disheveled old man was rifling through the trash can at the bus stop. Jonah turned back, his lip curled in disgust. Beth waited. He shook his head. "I don't know. It just seemed like life became boring. Rote. My job. The routine. The dogs. The constant socializing."

Constant? I see my friends once a month and you stay home except for the summer cookout, Beth thought.

Jonah continued. "And, you know, I thought marriage would be... different. You know, hanging out together. Not having to work so hard."

"What hard work, Jonah?"

He frowned. "You know."

"No. I don't." Beth was surprised to feel herself beginning to enjoy this. It didn't matter if he got angry, or walked out, or made a scene.

"Fine." He scowled and lifted his glass, put it down. "I thought marriage would be, hang out, relax. Sex without a lot of aggravation."

"What aggravation?"

He rolled his eyes. "The having to talk about stuff. Your endless feelings. And then the whole baby thing, I mean, Beth, seriously."

"Right. The whole emotions and a family thing. Normal marriage stuff, in other words."

"Yeah, I know. Blah, blah, blah. But I mean, seriously. We're not parenting material, you and I. I didn't want kids."

"But you lied. You let me think—"

Jonah held up one hand. "Stop it, Beth. I get it. I left out information. Yeah, not likely to have kids. But I really didn't think you were so gung ho. I thought you would just prove to yourself you'd tried and we'd be off the hook. Able to just enjoy our lives. Be free. You know, even to do this." He shrugged toward the rest of the Italian restaurant.

"Just pop out for a bite without having bring all sorts of accessories or hire extra help."

Beth rubbed one temple. "You thought I didn't really want kids, I just wanted to make a good show of it to ... me? To who?"

He shrugged. "Who knows? Your parents? Your friends? I mean, really, who wants kids?"

Beth sipped her water, her eyes fixed on his face. She felt cold, colder than the water, colder than the relentless air conditioning blasting from the vent overhead. "Is that how you feel, like no one really wants kids?"

He didn't even hesitate. "Crap, yeah. Absolutely." He snorted. "Kids? To put it in religious terms—for my mom, you know—it's a lifelong cross to carry." He shook his head. "So glad we dodged that bullet."

Beth felt her stomach twisting. She was completely honest when she said, "Me, too, Jonah. Me, too."

He looked at her surprise and then up at the waiter, who was carrying their pizza. "Did you guys put enough pepperoni on this for a change?"

Chapter 31

It had taken nine days to wrap up the signatures—just days before Jonah and Anastasia set off cross-country to start a new life, where Anastasia could rule the domicile and Jonah would have no demands placed on him by a needy wife, annoying sibling or addle-brained parents.

The first attorney advertised heavily in representing men's rights in divorces. He had looked over the pre-nup and the divorce agreement, rubbed his forehead, looked over his glasses at Jonah, and shook his head.

"What, exactly, is it you want from me?"

"To make sure I'm not getting ripped off," Jonah had said, barely containing an eye roll at the vapidity of this self-described tough lawyer.

The attorney had snorted contemptuously and said, "I can't believe you're letting this girl slip through your fingers. She's rich and generous, and clearly no fool. But, hey, suit yourself."

"So, it's fair?"

The attorney had leaned forward, elbows on the desk, forearms crossed, shaking his head. He looked Jonah right in the eye and said, "Son, no, it's not fair." Jonah started to smile, but then the attorney went on. "Your wife could clearly get away with just buying you out for your, what, twenty percent of the house? But she apparently wants you to have a secure start. No, it's not fair, it's in your favor. I'd shut up, take the money, and run if I were you, given you're foolish enough to let her go."

The second attorney had reviewed the paperwork and looked Jonah up and down skeptically. "And you're here ... why, exactly?"

"To see if I'm being ripped off."

The attorney had shaken his head and said, "Mr. Bonhall ... you're getting bought out very generously. It seems crystal clear; I mean, here's the pre-nup." He waved one packet. "And here's your letter from Santa telling you what you're getting." He waved the other. He placed them both down, stacked them neatly, and said, "You're getting a good deal and I guess it's just a mystery as to why she's so eager to get rid of you."

Jonah had pressed his lips together, and then said, "Well, the feeling is mutual. She's just never happy. She wants kids, and to spend time with the family ..."

"I see," the attorney had said crisply. "Well, usually things make sense if you poke around the edges enough. Fine, then, you're getting a good deal and good luck to you."

The third attorney had pretty much said the same thing, and added, "Jonah, I'm number three in your second opinion poll, correct? How much of that generous settlement do you plan to burn up getting the same answer at our usual hourly rates?" Jonah had nodded and paid his bill and then called Tara Mallory's office to arrange to sign off on the papers.

And so ended the marriage of Jonah and Beth Bonhall.

Chapter 32

Beth opened her eyes, staring at the ceiling. Sol was resting his head on the bed, inches from her face. She smiled, sitting up and rubbing his head. "Happy New Year, Naughty Sol." She rolled her shoulders, looked around the room. The sun was not quite up; the first light was peeking through the blinds onto freshly painted walls. There was time to get to morning Mass. She'd be meeting Alex and Alex's mother, stopping home to pick up Sol and the plate of homemade cookies she'd prepared, which were in the refrigerator where Sol could not get them. Then she and Sol would head over to Matt and Tim's to join their traditional New Year's open house for their neighbors.

Taking Sol for a brisk walk, she breathed the crisp, dry air. *These cool days are a great treat*, she thought. She looked around the neighborhood, feeling as if it were new, yet she'd been here for years. Sol, as if he sensed her mood, occasionally slowed, so she also slowed, lingering to soak in the fresh day.

She shook her head. *What a weird few weeks*. Jonah had signed off on the divorce and taken the settlement on the house as if he were afraid she might change her mind; he had actually arranged for a storage container to be delivered and put his things into it, except for two suitcases to go with him and Anastasia in his car. Izzy, Ozzy, Courtney, Sandy, Cody, and the twins had descended on her home the day after he left to help clean, paint, and push furniture around. Cody had happily taken Apple and Mac, and the dogs rotated which one slept with which twin on a nightly basis.

And then Christmas ... Beth had planned to be alone Christmas Eve, but Alex and Joe had been insistent: She was family, whether Jonah was here or in Austin. She joined them for Mass, as always, and then they all descended on Gloria and Bob's home. Kevin and Veronica had their hands full; baby Grace was only two months old, Gina was ecstatic about Santa coming, and Bobby was being ... Bobby. Beth made herself useful by keeping Gina occupied; the little girl was a lot calmer when she was at least a few feet away from Bobby. Beth had hoped to be able to spend time with the baby, but Veronica, as always, was glued to her infant.

Rachel and Aidan announced their engagement after Mass on Christmas Eve, and, despite it being perhaps the worst-kept secret in either family's history, Sandy and Cody also announced their engagement after Mass, which led to a long family discussion about how Marta and Sean would address Aunt Sandy when she was married to their dad. Sean didn't see why they should change anything. "We call her Aunt Sandy now," he said. "Why mess things up?" Alex and Gloria worried what people would think about their dad kissing their aunt. "He does already," Sean said, matter-of-factly, and Alex muttered, "Oh, God, here we go," as Gloria frowned and began waving her arms, emphasizing that Cody's annulment hadn't come through yet. "Oh, please," Alex interrupted her. "They've already said the wedding hinges on the annulment. Stop it." Gloria had widened her eyes and clamped her lips together.

Marta waited for a pause and then said, clearly and thoughtfully, "I'd really like to call Aunt Sandy 'Mom' once she marries Daddy." She looked at the adult faces, her sweet, serious expression silencing everyone." Other people call stepparents Mom and Dad. Well, Aunt Sandy is more family than other people's stepparents. And it would be nice." She paused, and then started again, with a slight break in her voice. "It would be nice to have someone who was, you know, a mom." Cody pressed his lips together, hard, and put an arm around Marta's shoulders, looking over at Sandy with eyebrows raised.

"Of course," Sandy said, without missing a beat. "Besides, if we get our way, that makes it easier. Everyone in our home besides Cody will call me the same thing."

Marta almost tackled Sandy. "Everyone? Really? Will we have a new brother? Or sister?"

"I hope so," Sandy said. "But we're not married, and it won't happen until at least nine months after that."

Alex said she hoped Sandy wasn't going to launch into a biology lesson.

"Why that long?" Sean began and Marta elbowed him.

"You remember. From science class."

"Oh. Yeah." Sean frowned. "Okay."

"Can we talk about this some other time?" Cody asked. "Don't you two have Christmas cookies to eat or something?"

"The only ones left have yellow sugar. Like pee," Sean explained.

Cody rolled his eyes. "Mom. Seriously? Can't you get Bobby to stop that part?"

Gloria shrugged. "I'm tired. I was glad he didn't decide to use chocolate chips as poop and that he didn't suck the color off any of the red hots this year."

Kevin and Veronica pretended not to hear their son's chronic misbehavior described. Instead, Veronica attempted a diversion by describing the wonderful job she would do as their wedding photographer. "You both are going to be such beautiful brides. We can start at the prayer garden outside of the church. Or maybe during dressing up. I know someone who does hair and makeup for the wedding party." She looked confused when Sandy vigorously shook her head.

Sandy explained that the weddings would be in the chapel, not the church, and very small, so there wasn't going to be any big production with lots of formal photographs. Rachel added that it would be a double wedding and the girls would stand up for each other. It would be at her and Sandy's home church, Blessed Sacrament, but Aidan's uncle Seamus, the pastor at St. Stephen's, would officiate. Cody would have Matt as best man, and Marta and Sean would be junior members of the party. Aidan's next younger brother would flyover from Ireland to be his best man. They would have a nice meal at Alex and Joe's place afterward. "Organic, of course," Alex interjected. Rachel and Aidan would have another blessing in Ireland during the summer trip home, with Uncle Seamus in tow to do their blessing and baptize a great-niece who had been born in the past year. Veronica looked confused, Tim rubbed Matt's shoulder happily, and Kevin nodded and said it sounded like a perfect wedding. His wife gave him a sharp look, and he shrugged.

Beth smiled, remembering it, and thought, *Maybe someday I'll be there. I'm not even thirty. There's time.*

Sol stopped and gave a short, excited snort. Beth brought herself back to the moment; approaching them was a pale golden retriever leading a man. "Be good," Beth said quietly, giving Sol a gentle tug.

The man grinned. "Happy New Year! Good morning!" He approached, his dog leaning out toward Sol and Beth.

"Happy New Year." Beth petted the dog, and Sol and the pale retriever sniffed each other's faces and then proceeded to inspect one another thoroughly. Beth looked at the man. She didn't recognize him. "A beautiful dog. You're up early for New Year's."

He nodded. "Yes, but you know how it is." He looked toward the dogs. "No rest for the weary."

"I haven't seen her before." Beth paused. "Are you visiting family?"

He shook his head. "No, I've just moved in. I know," he added. "Heck of a time to relocate, but I have a new position at the state college starting in the January term."

"Nice," Beth said. "What position?"

"History faculty," he said. "I was lucky. These positions almost never open up. But there's a professor who's on sabbatical, so I'll be covering his courses this term and then they're looking to boost up the department. More history, more U.S. government classes."

"Congratulations," Beth said. "I think you're talking about my family."

"Your family? Your dad?"

She almost said, "My ex-father-in-law," hesitated, and said, "No, I guess friends of the family. You know." She paused. "Well, moving this time of year must have been tough for your family."

He shook his head. "Not so much. I was divorced a year ago. Just bought a place in this neighborhood, about three blocks that way." He gestured in the general direction of her house. He put out his hand. "I'm Sam. Samuel. Samuel Karlinski."

Karlinski. Polish? Probably Catholic, Beth thought.

"Yes, actually."

Beth cringed inside. *I have got to stop thinking out loud.* "Me, too. Catholic, that is. Not Polish. And, um." She hesitated. "I'm meeting some people from my family for Mass in about," she glanced at her wrist, "an hour. If you're heading over to church to start the New Year right, feel free to join us." She added, unnecessarily, "Usually one of them goes at seven, but we talked her into the nine a.m. Mass this year. Just for a change. Oh. And I'm Beth. Beth Bonhall. And this is Sol. Solar, actually, but he goes by Sol."

Sam Karlinski smiled and said, "Church sounds good. Everything here is still ... unfamiliar." He fell into step beside her. "And this is Deborah." He caught Beth's quizzical glance. "Deborah Sampson in her official papers. I named her for the woman who disguised herself as a man to fight with the Americans in the American Revolution."

"Interesting," Beth replied. *Joe is going to love him.*

"I thought it fit her," Samuel continued. "Debbie here is full of spirit, she isn't afraid of anything. She can be a bit ... feisty, I guess." He continued describing the assets of Deborah Sampson while Beth mused on the weirdness of this encounter. Joe's probable future replacement ... She thought of Courtney asserting, "I don't believe in coincidences."

They reached the corner near her home and Beth said, "Well, I'm about home. So maybe we'll see you at Mass in a bit?"

"Absolutely."

"One little thing ..." Beth thought of Dr. Garnette and his assignment to be honest. She decided it wasn't fair to have Samuel be totally blindsided. "That professor who's on sabbatical? That's my ex-father-in-law. And the people I'm meeting for Mass are my ex-mom-in-law and her mom. I don't want it to be too ... weird. When you find out, I mean."

"Interesting." He nodded thoughtfully, and added, almost to himself rather than to her, "Well, I don't believe in coincidences."

"Did I already say that out loud, too?"

"Huh? No. No, I say that all the time. Why?"

"I just was thinking it. A friend of mine says that whenever the rest of us are tempted to just shrug something off as random."

"A wise friend." He laughed at his awkward self-compliment. "See you at church." He turned to continue his walk. She watched him turn the next corner—down Ozzy's street and heard the rumble of male voices and Izzy's higher tones. *Of course, he already knows Ozzy and Izzy ... and he's going to work with Joe ...* Beth shook her head, smiling, and went in to have a second cup of coffee while she prepared for church. She wondered, briefly, if Samuel Karlinski could pass the 'Do you like Matt and Tim?' test. And then thought, *Well, of course. He seems normal enough*. She wondered if it would be inappropriate to invite him along. He was new here and alone on a holiday.

Sol nudged her thigh as she headed out for church. She paused to pet him and kiss the top of his head. "Try to not be naughty," she said, not succeeding in sounding stern. "I'll be back after church and then we'll go visit Matt and Tim." Sol woofed with approval and went to rest on the living room rug, settling with a satisfied huff.

"You got that right, Naughty Sol," Beth agreed, and stepped out into the sparkling day.

Book Club Conversations

1. Chapter one opens with Beth and Veronica both lying. Later, Alex remarks that, when it comes to lies, "There's never just one." How does lying impact the characters?

2. How might the story have been different if, from the first pages, no one lied? If one person instead told the truth?

3. Are there any characters who don't lie? If so, who? How does that honesty impact events?

4. Were any of the lies helpful in the long run? If so, how?

5. What other lies do you wonder might be simmering under the surface among the characters?

6. Which character resonated most with you? Why?

7. Did you dislike any of the characters? Which ones, and why?

8. If you were casting this book for a movie, which character would you want to play? Who plays your least favorite, and who is cast for your favorite? What contributes to your decisions?